HIDDEN DOORS, SECRET ROOMS

JAMIE EUBANKS

This is a work of fiction. Characters, names and places are either the product of the author's imagination or used fictitiously. Any resemblance to actual persons, living, dead, or undead, or to any establishments, locations or events is entirely coincidental.

The author does not have any control over and does not assume any responsibility for third-party websites or their content.

Cover Graphics by Michael Wilson

HIDDEN DOORS, SECRET ROOMS

ISBN: 978-1482356182

Special thanks to my friend, Linda Fields Gold.

"Vast is the void. Wicked, the curse..."

CHAPTER 1

The young woman staggered, leaving tracks through the deep snow, hugging an unconscious child to her breast, shivering, exhausted. She paused, gasping, attempting to gain her bearings. She turned to the left, the right, whirls of snow casting the high desert into a blinding rage of white. Everything was white, cold. The blizzard air turned to fire in her lungs, seared her throat with each ragged breath. Her legs were past the point of aching; they felt numb, heavier, and stiffer with each stumbling push forward. She could go no further. She pushed on.

An hour earlier, the question had been one of escape. Now, it was one of survival. After the van had been left behind, its front-end buried in a snow embankment, rear wheels spinning uselessly when she'd attempted to rock the vehicle back and forth and out of the snow wall, the Ski-Doo had slid from the back of the van without too much trouble. Its engine turned over on the first attempt, and hope once again reared its wondrous head, though only too briefly.

Even with no helmet or face shield to protect them from the elements, she'd made due, turning her collar to the wind, and holding on to what little bit of hope she could grasp as her face went from stinging cold to numb. All the while, little Valerie rode at her back, mittened hands clinging tightly, her red-cheek face pressed against her mother's back, fighting the icy cold wind. Even with no destination in mind, with no idea what direction they were heading – even in a blinding blizzard – there was hope: as long as they kept moving, they'd eventually run into a house, a street, a passing vehicle, a gas station, someone whom she could flag down and beg for mercy. That hope, however, ended when, after the snowmobile took them perhaps three or four miles further into nowhere, the machine simply died.

If she'd thought things couldn't possibly get worse after that, she'd been wrong. The nightmare crept up on her again. And it was too late; she was too tired. But her child...She had to protect her baby.

She knew the signs that preceded the attacks: An acrid smell, like burning rubber, growing stronger. The air came alive as if electrically charged. And the sound it made was that of an angry swarm of bees defending the hive. It drew closer. She knew of no way to stop it. But her little girl...

Her resources were nearly depleted, yet she had to try. The woman fell to her knees, dropping the little girl in the snow as the scent of burning rubber overtook her. There was only one way to save the little girl, one last resource left to tap. The effort alone could prove deadly to the woman; it would magnify the attack tenfold.

The woman dropped her head back until she gazed straight up at the overcast sky. The blood drained from her face, leaving her complexion as pale as the snow around her. Her breathing became increasingly slower, shallower, sending small frosty plumes into the air. A light scent of roses replaced the stench of burned rubber. She pushed the buzzing sound to the back of her mind. The air became soft and mellow, neither hot nor cold. She muttered an oath beneath her breath. Her expression went funny, upper lip snarling, body twitching, eyes rolling back until only the whites could be seen. Every muscle tightened, pulling inward. Moments passed, bringing a greater pain. Then all at once, the pain eased.

The child's eyelids fluttered and came open. "Mommy...? Mommy!"

The woman crumbled over on her side, losing her grip on the child, nearly losing her grip on consciousness. "Go, sweetheart," she said, lips trembling in a stammering whisper. "Hurry. It's coming."

"*No!*" the girl shrieked. She shook her head in disbelief. "I won't leave you. *No!*"

"Look for shelter, a light. *Run!*"

The child got to her feet, not bothering to wipe the snow from her coat or jeans. Tears welled up in her eyes and clung to her long lashes. Both mittened hands balled into desperate fists as she looked around her, taking in the blinding snowstorm. Her bottom lip quivered as she hitched for air. She was only five years old, but old enough to understand the danger. It was one she'd lived with for more than half of her life.

She grabbed her mother by the wrist and pulled back using all her might, crying, feet slipping in the snow. Her face was red and stinging from the cold. Her voice shook. "Mommy, I can't! Please. Please. I can't leave you! Mommy...Mommy! *Please! You gotta WAKE UP!"*

Shortly after dark, John removed his wool trousers and turtleneck sweater and slipped into silk pajamas. He extinguished the flame of the last candlestick and now stood, cane in hand, staring into the warm glow of the fireplace.

The blizzard was forecast to hit the northeast portion of Arizona late tonight and had arrived a bit early. Due to the last several days of overcast skies, his electrical supply was low. The solar panels had been rendered all but useless, and the numerous candles placed throughout his home, though not quite an absolute necessity, presently served as his main lighting. There was, however, a gas generator for back up and enough fuel – if rationed carefully – to take him through the next few weeks.

He'd grown accustomed to inclement weather. His hometown of Dover, located a couple hours outside of London, had left him with a full appreciation of all four seasons. Here, however, in the upper desert region of northeastern Arizona, the snow meant total isolation. There were no stores within reasonable walking distance. No gas stations; not even a police station. The closest neighbor resided over a mile away – as the crow flies. With the way the snow was coming down, his Land Rover, parked across the yard in the garage, would not see daylight for at least another week.

The bedroom he had claimed as his own was a generous thirty by thirty-five and made the king sized, four-poster bed seem almost insignificant.

Standing before the stone fireplace, he stirred the embers, tensing briefly as sparks jumped then briefly danced like fireflies. John bent low, grasped and tossed in a couple of sticks of wood, one at a time. He lingered for a moment to bask in the dry, crackling heat.

Across the stone mantle, rested several snapshots of his wife and young son. One by one, he gave each of the six photos his full attention, wanting – needing – to remember their every detail. Each evening, each morning, the ritual was the same. He was alone. The photos were all that was left of the ones he had loved most.

Times such as this, if not for the hiss and occasional snap of the fire, the silence in the house would surely consume him entirely. John dropped his gaze to the gray slate hearth, watching as it reflected a muted glow from the fire. The flames popped, crackled, and the lyrics to one of the songs he'd written some twenty years before came to mind. His grip tightened on his cane as he recited the first passage of *Yesterday's Dreaming of You* softly to the fire.

Two hundred sixty acres of desert wasteland had been purchased and the house had been built about two years after the helicopter accident and after one quasi-successful attempt at an on-stage comeback. Quasi, because his heart had not been in it. The property was situated twenty miles from the nearest town, nine miles from the nearest paved road, and was just about the furthest he could get from civilization in this desert state, and still have access to the town's supplies.

"Bear" padded into the room, curling up on the braided rug at the foot of the bed. The old dog whined and regarded his master with large soulful eyes as if troubled by the storm.

"Merry Christmas, Bear," John said as he turned from the fire. "Looks like we're going to be snowed in for a while." Christmas – he'd almost forgotten. It was strange how the days all blended together and passed so quickly. How a single day could seemingly stretch into eternity.

He scratched the black chow behind the ear, then turned down the sheet and slipped into bed. He listened to the wind shriek and howl as if it were a living thing. The storm had moved in with great intensity. A distant loose shudder flapped and banged against a stone wall. In response, Bear's whining grew louder, more desperate. And despite it all, John drifted off to sleep, returning to a time before Rap music, before Disco, to an era when Rock 'n' Roll ruled the charts with open defiance.

CHAPTER 2

John awoke and sat up in bed, eyes stinging, dry. Smoke filled the air. His throat felt sore, parched. He got to his feet, using the five-foot-high posts and frame of the bed to maneuver his way to the wall, where he drew up a nearby window. Outside, the storm waged war, spitting snow into the room, backing up the chimney. He reached the fireplace just as he heard Bear barking from halfway across the house. Judging by the sound, the dog was in the foyer, wanting to go outside.

"Bear!"

A moment later, the dog came and stood in the doorway, then edged into the room at a reluctant pace, looking towards John, then back towards the doorway, then back at John again. Bear whined, nudged John's hand with his muzzle, then took hold of his master's pajama sleeve with bared teeth, tugging, as John attempted to throw open another window.

"Patience, Bear."

The dog whined again, but refused to give up its hold on the silk sleeve.

"All right, all right. Let me get my cane, and I'll let you out."

It only took a moment of gentle persuasion and Bear let go. The dog returned to the doorway, stopped, and turned around, issuing a quick bark as if he didn't quite trust the situation.

"Go on, boy. I'll be right there."

By the time John had the smoke mostly under control and reached the living room, Bear was already in the foyer, pawing at the large oak doors.

"You're going to freeze out there," John grumbled, tucking a flashlight under his arm. "You sure this is what you want?"

Bear turned around, meeting John's gaze with a pair of urgent dark eyes. The dog issued another bark in response.

John retracted the deadbolt, pulled open the door, pointed the flashlight's beam outside and said, "Off with you! And hurry!"

Bear started into a fit of barking as he edged further onto the porch. Instead of continuing his advance, the chow started backing slowly towards the doorway as the storm spit icy bits of snow into the foyer. As Bear moved back, John moved forward, going out into the storm. Halfway across the snow-covered porch, he dropped the cane and went to his knees. A spike of pain shot up his bad leg, yet the agony was secondary to a different kind of distress.

He shone the flashlight upon the object in question. There was a beige overcoat. A child's coat, dusted with snow. Huddled within was the owner. *Too small to be an adult. Too small to be a young teen.*

"Dear Lord." Dropping the flashlight, he scooped up the child – a little dark-haired girl. She fell pliable against his chest and he held her close against him as he struggled to his feet *sans* cane. "Can you hear me?" John attempted to rouse her, his warm hand holding her cold face. She wasn't conscious. But as he pulled her closer, he could feel her warm breath against his neck as he made his way inside. "Bear, get a blanket! *Hurry*!"

She couldn't have weighed more than forty pounds and yet getting her through the living room without the aid of his cane was a struggle. John silently cursed his mangled leg. He cursed the helicopter accident that had left him this way, and then gritted his teeth against the pain as he made his way past the Steinway, to the couch in the main sitting area. He gently set the child down and brushed a hand against her icy red cheek, while his other hand searched for the lamp switch.

The little girl was about the same age as his son, Ryan, when the boy had died. Four, maybe five years old. The situation was beyond imagination. The child had to have parents, guardians, someone who was supposed to be in charge of her welfare, and yet here she was, nine miles from the nearest paved road, left in a blizzard. And the nearest hospital was over twenty-five miles away. No snowplows would be out in this kind of weather. Neither ambulance nor police would be able to make it here through the blizzard. The roads would be closed, possibly for several days. The Land Rover would never make it up Disaster Hill, upon which his property bordered, not even with a set of chains. Not only was the hill steep, but it was also filled with deep ruts and littered with boulders – both large and small – and one wild curve where the land fell sharply away into oblivion. A slip of the tires at the wrong moment and there wouldn't be enough left of his Land Rover for a tow truck to pull away, or enough of the vehicle's occupants to warrant an ambulance.

When Bear returned dragging a blanket, John sent the chow on another errand for a pillow. Now that she was inside, and the snow on her shoes was melting, John could see that they had become soaked clear through. He slipped them from her feet, removing a pair of wet socks. Thankfully, both feet were a healthy shade of pink. He noticed no whitish discoloration around the toes, no signs of frostbite, which was a miracle in itself. He had no idea how far this little girl had walked, but it was probably at least nine miles. Because the dirt cutoff from the highway that led out here had been impassable by car since the snowfall of last week, and her face wasn't one he recognized from the area.

She may have fainted from exhaustion. Then again, it could be something much more serious. Whatever the reason, he had to get her body temperature back to normal. He quickly undressed the child to her underclothes and had her wrapped in the blanket by the time Bear came dragging a pillow.

"Thanks, boy," John said, scratching Bear behind the ear. "I'm going to grab my cane and draw a cool bath. Watch her for me."

John struck a match to the stovetop and set three kettles to boil. For the first time since he'd moved out here, he battled fear. Prior to tonight, he had considered himself prepared for any eventuality. The pantry stood stocked with a year's supply of food, some of which he had canned himself. The chest in the master bath had a wide assortment of medicines. He had solar panels to take advantage of the Arizona sun, a gas generator for back up. He had a library of books to challenge the mind and keep him amused. A generous stash of pain medication for when his leg acted up or when he was just plain bored. What he did not have was a telephone or CB, or Internet, or transmitter of any kind. It had never seemed necessary before.

While the water heated on the stove, John went into the guest bath and lit the gas heater to take the chill from the air. He left the bathroom, closed the door behind him, and went into the living room to check on the girl. A few feet from the couch, he stopped short, eyes still red and watering as the scent of smoke hung in the air, meeting the child's gaze. She had awakened and lay trembling beneath the blanket, eyes wide, and teeth clattering.

"My name is John. You're safe here. How are you feeling?" he asked, edging closer. "Are you hurt?"

"My mommy," she uttered in a voice so small that John found himself leaning closer. "She's hurt."

Until the child spoke, it hadn't occurred to him that there was someone else in need of rescue. Hurt. Somewhere out in the blizzard. John attempted to maintain some semblance of composure, as much for the child's sake as for his own. He eased into a sitting position next to the child, maintaining a grip on his cane. She was definitely not one of the children from the five-mile stretch he referred to as 'the neighborhood.' He couldn't imagine why this little girl was so far from home – especially on Christmas and during a blizzard. "Where is your mother?"

"Outside. She got hurt."

"How far?"

A tear slipped down the girl's chipmunk face. She swallowed hard, wincing, shivering, teeth clattering. "By the big hill. Flat hill. Mommy...fell down."

"Bear, get another blanket! Hurry!" He turned back towards the child and rose to his feet. "I need to know which mesa...hill. Where's your mother? What direction were you heading?"

The child hesitated a moment, then shook her head.

"Where do you live?" he asked.

"San Diego."

"California?"

She nodded, momentarily closing both eyes against the tears.

"How long has your mother been out there?"

The child stared vacantly.

"Did you follow the road directly here?"

"I don't know."

"What's your name?"

"Valerie."

"Okay, Valerie, I want you to listen closely. I'm going to find your mother. You stay here with Bear. You'll be safe and warm as long as you stay inside." He paused for a moment, searching the child's red-cheek face for a sign of understanding. "I'll be back as soon as possible, but it may take some time."

CHAPTER 3

John quickly dressed in warm boots, heavy clothing and donned a fur-lined parka for the hike. After filling, then slinging a knapsack over his shoulder, he repeated his order for the child to stay put, slipped on his gloves and headed out into the storm.

The stairway leading off the porch stood hidden deep beneath the snow. The boundaries of the dirt road were no longer discernible. He could see no tracks in the snow, no indication as to what direction the child had travelled. Several inches of snow had fallen between now and the time when he'd first retired for the evening, which was less than two hours ago. And it still fell – whipping with the winds, pummeling out of the sky in embattled whorls – impeding the view despite the five-cell flashlight he carried.

The going was slow. A man with two good legs would have had trouble getting through the deep drifts, which at times swallowed him up to his waist. Biting cold winds whipped at him from several directions at once. He kept his face down, his hood up, and the all but useless beam of the flashlight scanning the snow in front of him.

The first mesa he would come to stood less than a quarter of a mile away. It was the closest thing that could fit the child's description of a 'hill.' If luck were with him, he would find the woman there. But tonight, he did not feel lucky. The below freezing weather played havoc with his bad leg. Already, the tips of his fingers, lips and nose had begun to go numb. Despite the cane, he slipped twice, getting snow up his sleeves and in his face. Even if the woman were in the vicinity of the closest mesa, he had no guarantee he'd find her. Left in a storm like this, chances were she was dead by now. And like the dirt road, her body would be lost beneath the snow for days to come.

John began to regret leaving Bear behind. When he trudged around to the other side of the mesa, he also regretted leaving his shotgun behind. John hunkered down briefly, extending a gloved hand towards a reddish blotch in the snow. Although his mind initially tried to reject it, he knew what it was. Blood. Fresh blood. And there seemed to be a lot of it.

He pressed on further, coming to the top of a rise. He gazed down at the other side of the hill, unable to see clearly through the blizzard's blur. But something was there. Just down below. The next few feet of snow he crossed were mottled with large blotches of dark blood. It appeared as if something had been thrashing around, leaving evidence behind that a fight had taken place only moments before; for the imprints were too crisp, too deep, and otherwise would have been buried.

He shone the light to his left, to his right, and saw what appeared to be an article of clothing. He reached for it, shaking it free of the snow, and held it up for a brief inspection: A woman's lightweight coat.

The collar had been torn off. One sleeve was missing. For the most part, it was beige, the same color as the little girl's coat. The rest of it, however, was blood red.

He made his way to the woman's body less than a minute later, just a few yards down the hill from where the coat had been found. Her blouse had been ripped open. What appeared to be claw marks had parted skin and muscle from her throat to her bare stomach. Her arms were slashed all the way down, still oozing blood. Snow covered her feet and lower legs.

John removed his left glove with his teeth, reaching for the woman's blood-smeared face. She was cool to the touch. He started to reach for a pulse, but instead dropped his hood and leaned his head to her chest, listening to the weak but steady beating of her heart.

Without wasting another moment, he stripped off his parka and flannel shirt and began tearing his over shirt into strips for tourniquets and bandages to slow the worst of the bleeding. Covered from the waist up with only a thin T-shirt, his flesh gathered into goose bumps. He shuddered uncontrollably, and then slipped back into the parka. The woman was a mess, but alive. He had to hurry, not only for her sake, but also for his own. Whatever beast was responsible for her condition was probably still out there and by all indications, close by. He brushed the snow from her bare legs, removed the blanket from his knapsack, and wrapped the woman as best he could, running a length of rope around several times to keep the blanket in place for the trip home.

Finding her had proved to be the easy part. The most difficult part lay directly ahead: getting her to the house through a blinding blizzard, and getting her there alive.

Still shivering beneath the blanket, Valerie managed to sit up. Bear barked and ran for the door. She could only hope the dog acted that way because the blond headed man had returned with her mommy. When the door flew open, her heart raced. She wanted to run to him, but barely had the strength to hold her head upright. Her head felt funny, tingly. As if succumbing to a powerful tranquilizer, her eyelids closed, her head tipped to one side and she remained lost to the world for several hours.

For John Mills, the night seemed endless. The throbbing pain in his right leg alone proved to be more than enough to keep him awake. He grew optimistic concerning the child. She had no signs of fever or any other malady, and rested soundly enough in the living room with the benign expression that most children wear in their sleep. The woman, however, remained critical.

Using a sewing needle and ordinary household thread, he'd stitched up the more serious gashes, dressing them with a triple antibiotic ointment and gauze. Despite his efforts, it didn't look good. Her breathing became even shallower. Her coloring had gone from pale white to ghostly gray. Each time he returned to the guest room with more gauze or clean towels, he expected to find the woman dead.

As he stood in the bathroom, lathering and scouring his hands, he stared into the mirror as if the reflection he faced was that of a stranger. Ragged, pale, two days in need of a shave. His blond hair was a disheveled mess, falling in thick, tangled locks an inch or so below his collar. Tonight, he looked every bit his forty-two years. It had been a hellish evening. Watery blood ran down his wrists and along the length of his forearms, dripping from the tips of both elbows and spilling into the porcelain sink. John grabbed the scrub brush, soaped it up, and focused his efforts on the red grime staining cuticle and fingernails. The future seemed as bleak as his weary expression. By daylight, the woman would be dead and her corpse would be left in the guest room until he gathered the gumption to do something about it.

And the girl, what would he do with a motherless child? It would be at least a week before the snow melted enough to get the Land Rover into town. He would turn the little girl over to the local authorities then. But in the meantime...

John searched the medicine chest and pulled a prescription bottle of Norco. He kept a heavy supply of pain medicine around the house; it would help if the woman were to wake in agony – if she awoke at all. What he needed was an antibiotic to start the woman on before an infection set in. And somewhere he had at least five days' worth of penicillin. The problem would be in getting an unconscious woman to swallow a pill.

Sometime after five o'clock the following morning, John brought a candle, went into the kitchen and poured himself a glass of cool tap water. Even now, the picture remained fresh in his mind: pinching the woman's skin together with fingers and thumb, puncturing living tissue with a needle and pulling cotton thread through the snug holes. He had tried to tell himself that it was no different than sewing closed a Christmas goose once it's been stuffed for the oven. One thing was certain: If the woman survived, she'd be in desperate need of cosmetic surgery.

At the sound of footsteps, John turned towards the doorway. Wearing the blanket like a hooded cloak, the child stepped into the room.

John rose to his feet. "How are you feeling?"

"Did you...Where's my mommy?"

"She's in the guest room, resting. She needs all the rest she can get. So we don't want to disturb her."

"We don't?"

"No. She mustn't be disturbed. If you're hungry, I was about to make breakfast."

"I have to go to the bathroom."

"It's down the hallway, second door to your left. I'll show you."

She walked at his side, not watching where she went, but eyeing his cane. The stone floor felt cold beneath her bare feet. And every few seconds, she'd glance down, trying to find a pattern to the placement of the large, smooth stones.

"How come you have so many candles here?" she asked when they reached the bathroom door.

"It saves on electricity." He ran a hand along the inside wall, flipped a switch, flooding the bathroom with light. "There's soap in the dish by the sink. The towel on the far left is for you." Noting the confusion on her face, John pointed to the white towel he'd previously placed there for her use.

When she came out of the bathroom, she looked up at his face, then down at his cane. "How come you walk with a cane?" she asked as they passed down the hallway.

"I hope you like oatmeal," he said, ignoring her question. "I've no milk."

"Got any raisins?" she asked. "Mommy always puts raisins in my oatmeal."

"I might be able to scare up a few."

"Mommy says raisins have vitamins in them, only you can't see the vitamins 'cause they're real little."

John went to the kitchen counter and pulled a canister of dried oats from a cupboard. He had several questions to ask of the child and he wanted to go about the task without it appearing to be an interrogation. The poor girl had been through enough.

"I take it you and your mother are travelling alone?"

Valerie nodded, pushing her dark hair from her face with both hands. "The van got stuck. So my mommy got the snow rider machine out of the back. But then it broke, so we had to cover it all up with snow and walk."

He measured a cup of water into a small saucepan and set it to boil. "A snowmobile? Why did you have to cover it up with snow?"

"'Cause Mommy said so."

"So you started walking," John prompted.

"Yeah. We walked real, real far. It was so cold. Then my legs hurted me and Mommy had to carry me."

"What about your father? Does he have any idea where you and your mother are?"

She shook her head and gazed briefly upward as she spoke. "He's gone up to Heaven. Mommy says he can see me, but I don't think so." She looked at John from the corner of her eyes. "Kimberly Shelter says that once you're dead, you're dead. They just put you in the ground and you stay there until the worms eat you down to the bones. I know bones are white. All people have white bones. Don't matter what color their skin or hair is or if you got brown or blue eyes. Did you know dogs and cats have white bones. But bugs don't have no white bones.

If you step on one they scrunch. And that's really yucky."

He looked down at the small child, who was all but hidden under the blanket. Her thoughts were forthcoming, readily spoken. Yet there seemed to be a morbid streak there, one he considered strange for a child her age.

"While we're waiting for the water to boil, let's find you something a bit more suitable to wear."

CHAPTER 4

The guest room had a four-poster bed quite similar to that in the master bedroom, its own private bath, a stone fireplace, and a bookshelf filled with reading material, mostly of high literary quality: works by authors such as Charles Dickens, Edgar Allan Poe, Fyodor Dostoevsky and Thomas Hardy. Like the rest of the house, the floor in here was made of large, smooth stones. It appeared open, spacious, with a high vaulted ceiling and exposed wooden beams overhead. A portrait of John's deceased wife reigned above the mantle, having sea green eyes that pierced his soul, even when the room lay in gloomy shadows as it did now.

He went to the window and drew open the drapes. A light stirring of dust caught a thin stream of light, scattering then disappearing around him. For the most part, the blizzard was over. Yet the skies remained mostly overcast, dark, leaving the room a lackluster shade of gray. Out of necessity, he turned on the lamp beside the bed, then went into the bathroom and poured a glass of water. Six hours had passed since the woman's last dose of medicine, so he mixed the powdery contents of one crushed penicillin tablet and two crushed acetaminophen tablets in with the drink.

As he had done every hour on the hour since midnight, John administered water to the unconscious woman with a turkey baster. He felt her forehead and found it mildly warm, but not alarmingly so. Her face was pale, ashen. She had lain in the same position all night, not moving. Yet for the first time since he'd found her, with morning having arrived without further incident, he felt hope that she might survive.

He drew back the quilt to make sure the stitches had held, and his breath caught in his chest at the sight of the injuries. She couldn't have been more than thirty years old, probably closer to twenty-five, small framed. There were a great many bruises that had not been visible before, much swelling beneath the skin. A few of the injuries didn't appear to be claw marks, but appeared as if someone had taken a whip to the woman. These were red and inflamed, though likely not life threatening. The stitches seemed to be doing their job. Scabs had formed along the wounds and the bleeding had ceased. John straightened the quilt, added another log to the fire, and left the room, closing the door behind him.

The child stood waiting for him in the hallway, eyes widening the moment she saw his face. "Is Mommy awake?"

"No," he said, leaning into his cane. "She's very tired. It may be a few days before your mother wakes."

"She's sick, huh?"

"If it were possible, I'd take her to a hospital today. But it'll probably be a week or two before I can get her there."

"No!" Valerie said, shaking her head. "Don't make her go there!" Her eyes went glossy, wild. Her little hands tightened into fists.

He considered the child's reaction for a moment, drawing his own conclusion that it had something to do with her father's death. "In a hospital your mother can get the kind of treatment she needs. She'll have doctors to care for her and the proper medication. We have no choice. And I'm sure she would be much more comfortable there."

"No," she said stubbornly.

"I'm afraid the decision isn't yours to make."

He turned away and headed down the hallway. He entered the living room when Valerie ran up behind him and stopped suddenly in her tracks.

"I thought you were gonna help my mommy!" she cried, hands still balled into fists. "But you're mean, just like everybody else!"

He shot a glance over his shoulder then continued into the living room, seemingly unaffected by the child's outburst. John leaned his cane against the wall and settled into a padded armchair. The child walked right up to him and stared as if she had something else to say – something unpleasant.

"Are you afraid of hospitals?" he asked, eyes narrowed.

"No."

"Then what's the problem?"

"I'm not apposed to tell."

"If I don't know the problem, how am I supposed to fix it?"

"You can't fix it."

"What? What can't be fixed?"

"The problem."

"Which is...?"

"I'm not apposed to tell."

"I don't think you understand the situation here. Your mother was attacked by something. She sustained some rather nasty cuts that require medical attention. I'm not a doctor. I've done the best I could, but sooner or later, a doctor must look at those cuts or else she'll be left with terrible scars."

"No."

"Listen to me. The doctors won't hurt your mother. They're good people. Of course, they give shots, and those hurt. But that's for your own good."

"I'm not ascared of all doctors," she said and pursed her lips.

"Good."

"Just the bad ones."

John suppressed a smile. Like most children, this little waif seemed to have watched too many movies, which was probably where she got her morbid fixation. Good doctors. Bad doctors. Such an intriguing little creature. He wasn't at all sure what to make of her.

"Why do you think some doctors are bad?"

"I'm not apposed to tell."

"Then I won't be able to help."

John reached over the arm of the chair, pulling a book from the magazine holder on the floor. He flipped through the pages, not reading, just biding his time, listening to the grandfather clock tick away the seconds. A few minutes passed and he looked over at the girl, who now wore one of his T-shirts and stood by the piano. The clean, white shirt fell well below her knees; the sleeves went past her elbows, nearly to her wrists. If nothing else, she appeared comfortable in her new attire. She also appeared quite bored.

"Little girl." He paused, waiting until he had her full attention.

Her eyes curled upward, and she crossed her arms sulkily, as if challenging his authority. "Don't call me little girl. I'm a big girl. I'm Valerie," she replied.

"Well, Valerie, do you know how to read?"

She nodded slowly with uncertainty.

"Good. I have lots of books. Have you read *Treasure Island*?"

"No."

"If you sit by the window, I'm sure you'll have enough light. Are your hands clean?"

She hesitated a moment, then walked closer, holding both hands up for his inspection.

"They'll do. But before I get the book, I want your word that you won't bend the pages. If you get tired of reading, use a bookmark. Do you understand?"

He heard the woman's screams halfway across the house and grabbed for his cane. The child was already to the guest room, reaching for the door when John rounded the corner at the top of the hallway. Bear barked, danced in circles around John's feet as if unsure of what to do.

"Out of the way, boy!"

When John got to the room, he was stunned at what he saw. The woman thrashed her head from side to side against the pillow, as if having a seizure. Both of her hands were clenched around fistfuls of quilt. And the child sat calmly on the bed, hand placed against her mother's forehead, gently whispering, "It's okay. It's all over. The monster's all gone. I won't let it hurt you any more."

This was not a reaction he'd anticipated from a small child. So calm, as if the role of caretaker came perfectly natural to her. And in that same gentle tone, the child started singing to the woman:

"*This ole man*
  He played one.
  He played knick-knack on my thumb,
  With a knick knack paddy whack,
  Give a dog a bone.
  This ole man came rol-ling home."

Even when he walked to her side and placed a hand on her shoulder, the child continued her singing. The entire scene was remarkable. Within moments, the woman fell into a peaceful sleep. Valerie then got to her feet and straightened the quilt, saying confidently: "She's okay now."

John looked down at the woman, noticing a jagged scratch mark to the left of her nose, one that wasn't there earlier. He took a Kleenex from the dispenser on the night table and wetted it with hydrogen peroxide. While the child watched on, he carefully cleansed the wound then applied a thin coating of antibiotic ointment. "That should do."

The child regarded him with apologetic eyes, shifting from one bare foot to the other. "You're not mean. You're not mean at all."

"Now that that's been established, it might be best if I were to ask you a few questions regarding your mother. First, I'd like to know her name. Not the one you call her, but what everyone else calls her."

"Jill."

"Your mother, Jill, is she on any regular medication?"

"I don't know what that means."

"Was she ill before all this happened?"

"A long, long time ago. But not any more."

"The reason I'm asking is that you seem to know exactly how to calm her down, as if you've been through it before. If she has a medical condition, epilepsy or what have you, it's important I find out now. If she takes pills or injections regularly, then it would be wise for me to go back to where I found her and look for her purse. So, I want you to think very hard. It's quite important. Have you ever seen your mother taking pills or injections?"

"I don't know."

"Does she frequently visit a doctor?"

"No."

"Has she had bad dreams when you've had to comfort her before?"

"Only after."

"After what?"

"I'm not apposed to tell."

John exhaled sharply and took a seat on the edge of the bed, leaning forward until he was eye level with the child. "Is this secret of yours more important than your mother's life?"

Valerie shook her head slowly, her eyes glistening with tears of frustration. "Mommy said never tell or the bad people will come."

He braced her by the shoulder, brow raised. "And just who are these bad people?"

"I don't know. I only know when I see them."

"Then let's start there. What do they look like?"

Valerie reached above her head and stood on her toes, stretching to reach higher. "They're tall," she said. "And sometimes they wear two coats at the same time."

John nodded his understanding. The men wore suits and overcoats. It made sense.

"And they have radios like Space Ghost talks on, 'cept bigger." She swiped a hand across her cheek, brushing away the tears. "They have guns, too. Mommy says if I ever tell…"

Behind him, the woman moaned in her sleep. He shot a glance in her direction then returned his attention to the teary-eyed child. "I want to help your mother. But I can't unless you help me first. Regardless of what you tell me, I have no intention of letting anyone hurt her. Whatever trouble your mother is in, it's none of my business. Understand? My only interest is in her health, in making her well."

His little speech wasn't doing any good. The child just stood there in silence. "You're strong willed. I'll give you that. Would you care for some lunch?"

Shortly after lunch, the bad people came.

John sat in the armchair and found that the girl could not read. *The Scarlet Letter* by Nathaniel Hawthorne was open on his lap. Valerie stared at the book she held, *Treasure Island*. When he turned a page, the child followed suit, matching him page for page. He placed the bookmark and closed his book; the child did the same.

"Do you find the book interesting?" he finally asked.

Before she had time to reply, Bear started barking. The dog went to the center of the living room, spun in circles, dark eyes directed upward as if noticing a bird or squirrel nesting upon one of the wooden beams overhead.

"What is it, boy?"

John stood, hearing a faint thumping of a helicopter rotor in the distance. He visibly tensed. The sound brought back grief and painful memories of death: His leg had been crushed and trapped in the wreckage of such a machine. His wife and five-year-old son were not so lucky. Vickie remained alive for about two minutes, unable to move, her neck broken.

Little Ryan, the boy who wanted to grow up and be a musician like his father, fought for his life for nearly an hour, not once crying, although in agony. And then the fight was over. In all, five people had died in the crash. Only one survived. The accident had occurred at four-thirty in the afternoon. By nightfall, after an eternity of staring into the faces of his dead wife and son, the rescue team arrived. Up until that moment, John had held on to his sanity fairly well. Then one son of a bitch had the gall to ask for an autograph while he was loading John's stretcher onto the rescue helicopter – which was when John Mills realized an important truth: The world is filled with thoughtless bastards.

Now, the roar of the helicopter grew louder, muffling the sound of Bear's barking.

"It's all right, boy," John said tensely. "It'll be gone in a minute."

Following the sound, he went to the nearest window overlooking the front yard. He raised a brow and turned to his dog. "I believe we have visitors."

As soon as the craft landed, one man jumped out, falling up past his knees in snow, talking into a two-way radio. John turned again, this time talking to the child. "Overcoat. Black suit. Two-way radio...Sound familiar?"

Valerie nodded, frozen to where she stood.

"Why don't you go into the guest room and sit quietly with your mother for a while."

"Please. Please don't..." Valerie cut off in mid-sentence when the knock came at the front door. Her eyes flashed with dread and worry then she turned on her heels, running silently down the hall.

CHAPTER 5

John opened the oak door with Bear directly behind him. He had a skeptical glint in his eyes. His blond hair danced lightly in the icy wind. His right hand remained firmly on his cane, knuckles showing white. The show had begun. And he wanted to do it right. A badly frightened little girl depended on him.

"You're trespassing on private property. This had better be important."

The man standing a few feet away on the porch removed his sunglasses, tucking them neatly into his inside jacket pocket. A polite smile crossed his thin lips. He had an average build, but tall – at least three inches taller than John.

Talking over the high-pitched whine of the helicopter, the smiling man said: "Mr. Mills?"

"Yes."

"*John* Mills?"

"You seem to have me at a disadvantage."

"I won't take much of your time. You are John Mills? *The* John Mills?"

"If you're here on behalf of a recording company, the answer is no. If you're a journalist, I don't do interviews. I seriously doubt a run of the mill salesperson would go through the trouble and expense of flying out here just to sell a vacuum cleaner."

"My name is Brewster, Special Agent Kevin Brewster. FBI." He reached into his breast pocket and then flashed his credentials.

"FBI?" John repeated. All pretense of being annoyed by the man's intrusion had left him. This wasn't at all what he'd expected. But what had he expected? Mafia, maybe? A loan shark bent on revenge? A jilted lover hiding behind private investigators? The police?

It was like downing a glass of water, only to find out it was actually vodka. And yes, it took his breath away.

"How may I help you?"

"I'm looking for a woman and her small daughter who've been missing in this area since yesterday afternoon." He reached beneath the flap of his overcoat, and slipped a five by eight glossy print from a manila envelope. "I have reason to believe they're still in this area. Have you seen this woman?"

John shook his head slowly, reluctantly, as he studied the photograph. He thought about the woman who lay unconscious in the guest room; about the helicopter that could get her to the hospital within minutes; about the little girl whose fear of this man was stronger than the fear of her own mother's death. He tried to view it all objectively, logically, and decided this was the opportunity for which he'd been waiting.

"I can scarcely hear you. Please, do come in."

John gave the man enough room to enter then closed the door against the noise and icy air. "As you were saying?"

"I'm looking for the woman in this photograph. We located the abandoned van she was driving about eight miles south-southwest of here. Unfortunately, after last night's snowfall we couldn't pick up their trail, but we believe they may have been heading in this direction."

"How long did you say they've been missing?" John asked.

"Since yesterday afternoon."

John ran a hand back through his hair. Indecision had his stomach tied in knots. The simple solution was to turn the woman and child over to this man. And he would have, had it not been for the dread he had seen in the little girl's eyes. It was the same look his son Ryan had whenever he thought a monster hid in the bedroom closet. The girl was terrified. Understandably so. The FBI wanted her mother. And John wanted some answers.

"I'll certainly keep an eye out for them on the chance they survived the storm, which is highly unlikely if they were outside. Is there anything else I can do for you, Special Agent Brewster?"

"No. But there is something I can do for you. I can give you a little warning, a little piece of advice." He turned the picture over in his hand, regarding the plain white backside as if something interesting had been written there. "If you do run across Jillian Braedon, be careful. She's wanted for the murder of two of our men. Do you own a gun?"

"Yes." John's eyes narrowed sharply. It was one stun on top of another. "Surely, you're not suggesting I'll need to shoot the woman?"

"Just a precaution, given how remote this place is, Mr. Mills. But as I was saying, she's wanted for murder, among other things that I am not at liberty to discuss. I don't want you or anyone else taking chances, especially when the stakes are so high. You have a gun. Defending yourself is not a crime in this country."

Having heard enough, John opened the front door for the man to leave. He couldn't picture himself killing a woman, not any woman. And yet he knew he stood eye to eye with a cold-blooded bastard who could pull the trigger with ease. It was cause enough to believe the woman would not live long enough to see a hospital, should the trip be made alongside this man.

She was a stranger, a dangerous stranger who happened to be incapacitated in his guest room. Yet, he had saved her life, or so he hoped. After spending over two hours finding and dragging her back here, two and a half hours stitching the woman up, hour upon hour of sitting at her side feeding her water through a turkey baster, he wasn't about to hand her over to a man who'd undoubtedly take revenge for the two men she had allegedly killed.

"Sad to say, especially with a child involved, but doubtful they survived the blizzard," John said. "On the off chance they did, rest assured, I'll keep a watch for them. Good day."

John stood watching from the doorway as Brewster trudged through the snow to the helicopter. He wasn't out to defy the United States Government. He didn't doubt the validity of what he'd just heard. From what the girl had disclosed thus far, the two stories fit together neatly. However, although he hadn't come right out and sworn allegiance to the girl, it had been implied. The weight of that responsibility held him back, responsibility for both mother and daughter.

He waited until the chopper rose high above the house then he closed the front door against the wind. Bear whined at his heel. John absently reached down to scratch the dog behind the ear. He had a feeling Brewster would return. If not tomorrow, perhaps the following day. Hopefully, by then, he would come to a decision as to what to do with his two houseguests.

John had no doubts that the child had caught at least some of the conversation between himself and Brewster. Her behavior was indicative of an inner turmoil – something a child so young could not easily hide. For several hours afterwards, she moped around the house, keeping her head downcast as if in doubt of her own sense of reality. Her appetite was poor. She was peaked, restless.

And when given the choice between tea and water with her meal, she broke into tears and said: "My mommy didn't kill *anybody*!"

He hated to press it, but with the situation so dire he asked, "Do you have any idea as to why those men are looking for her?"

She drew in a shuddering breath, holding it for a moment, bottom lip quivering. "I...I'm not apposed to tell. I promised. It's wrong to tell!"

He pulled out a chair and sat down beside her, both brows raised inquisitively. "How old are you, Valerie? Four? Five?"

"Five."

John used her napkin to dab the tears from her face. "Then I think it's time for you to learn an important truth. Sometimes, life isn't about what's right and what's wrong. No. It's about what's best. When a promise is made in good faith, the only way it should be broken is in good faith, by doing what's best for all concerned. Your mother probably hasn't told you this yet, because it's difficult for a child your age to know what's best. But I believe you're old enough to understand that I mean you no harm. I'm on your side, whatever that side may be. I sent that man away. I told him nothing. Doesn't that prove something to you?"

The child stared blankly.

"Valerie," he began again, realizing the need to pick his words more carefully. "I want to help you. I want to help your mother, too. But if I don't know what's going on, then how can I help?"

"They," she said, then paused, swallowing hard. "They want to kill Mommy. And they want to kill me, too."

"Valerie, listen to me. The man who came to the door works for the government. They don't go around killing innocent people. Why on earth would you believe they'd want to kill a little girl?"

"Because I know things. I know about the monster that keeps chasing my mommy. And I sorta know why the monster comes: Something bad has to happen every time you be good. If it wasn't that way, it would be too easy to be good. And God wouldn't be able to separate the sheets from the coats."

"Sheep from the goats," John corrected.

Valerie paused for a moment, pushing the peas around her plate with the fork, tears slipping from her eyes. "Mommy and me move a lot. Once, a long time ago, she cut her hair real short and painted it blonde, like yours. She made me say that my name was Jane. But they always find us. Always! They found Uncle Richard...and he's dead. When the house got on fire, they thought they'd killed me and Mommy. Daddy was the only one home. I don't remember him, 'cept that his hair was brown and his shoes were real big and he used to drink hot coffee. It was a long, long time ago when I was little."

The child wasn't lying, at least not intentionally. He understood honest conviction when he heard it. And those tears. Her father was dead. Her uncle, dead. John momentarily lowered his gaze, finally understanding how someone so young could have developed such a morbid outlook. Her life had been one long nightmare. She was a little girl who had to grow up quicker than most, because she saw monsters and bad men around every corner.

"If the government is responsible for your father's and uncle's deaths, what reason did they have to do that? Think real hard. Because people don't kill without reason."

Valerie set down her fork and pushed her plate forward, folding her arms up on the table. The tears began to dry on her face. She sniffled, running a bent finger back and forth beneath her nose. "Do you know what would happen if everybody in the whole wide world was all healthy forever?"

"Tell me," he said to humor the child. Yet his mind was elsewhere, conjuring up a list of possible crimes the woman might have committed against the U.S. Government.

"Mommy says that after a while, there'd be too many people and not enough food to eat. Do you know what would happen if just some of the people in the world was all healthy forever?"

"They'd rule the world," John said with a nod. Still, his mind was elsewhere. It was difficult to fathom a crime worse than murder. Although, what he viewed as worse and what the FBI viewed as worse, could be two entirely different things. So what was it? Espionage? Was it possible for a five-year-old child and her mother to be a threat to National Security?

"That's what Mommy says too," Valerie said. "Those people would rule the world. And she says that would be very, very bad."

The girl seemed to have calmed down enough for him to ask about Brewster again. "Those men who are following you and your mother, why are they doing it?"

"I just told you."

John shook his head lightly, as if trying to rid his mind of fog. "Told me what?"

"They want to rule the world."

CHAPTER 6

Jillian Braedon opened her eyes briefly, not knowing where she was or who, then slipped back into a world of dream images. The mistakes of the past haunted her subconscious. They came to her, each one a still-life scene of black and white, blending together in a chain of events. There was the doctor's office, where she'd received a death sentence nearly five years ago.

Next came the dinner scene, when Jillian disclosed to her husband the news of the doctor's frightening prognosis. There were a dozen different angles of the hospital room in which she was prepared to die. A quick flash of her brother's guest room, where the plans were finally implemented, giving first hope, and then life. She gazed at the charred remains of the townhouse in which she had lived.

The next four pictures flashing in her mind were those of dead men: Jim, her husband, scooping the leaves from the pool with a long-handled net; Richard, her older brother, dressed up as a much too skinny Santa for a Christmas party; and two men whose names she did not know, but whose bodies had been clawed and mangled, whose eyes had been ripped from their sockets.

Suddenly, she felt herself running down a long corridor, lined with many doors. Walls, no longer perpendicular to the floor, oozed a sickening shade of red. Doors bulged and bubbled towards her as she raced through the hallway. She could sense something coming up from behind. Something she dared not look back to see. From far in the distance, came music. It was soft, relaxing, taking away from the threatening feeling. She stopped in her tracks and listened. A single instrument. A piano.

Then the corridor disappeared and was replaced with reality: a high vaulted ceiling and a four-poster bed. The haunting music, however, continued uninterrupted.

Her eyes connected with the eyes of the portrait that hung above the mantle, feeling as if the woman's strong presence resided within the richly painted canvas. Below it, in the fireplace, a flame crackled and popped, casting a flickering orange glow against the gray shadows of the room. At first, it seemed as if it were just another dream. Thick velvet panels were drawn against the night, leaving but a narrow parting where a slanting of pale moonlight cut into the large, stone walled room. Yes, it had to be a dream. But she wasn't asleep. When Jill lifted her head from the pillow for a better view, she had a throbbing headache to prove it.

Her recollection was clear – up until the time of the attack. And there had been an attack. She didn't need to examine her arms; it wasn't necessary to look beneath the quilt. The pain spoke loudly and kept her from leaving the bed.

"Valerie!" she cried, panicked, almost certain her voice had not carried over the music. "*Valerie*!"

John played the Steinway and Valerie stood there in fascination, following his hands with her eyes. When she thought she had the hang of what he was doing, she edged a little closer, biting down on her bottom lip, and a little closer, until she stood with her chin just above the keys.

"Can I play a song, too?"

The music stopped and she knew what was expected of her. Valerie held up her hands to show they were clean.

"I don't know, can you?"

The child nodded, eager to try.

The music ceased. The house fell quiet. Jill frowned while looking at the large, arched door that sealed off the room. "Valerie! Someone! Anyone! *Please*!"

Within moments, the door swung open on silent hinges. And Valerie, practically swimming in the white T-shirt she wore, rushed to her mother's bedside, smiling. "You're all better!"

"Oh, honey, I was...so worried about you." Jill reached up as if her arms were made of rubberized lead, brushing the dark bangs from her daughter's eyes. "Honey...whose house is this?"

"Mine," came a voice from the doorway. He moved into the room at an awkward pace, striking a match to the candle by the bed. "Good to see you awake, Mrs.

Braedon. Valerie and I were rather worried about you. How are you feeling? If the pain is bad, there's medicine for that."

She didn't answer, but painfully scrutinized the man who leaned into his cane. His accent was more than slight, but very smooth. The way his words flowed into sentences was almost poetic. Despite the cane he leaned into, his posture was that of a man of distinction, shoulders straight, head cocked slightly to one side, brows raised. She couldn't swear to it that he played the game, but he had the composure of a chess player, calm on the surface, intense beneath. His expression revealed no hint of emotion. If he was worried, angry or simply amused by her intrusion, she couldn't tell. Neither could she decide whether his cane made him less or more of a threat. His hair was a pale shade of blond, neither long nor short, but tapered back, surpassing the stiff collar of his shirt by an inch or so. His clothes – a crisp, white shirt and a pair of dark trousers with a thin leather belt – appeared to be tailor-made for his lean body. Most intriguing, however, were his eyes. She'd never seen any quite like them. They were blue, a strong shade of clear blue, with little flecks of dark blue giving remarkable alacrity.

"Mrs. Braedon, can you speak? How are you feeling?"

"Like I've been mauled...by a bear. Who are you?"

"John. John Mills."

"How did I...get here?"

He tightened his grip on the cane. It seemed as if the woman had never heard of him. Relief, in the form of a smile, swept over him. For once, it appeared he was about to be taken at face value. "I brought you here, last night."

"Where is here?"

"The desert, Mrs. Braedon. About twenty miles outside of Sandstone. May I get you anything? A glass of water? A cup of tea?"

"Water. Please."

After pouring a glass of water from the bathroom faucet, John tipped it to her lips. She drank a little less than half before guiding it away with an unsteady hand.

"Mommy, the bad people came today, but John made them go away."

"Bad people?" Jill repeated, eyes narrowing. She looked from her daughter to John, then back to her daughter, all without moving her head. "Honey," she said, taking on an anxious tone, "you didn't..."

"Relax, Mrs. Braedon. You've nothing to worry about for the time being, except getting well."

His reassurance had little, if any affect. She pressed her lips firmly together, drawing breath through flaring nostrils, and said, "What did they say to you?"

"Only one man came to the door. Kevin Brewster, as I recall. He had a picture of you, asking whether I'd seen you or your daughter."

"And then?" Jill asked, voice wavering.

"Then I told him I'd keep an eye out for you."

Valerie took hold of her mother's hand, squeezing tightly. "They won't find us, Mommy. Not this time."

Jill smiled weakly up at the little girl, then, with a roll of the head against the pillow, returned her attention to John. "You don't even know us."

"I know you're wanted for murder and probably for a lot worse. One of the things that make this country great, Mrs. Braedon, is that a man – or in your case, a woman – is considered innocent until proven guilty." And yet, she was guilty. Perhaps not of murder, but of something worse: the lifestyle she had given an innocent little girl.

"Thank you. You probably saved my life."

"Don't thank me," he said, no longer smiling. "Thank your daughter." He wanted to smile. Not only was she alive, but was also well enough to speak. Regardless, he wanted to be cold, angry. He wanted to explain to the woman – clearly as possible – that the only reason he hadn't cheerfully turned her over to Brewster, was for the sake of a five-year-old child. A child, he might add, whose life was being ruined by the irresponsible ventures of her own blessed mother. As far as John was concerned, any woman who'd expose a little girl to the fugitive lifestyle Valerie had described probably deserved whatever Brewster and his ilk had in mind for her. He wanted to point out that an orphanage would have been a better alternative to day after day of putting the child's life in jeopardy.

There were other things grating upon his ire: the lies that woman told her daughter. Valerie seemed to be of the opinion that it was she and her mother against a wicked, wicked world. While most parents assured their offspring that monsters do not exist, Mrs. Braedon stayed busy convincing hers that the bogeyman was very real, and that its job was to hunt down and destroy anyone who does a good deed.

He didn't want to sympathize with the woman. And he most certainly didn't want to like her. There had even been a time or two when he had considered how the child might actually benefit if her mother were never to regain consciousness. The woman's past actions were unacceptable by any standard.

Despite the onrush of anger of moments passed, he found himself sympathizing, anyway. Each time she flinched or winced in pain, his hand tightened on the cane. He worried that a stitch might break and hoped that the pain medication would soon take effect. She was pale, weak.

Standing here, gazing down at the woman, he found it preferable to believe a five-year-old's fairy tale of monsters and eternal life, than to consider this woman capable of murder. Everything he saw contradicted the self-absorbed image he'd perceived of her.

"I'd like to speak with your mother, Valerie. Why don't you wash your face and hands and use your new toothbrush. It's time for bed."

Valerie leaned forward and kissed her mother's forehead. "Goodnight, Mommy."

"Goodnight, honey."

John stood in silence until the child left the room, then said: "You've lost an awful lot of blood, Mrs. Braedon. You're fortunate to be alive."

"I want to thank you, Mr. Mills."

He nodded slightly, acknowledging, yet not wanting to accept her gratitude. "There are certain *things* you won't be able to do on your own during the next few days. If I were you, I wouldn't try getting out of bed without help. Some of your wounds went very deep."

The expression on her face was bleak, as if she were staring off into oblivion. She whispered, "It didn't kill me."

"Unless you need me for anything, I'm going to leave so you can rest. We'll talk in the morning."

"There is something –"

"Yes?"

"The ladies' room."

CHAPTER 7

He awoke long before the helicopter landed in the front yard. The breakfast dishes had been washed and put away. Firewood had been brought in from the garage. He'd completed four sets of leg lifts at the weight bench. Yesterday's clothes hung drying on a wooden rack near the living room fireplace. For the past twenty minutes or so, John and Valerie had sat at the kitchen table. He held up homemade flashcards of the alphabet. The child already knew the names of each letter; now, she learned the sounds they made. She had a little difficulty with the C, W, and all the vowels.

He started pairing up the letters, making the words NO and GO. The girl caught on. He added a T at the end of those words. Valerie said, "Note," and "Goat."

John pronounced the first word, "Not,"

Valerie pronounced the second word, "Got."

He offered her a smile of approval.

She paid him back double.

"You're doing well."

"Can I play the piano now?"

"Show me your hands."

She displayed first the palms, then the backs, fingers splayed.

"You may, but no banging the keys."

Valerie scooted out of her chair. As her sock clad feet touched the stone floor, Bear started barking. The dog dashed into the kitchen then went right back out, whining, barking, glancing around in all directions before returning to the kitchen.

The child's chipmunk face went pale, while one small hand clung to the back of the chair. Her mouth fell open and her eyes curled upward as she looked to John for some kind of direction.

John hushed the dog, and then listened intently to the distant thumping of the helicopter. "Valerie," he said calmly, "take the flashcards to your mother's room. Don't come out until I say."

Valerie collected the flashcards without hesitation, then rushed off, just as John had instructed.

He grabbed his cane and headed into the foyer, where he stood before the open doorway while the helicopter finished its descent. He then stepped out on the porch, already chilled by the stiff winter breeze.

Brewster approached in a brisk stride, removing his sunglasses. He carried a briefcase, this time, and greeted

John with a stiff but friendly: "Good morning, Mr. Mills."

"Special Agent Brewster," John said with a nod.

"Sorry to keep bothering you like this."

"Did you find the woman and child yet?"

"Not yet, Mr. Mills. I was wondering if I might ask a favor of you. Could I talk to you inside for a minute?"

"Certainly."

John showed Brewster to the living room. Bear circled around their feet, then the dog sat back on his haunches, keen eyes fixed on the intruder.

"What can I do for you?"

Brewster's gaze rested briefly upon the clothes rack by the fireplace. Both eyes then made an analytical sweep of the living room, lingering here and there, as if making a mental note of all he could see. "It's come to my attention that you and a few others out here have no means of communication." He opened the briefcase on the coffee table. "Since communication is important, I'd like to leave you this."

John stared at the object Brewster now held, but his thoughts were focused on the clothes rack behind him, where the child's mittens hung along with other items of clothing.

"It's a transponder," Brewster said. "Very basic. Turn it on and it sends a beacon. We get a fix on your location and we're here. By the way, if you find the woman, there is a reward."

"I'll keep that in mind."

"But only if she's alive."

"Yesterday, I was under the impression you wanted her dead or alive."

"That was yesterday, Mr. Mills. A lot can change overnight. Keep your doors locked. How good of a watch dog is that chow?"

"Excellent."

"If it starts barking, activate the transponder by flipping this switch. We can be here within twenty minutes, probably closer to five minutes. Don't worry about false alarms. We can deal with them. Don't try to approach Jillian Braedon. It's too risky. And for God's sake, don't let her inside."

John opened the hall linen closet where he stood for a moment, listening to the distant thumping of the departing helicopter, turning the transponder slowly in hand. If things went from bad to worse, he now had a way out. Help was only twenty minutes away at most. It should have made him breathe easier. It did not. He felt like a man under house arrest: the woman and child, his cellmates.

Leaving the transponder out in the open where the child might find it could prove disastrous. With that in mind, he placed it between two blankets on the top shelf then closed the closet door.

Three miles away, in what was once an abandoned shack, a soft hissing noise came over one of many speakers set up in the room, registering on a computer screen. It was followed by a muffled thud then all was quiet at the Mills' residence.

After dragging the padded chair from the bathroom vanity into the guest room, John positioned it by the woman's bedside and took a seat. Some color had returned to her cheeks. A thin scratch on her face glistened beneath a coat of antibiotic ointment and was the only cut, aside from the one that ran the length of her neck, not covered by either the quilt or the blue silk pajamas she now wore.

"Mrs. Braedon..."

"My friends call me Jill."

He cleared his throat and began again. "Mrs. Braedon, why are you wanted by the FBI?"

"You get right to the point, don't you?"

He smiled. "When it's important – yes."

"If I told you the truth, you wouldn't believe me."

He nodded with amusement. "I'll try not to be skeptical of what you have to say, if you'll try not to be skeptical of me."

"Mr. Mills, I appreciate your hospitality. Valerie and I would be dead if it weren't for you; I know that. I owe you. I'd like to pay that debt. And I will...by not answering your questions." She closed her eyes tightly, then pinned him with a steady gaze. "If you knew what I know, they'd want you dead, too."

Damn if he didn't like her. Here she was, a suspected murderess, and she had the most compelling blue eyes he'd ever seen. "They don't want you dead, Mrs. Braedon. They want you alive and are willing to pay for it."

The woman slowly turned her head on the pillow until she stared straight up at the wooden beam overhead. She lay so still for so long, had her eyes been closed, he would have believed she had fallen asleep.

John leaned forward in his chair. "Mrs. Braedon?"

She met his gaze directly. "I need a way into town."

"Even if the roads were passable, you couldn't make the trip. You're in no shape to travel, and there are people out there looking for you."

"You don't understand. I have to find out what's going on."

"That makes two of us."

"Do you have a computer?"

"A laptop. No Internet."

"Damn!"

"Mrs. Braedon, don't you think I have a right to know what's going on? The fact that you're here in my home makes me an accessory. If I'm going to be tried, convicted, and forced to serve time on your account, shouldn't I at least know why?"

"You wouldn't believe any of it."

"Try me."

Jillian Braedon asked for a glass of water. She drank a few sips then placed the glass on the nightstand. "My husband was a psychiatrist, Mr. Mills. He used to say that if you want someone to believe the unbelievable, and it's important enough, then you'd better have proof."

She pulled the silk sleeve up, studying her left arm. "This is probably the least of my injuries this time," she said, pointing to an inch-long gash just above the inside of her wrist. "It's not very bad, but it's enough to demonstrate my point."

"Which is?"

She gently massaged the wound with her thumb as she spoke. "My brother was a neurologist. He believed that if the conscious mind could assume full working control of the brain, hospitals would become almost obsolete."

Jill let go of her wrist. She brushed away the flakes of dried blood with her fingertips. The cut was gone, leaving behind nothing but smooth skin.

She continued talking in a calm manner, as if nothing at all had happened. "The healing process could be speeded up at will; the aging process could be stopped, reversed even. The more it's used, the more important sleep becomes. Some people might argue and say sleep should become nonessential. But it's proven to be even more essential than before the process...and more dangerous. Energy doesn't appear out of thin air. It's physically draining."

He reached out slowly, lightly touching her arm, letting his fingers confirm what his eyes had just seen. "My God," he whispered.

"Pain can be controlled through hypnosis. Physical urges such as cigarette smoking, over-eating, can be controlled through hypnosis. Under hypnosis, someone could suggest to you that caterpillars are crawling all over your body. And you'd feel those caterpillars, Mr. Mills. You might even claw yourself up trying to get them off. In a hypnotic state, men have been able to control the beating of their own heart, slowing it down until it appears to have stopped. The respiration process can be all but stopped...for a very long period of time."

"So I've read," John said, raising a skeptical brow. "But that...that doesn't explain what I just saw. You...Mrs. Braedon, if a person could heal their own body through simple hypnosis, everyone would be doing it."

"It's not that simple. Hypnosis alone isn't enough. Some doors of the mind are locked. A hypnothcrapist can walk you down the corridors, but he can't always produce a key to locked doors. However, there are keys. And certain people dedicate their lives to finding them."

"Your brother, the neurologist."

"He died because of what he'd discovered. Men of science tend to overlook the bad in favor of the good. They see the positive uses for their inventions. They're out to make the world a better place by providing clean nuclear energy to power cities. But there's always someone out there who thinks atoms should be split so troublesome countries can be annihilated."

John leaned back in his chair, unable to believe, unable to disbelieve...for he had seen it with his own eyes. The answer to all the world's problems lay in a four-poster bed in his guest room. He was staring straight at her. No pain. No deformities. No diseases. Every man's dream. A blind man could restore his own sight. A cripple could mend his own leg. An end to all suffering.

Immortality.

It didn't seem possible for medical science to have progressed so far that it now had the capability to produce a race of gods. Life eternal was no longer just a concept of the Bible, but a reality. Reality hit hard.

It was like the little girl had said: For every good thing that happens, something bad comes along. A side effect of worldwide perfect health would be over-population. And the question remained: would it ever be worldwide, or would just a few in power use it to remain in power?

"Mrs. Braedon." He paused for a moment, still in awe over the possible ramifications. "Those men won't give up until they find you. They'll never give up."

"I know."

CHAPTER 8

It was after one o'clock in the afternoon when Valerie knocked on the guest room door, proclaiming her hunger. John had completely lost himself in the conversation. He could have sat there for several more hours, listening to the woman speak. One of his greatest passions was for knowledge. And Jillian Braedon had a way of presenting her knowledge with both wit and charm. She was disarming. He was captivated. In comparison to hers, his life of world tours and packed concert halls seemed dull, without purpose.

John fixed lunch for the woman and her child, and then retired to the library with a lot of heavy questions weighing on his mind. The library seemed appropriate for the occasion because several volumes of science fiction graced the shelves. He felt as if he might be living in one of them now.

It was a small room, only fifteen by eighteen. One window, which faced the east; a single hardwood chair; and a small round table draped in lace, upon which was a candlestick, a pen and a legal notepad. Like the rest of the house, the library was well organized, set up for not just functionality but to please the eye. The books, all of them hardbound, were arranged into three categories: fiction, nonfiction, and reference. The fiction was in alphabetical order according to author. Nonfiction, alphabetically according to subject matter. The reference books, according to volume or practical use.

He usually came here in the mornings, when the sun was at the window. This afternoon, however, he hadn't come in here to read, but to think.

Keeping more than two fireplaces going day and night was unwise. They could be out there, close by, watching his home even as he sat here questioning himself as to how best to handle this situation.

It was a wonder Brewster hadn't noticed. A single man living alone in a large home would be inclined to close off most of the extraneous living quarters during the winter to save on heating – especially if the heating was through a combination of solar panels, gas and firewood. It seemed as if Brewster had overlooked two things which should have alerted him that John wasn't in the house alone: the smoke from several different chimneys, and the little girl's white mittens that had been somewhat camouflaged by the T-shirt she'd worn yesterday.

The bathroom heaters worked fine in small quarters. He hoped they worked equally fine with the bathroom doors left open so to warm the bedroom each one adjoined. And the piano...Valerie would have to find other means of entertaining herself. The sound would carry. If they approached on foot instead of by helicopter it could prove disastrous. Anyone within earshot would know that a child and not an adult sat at the keys. Neither could he allow the girl to go outside. Bear was a good watchdog, keen hearing, and an excellent sense of smell. If anyone came into the yard or even approached from a visible distance, it wouldn't go without Bear's notice. If high-powered lenses and listening devices were used from one of the nearby mesas, however, they could have the house under constant surveillance without alerting even Bear, which, given the magnitude of the situation, seemed quite probable.

John took a seat at the small table and studied the wintry view outside the window. The snow glistened as if made of granulated sugar. Its top layer melted beneath the afternoon sun and would turn into a hard crust before morning. The sky was a troubled shade of blue, with only a few gray clouds. For the past few winters, he had welcomed the snow here. It had given him that added peace of mind that no one would disrupt his solitude, because dead men don't feel comfortable in the presence of the living. And he was dead – five years dead. Or so he had thought before a certain little girl showed up on his doorstep.

John struck a match and watched it burn. Of everything that had been said, either by Brewster or Jillian, there were only two facts he could verify. One: Brewster was after the woman. Two: she did possess a special talent. He could understand the government's interest in the woman. The killing of her husband, Jim, however, mystified him. Even if they wanted the woman dead, it would seem the government should have need of men like Dr. Braedon.

The house had burned to the ground and, subsequently, Braedon's medical journals had burned with it. If the FBI were involved, it would make more sense had they seized the house and all its invaluable contents and taken the man into custody. But they wanted him dead. They wanted all documentation destroyed. Yes. They wanted utter control. It gave credence to the woman's theory: Only select individuals would benefit from the healing technology. They would be picked secretively. Sooner or later, however, the secret would leak out. Which was when the trouble would begin: Millions upon millions of people willing to kill for eternal life. Millions more protesting the abomination that could turn men into gods. Mass disorder. The Third and Final World War. Armageddon.

He'd be doing the world a favor if he went into the guest room right now, slit her throat, and buried her body without a marker. Jillian was the only person who could give those men what they wanted. According to her, there was another man who had taken part in the experimental surgery: Dr. Carl Neas. But as Jillian had pointed out earlier, Neas was probably dead. If they hadn't murdered or otherwise disposed of him, he must have taken his own life, as her brother the neurologist had two and a half years ago. Otherwise, they would have no need to capture her alive. Or maybe...they had another reason. Perhaps they'd come to the conclusion the woman couldn't be killed.

John lit another match and again studied the small yellow flame. Sitting here like this, trying to contemplate his next move, was pointless. He was either going to turn the woman in, or he was not. Lousy as it was, he thought it better that the world should continue as it had over the millennia: no immortal gods in human form, just men who thought of themselves as such. John's reason for helping the woman, however, was a little more personal than that.

Whether the world blew up tomorrow, or whether it remained intact for all eternity...it didn't matter much to him. But, he once had a wife. He once had a child. Had the helicopter accident turned out differently – had John died and his wife and son survived – it would be nice to think someone out there would watch over them. Dr. James Braedon must have felt the same way about his own wife and child. Subsequently, John found himself bound by his own ideals to three people, one of whom was dead, two of whom might get him killed.

When John came into the room, he found Jillian sitting up in bed with the pillow propped against the mahogany headboard. Her shoulder length hair was brushed back away from her face. Straight dark brows, blue eyes, full-bodied lips. By American standards, she would be considered a bit peaked. John, however, was not American born and therefore had a different set of standards. Yesterday, he had welcomed her back to the land of the living. Even this morning, she'd been in a lot of pain.

Now, however, as John propped his cane against the nightstand and took a seat, he felt a little awkward. He wasn't at the bedside of an ailing patient who needed to be nursed back to health; rather, in the bedroom of a vibrant woman, a handsome woman. One who made him feel both twice his age and half his age – at the same time.

When she spoke, she spoke softly, thoughtfully. "The woman in the picture...she's lovely."

John gazed silently at the portrait, as if he'd never seen anything quite like it before. Then he lowered his eyes to the fireplace, staring at – but not quite seeing – the dying embers. "My wife, Victoria. She was twenty-eight when she died."

"I'm sorry for your loss. Jim was thirty-five. He and my brother were the same age." She brought a hand to her stomach, wincing slightly as she sat forward and adjusted the pillow.

"You're in pain?"

"Some."

"But I thought..." He paused for a moment. The scratch was gone from her face. No marks remained on her neck. If she could heal herself, then why was she in pain? He'd sat in this very chair just a few short hours ago and witnessed the miracle that had vanished the cut above her wrist. And yet... "If you need them, I have more pills."

"No. If I feel the pain, I'll be more careful about moving around. I don't want to risk tearing the stitches."

His eyes narrowed sharply. His first reaction was bewilderment, followed by a cheek burning rush of embarrassment for having been made a fool. Within moments, anger turned the tips of his ears a hot shade of red. He knew what he'd seen. She had rubbed the cut and it vanished, much the same way as one might wipe a smear of lipstick from the skin. Of course, she hadn't used lipstick.

Whatever she'd used, it wasn't ordinary makeup, for he'd cleansed the cut on her face with hydrogen peroxide and it hadn't washed off. No explanation came to mind as to how she'd done it. She'd been placed in the bed completely unclothed and wasn't carrying around a can of instant cuts – if they made such a thing. Of one thing he was certain: He had been duped. And consequently, he had believed in her.

"Is something wrong?" she asked.

He raised a wary brow. "Should there be?"

"Something's bothering you. I've upset you somehow."

John reached for his cane and stood up. His smile became one of sarcasm mixed with wry humor. "Ahh...a miracle healer *and* an empath. You're a woman of many talents." He made his way to the door then turned around. There were a lot of things he wanted to say, but now wasn't the time. The anger over having been made a fool remained too fresh. John Mills needed a few moments alone to put things into proper perspective. So he left.

He found himself in the library again. Although the temperature in here was much cooler than the room he'd just left, John didn't seem to notice. He didn't care. His mind was preoccupied. He took a seat in the only chair and unfastened the buttons at the cuffs of both sleeves, rolling them up against his forearms, exposing an inch long scar five years old. His good leg was sprawled under the table before him. His fingers drummed softly on the arm of the wooden chair. Though he appeared relaxed, content, he was not.

Outside, the shadow of the house grew long against the snow-covered ground. A half hour or so of daylight was all that he had left. If he were going to use the transponder to call Brewster, now would be the best time. Now, before that woman tried any more tricks. Not counting his Uncle George, Jillian Braedon was the best damn liar he'd ever met. He had been totally convinced. Had that ludicrous story about brainpower been told by anyone else, John never would have believed it. It seemed so strange; until a few moments ago, he'd been willing to harbor a suspected murderess in his own home. A murderess! He could almost accept it, because maybe, just maybe, she had had good reason to kill: self-defense.

She had, however, no good reason to lie, not with him already willing to help.

The sound of light footfalls caught his ear. John looked towards the doorway as Valerie stepped into the room, followed by Bear.

"Do you think the bad people will come back?" she asked.

He rubbed his face. More to himself than to the little girl, John said, "Probably."

Valerie lowered her eyes until she stared straight down at her sock-clad feet. "I hope they don't." A single tear left her lower lashes, spilling on the floor. "They're gonna kill me and Mommy, aren't they?"

Once again, his position on the matter changed. The woman could go straight to hell for all he cared. But the child...

John shook his head. "No."

"But you said they're gonna come back. And they keep coming back." Her bottom lip quivered as she hitched for breath. Then she broke down and sobbed: "I wanna go *home*! And I don't *have* any home!"

"Everything's going to be fine," he found himself promising. He reached for his cane, but remained in the chair. "You and your mother are going to stay here with me until we can figure out what to do. Even if they do come back a dozen times, they can't search the house without a warrant. I'll even show you a good hiding place where no one could find you. Would you like that?"

She sniffled a time or two and nodded.

"No more worrying about the bad people."

Again, she nodded, though apparently not convinced.

"Are you feeling a little better, now?"

A third nod.

"Good."

Weakly, she said, "Mommy's getting better."

"Yes, it does appear that she is."

"Every time the monster comes, I'm ascared she's gonna die. I tell her...I tell her not to make the monster mad, but she does it anyway. It wants to kill her. Just like those men want to kill her. And even though I'm not apposed to, sometimes I get in bed with Mommy. And if it looks like the monster's gonna come, I sing and make it go away."

"Valerie," he said softly, hesitantly, "monsters aren't real."

She walked up to the table across from where he sat, cocked her head to one side with a puzzled expression, and said, "They are so. Mommy says!"

"Have you any proof to your claim?" he asked, resting both arms on the table, leaning forward until he was at eye level with the girl.

She shook her head. "I don't know what that means. Sometimes you talk funny."

"Have you ever *seen* a monster?"

"No. Not really."

"Because there aren't any."

Valerie crossed her arms at the chest. Her nose crinkled, as if she'd bitten into something sour. "Then how come my mommy got all cut up?"

Not only did he sense her defiance, but he saw it brewing behind her troubled blue eyes. There was also a flicker of doubt. It was the kind of reaction a child her age might have if told Santa didn't exist.

"Valerie, your mother was attacked by a wild animal. Nothing more, nothing less."

She took a step in retreat, then another, shaking her head adamantly as she went. "No."

"Just an animal."

"No!"

"Think about it. What reason have I to lie?"

"You'll see," she warned, backing slowly out the door, chin held high. "When the monster comes, you'll see."

Bear issued a scolding bark at John, as if choosing sides and followed the child out. John leaned back in his seat, propping an elbow on either arm of the chair, hands folded and fingers steepled before him. It had seemed so damned important to set the little girl straight, that he'd overlooked one very important thing: no child that age wants to hear something bad about her mother – especially if it just might be true. He had said there were no monsters. In effect, he'd called Jillian Braedon a liar. The woman was a liar. He knew it with absolute surety. That, however, was beside the point.

CHAPTER 9

"It's in here," John said, and he flipped on the pantry light.

Valerie followed him partway down a narrow aisle. Straight ahead stood a smooth wall. To the left and to the right, were row after row of shelving, running the length of the pantry and encased in wood at both ends of the wall.

Saltine crackers were stacked four boxes high. Earl Grey tea boxes were stacked even higher. There had to be over a hundred cans of Campbell's soup, the majority of which was tomato. One shelf was lined with bottled juices, half of which were grapefruit juice. John had clear Ball jars filled with pickles and relish, and an assortment of vegetables from last year's garden. A gallon jar filled with a pink liquid and pink colored eggs. Several five pound sacks – some filled with sugar, some filled with flour. Three large canisters on the top shelf – one marked: RICE; one marked: N. BEANS; one marked: PASTA. All of which stood on the left side of the pantry. The right side was equally filled.

Valerie crinkled her nose. "This don't look like no secret hiding place. If I hide in here, they'd find me for sure."

"There's a door in here, leading to another room. Look around and see if you can find it."

John stepped back so Valerie could freely meander up and down the aisle. She scooted a few sacks of flour aside, studying the wall they previously covered. She got down on her hands and knees, peering under a bottom shelf that hung less than a foot above the cold stone floor. On her feet again, she re-stacked the spaghetti sauce to make room for her hands and pulled herself up, using the bottom shelf as a step. Filled with curiosity, she jumped down and cautiously stomped her chubby feet on the stone floor as if afraid it might give way to a secret entrance that could dump her into some dark, dank basement.

Finally, after inspecting practically every inch within her reach, she turned to John. Her head tipped to one side. "You're not trying to trick me, are you? Are you *sure* there's a door in here?"

The cynical way in which she pursed her lips while crossing her arms made him want to laugh. She believed in monsters, despite having never seen one. And yet that same brand of logic ruling her brain protested the possibility of hidden doors. John went to the far end of the pantry, leaning a hand against the wall. "Are you sure you want to give up so easily?"

She nodded, as if eager to find the door. Or perhaps, as her expression suggested, she was just eager to learn whether there actually was a door.

"Watch what I'm doing." He reached beneath the second shelf from the bottom and pushed aside a six high stack of canned tuna to leave room for his hand. To make sure she saw what he aimed for, he hunkered down, favoring his right leg. He pointed to the button. "You can't see it; you'll have to feel for it."

She crept closer and nodded. With the press of the finger, the end wall slid soundlessly away, revealing a triangular shaped room, roughly the size of a pool table cut diagonally in half. Inside, there were no windows, no other door. Nothing but bare stone walls, a low ceiling, and brown carpet covering the floor.

"If the bad people come back," John said, "you'll have a good place to hide. There's a little button on the wall, just inside the door. Push it, and the door closes behind you. Push it again, and it retracts into the wall."

"What's it for?"

"The secret room?"

"Yeah. What's it for?"

"It was designed to hold a water heater, but I went with a crude method of solar heating, instead, which means when it's overcast and cold, bath water is warmed on the stove like we've been doing the past few days."

"Wow," she said, venturing into the triangular room. "If any kids come over, we could play hide-and-seek and they'd never find me." She turned a slow circle, gazing around with wide-eyed wonder. "I wish I could live here forever and ever."

Since stepping into the pantry, he hadn't thought about the woman once. He was, however, thinking about her now. He'd brought her soup and crackers about half an hour ago and hadn't returned to collect the tray.

Neither did he want to collect the tray. Because whenever he found himself in the guest room, all logic seemed to be left behind the threshold. He wanted to expose her as a fraud, while dreading that she might perform another "miracle" which would once again mess up his equilibrium. So, aside from warning her that the tomato soup was hot, John had entered and exited her room without saying anything.

"...cane for?"

"Sorry. What did you say?" John asked.

"Why do you use a cane for?" Valerie repeated.

"My leg was crushed in an accident."

"Does it hurt?"

"Sometimes."

"Once I fell down and hurt my knee real bad," she said, bringing her left knee up as if the wound of long ago could be seen through her jeans. "Mommy kissed it and made it all better. Then she told me not to run down the stairs no more."

She hopped on one foot for a moment, nearly losing her balance before setting the other foot down. "John...?"

"Hmmm?"

"It's okay if you don't believe in monsters. Once, I didn't believe in God. I thought if there really is a God, how come He don't make the bad people go away forever. That's when Mommy told me about the sheets and coats."

"Sheep and goats."

"Yeah," Valerie agreed. "Sheets and coats. But I believe in God now. You wanna know why?"

"Why?"

"When the monster came the last time, I prayed. I asked God to help me find somebody." She gazed upward, first at the ceiling as if to acknowledge God was somewhere up above, then at John's face. "I think God heard me. That's how come I found you."

"I'm going to leave the door open in here. If the bad people come, just run inside and push the button." John turned and went into the kitchen. He thought about the last time he had earnestly prayed. And yes, help had arrived...after Vickie and Ryan were both dead.

Since Valerie would be staying in his home for at least a week or two, John decided it was best to invent some house rules. First, he took her across the house to the laundry room. He helped her climb up on the washing machine, so she'd have a better view.

"This," he said while pointing to the gauge upon the wall, "tells us how much power we have to run the house. You read it like a thermometer. If the green dot is lit up at the top where it says 'float,' we have full power. That means all the batteries behind that door over there are fully charged. The closer it gets to the red area at the bottom, the less electricity we have. And when it's in the red, we have to be careful about leaving lights on and we can't use the washing machine, toaster, or anything else that requires a lot of power unless I turn on the generator. I might ask you from time to time to come in here and check the battery meter. And it's very important you know how to read it. Do you know your colors?"

Valerie nodded.

"Do you know your numbers?"

Another nod.

"All right," he said, pointing to the fifty, "what number is this?"

"Five, zero."

"Very good. Now hop down from there and we'll go into the kitchen. I want you to know which appliances you should never touch."

After going over the house rules, John went into the living room to feed the fireplace. It was getting late. The child should have already been in bed. "Time to wash your face, and brush your teeth."

Valerie pointed towards the Steinway. "Before I hafta go to bed, will you play a song on that piano over there?"

Even as he tried to think his way out of it, he decided which music he would play. It was one he'd written some eight or nine years ago, when Ryan was only two.

He took a seat at the Steinway, handing Valerie his cane. Soon, music drifted throughout the house, bringing Bear into the room. It was a quieting, peaceful sound that complemented the night. A child's lullaby of the haunting variety, composed for one Ryan Peter Mills, who used to run about in a pair of terrycloth training pants. Ryan Peter Mills, who loved Rock 'n' Roll, and by the age of four, could sing every song on every album his father had recorded.

John stopped playing in the middle of the lullaby and looked up from the keys, startled by the woman who approached him.

Stopping at a distance of perhaps ten feet away, she tightened the sash on the robe, smiling. "That was beautiful. Please...continue."

John retrieved his cane and stood up. "You shouldn't be out of bed," he said, surprised by the concern in his own voice, for it bordered on anger.

Keeping her distance, Jillian pulled up her left sleeve, showing an arm that bore no gauze, no cuts, none of the stitches he'd sewn himself, not even a scar. "I'm feeling much better. Please, sit down. That was a beautiful song you were playing. What's it called?"

"It doesn't have a name," he replied, feeling as if he needed to shake his head to clear his mind. The woman had done it again, thrown off his equilibrium. He was lost somewhere between fear and relief. He felt his stomach tighten. His shoulders went rigid. His neck muscles stood out, well defined. He tried to swallow, but found his mouth had gone dry.

"You wrote it?"

He nodded, for the words were stuck in his throat.

"Have you written any others? Something you could sing?"

Another nod. "Y-yes. A few." It didn't feel as if they were holding a real conversation, but as if they were exchanging dialogue for a vaudeville act; soon, the punch line would be delivered and they would break out in song and dance before an applauding audience.

"Would you do one? I'd love to hear it."

She had to be playing head games again, using the poor lighting and distance to her advantage. No other explanation came to mind. No matter how ridiculous her ploy, no matter how unfounded her claims, she simply wasn't going to let it rest. She was as brazen as she was inventive. He had no clue as to how she'd managed to cover the stitches and wounds this time, but the woman had found a way. At first, he couldn't make up his mind as to which boggled him most: her strange and needless insistence that her fabrication was real, or the nature of the fabrication, itself.

For perhaps the first time in his life, John couldn't think of a single song he'd written. Worse: he couldn't think of a single song, period. She'd turned his mind into a vacuum and he couldn't understand how she could be so casual about it.

John reseated himself at the piano, passing Valerie his cane. As his fingers touched down on the keys, the music came. His mouth was still dry, his mind still dazed, yet the lyrics followed:

"Murky waters.
Envenom the shores.
For a thousand tomorrows
Of yesterday's dreaming of you.
Carving your name in a tree.
Wondering where you may be.
What solace I find,
Is a ruse of the mind,
When I dream of you.
   "Midnight finds me
Out for a walk.
Alone with my memory
Of yesterday's dreaming of you.
Counting the stars in the sky.
Watching as life passes by.
The haven I find,
Is deception of mind,
When I dream of you.
   "Vast is the void.
Wicked, the curse.
Eternity's haunting
Of yesterday's dreaming of you.
In darkness the future was cast.
Blinded, I turn to the past.
Where illusions I find
Sweetly torture the mind,
When I dream of you."

The last note faded like a drawn out sigh. Silence settled over the room. For a moment, no one spoke. Valerie stood at her mother's side, holding the woman's hand against her cheek, the baggy T-shirt falling below the knees of her jeans. Her eyelids were heavy. Her body still swayed to the soothing music that was no longer there.

"You have a lot of talent," Jill said. "I've heard it before, but never quite like that. I don't remember the name of the group who did that song. They were popular fifteen or so years ago. But your voice...It's so much like his, the singer for that band."

"They called themselves *Stretto*. The piece I just played was a cut from the album, *Hidden Doors, Secret Rooms*."

Valerie tugged lightly on the sleeve of her mother's robe. "John has a secret room. He says if the bad people come back I can hide in it."

Jillian placed a kiss on her daughter's forehead then gave the little girl a hug. "It's getting late, honey. You should be in bed."

"Are you really feeling better?" Valerie asked.

"Much. By tomorrow evening, I'll be as good as new. Hurry up and get ready for bed."

She watched the child trotting off towards the hallway then Jillian took a few steps until she stood next to John, who now looked down over the keys of the Steinway.

"I don't appreciate the game you're playing," he said, soundlessly tracing a finger across the keys of the piano.

"Game?" she questioned.

John shook his head, lips pressed firmly together. He had had enough of this woman's stories and was about to tell her as much, when he looked over at her and found himself once again speechless.

The woman no longer remained in the shadows a few yards away. She stood here, right beside him. John found himself lifting the sleeve of the robe she wore, exposing her left arm. Stitches he'd sewn himself were gone. The wounds there had completely healed. Her flesh appeared smooth and touchable. Unmarred. It was true. But it could not be true.

"Has Valerie been much trouble?" she asked.

"No," he said. He believed her now. What choice did he have? "None at all."

"She seems to have taken quite a shine to you."

"Your arm," he said, raising his gaze to meet hers. His mind kept rejecting what his eyes insisted to be true. "Are you sure you should be on your feet?"

"No. I shouldn't be. The music brought me out here. That, and I wanted to talk to you."

John walked her over to the couch. She took a seat, settling gingerly, then repositioning slowly until she could relax. John remained on his feet. From his vantage point, he could now see that all was not well with Jillian Braedon. True, she had erased the worst part of the wound that had started below the curve of her jaw and angled downward. But, she leaned forward now. The silk pajama top hung loosely, exposing more than she realized. The stitches he'd sewn and the scabs that had saddled around them, were all that held the skin together at the jagged seam slashing through her breast. He understood. As she'd said yesterday, healing doesn't come out of thin air. Sleep was perhaps even more important to her now. The woman could only do a little at a time, resting frequently to build up her strength.

Jill spoke up. "I can understand why you've been avoiding me. I put you in a position of either questioning my sanity, or questioning your own. I wouldn't have believed me either if I were you."

"I-I...It seems as though I owe you an apology."

"No you don't. I owe you my life. Valerie's life, too. And that supersedes anything else. You have every right to doubt me. Sometimes, I doubt it, myself. I keep thinking I'll wake up one morning and discover it's all been a terrible nightmare. Immortality is supposed to be beyond the scope of the imagination. But I'm living it.

The possibility of never being able to die scares the hell out of me. Granted, the average man may wish to live forever. But as the saying goes: Be careful of what you wish; it might come true."

John experienced a strange desire to reach out and touch her, just to make sure she was real. Only with great effort was he able to refrain, posing a question, instead. "Had you been left in the snow, would you not have died out there?"

"I honestly don't know. Even when a person is asleep, or in a coma, for that matter, the brain continues to function. It keeps the heart beating. The lungs breathing. In other words, the body fights to stay alive, until there's no life left – all autonomically.

"John, have you ever screamed during a nightmare, waking yourself up?"

He thought about the weeks and months after the helicopter accident. "More than once."

"What do you think would happen if, instead of lying in bed, you physically acted out those nightmares?" She lowered her gaze, studying her fidgeting hands in great detail. When he failed to respond, she inhaled deeply. "John," she said, searching his face with a pair of desperate eyes. "I-I don't know how to say this, except to come right out with it. Bad things keep happening to me. And as long as I stay here...you're in danger, too."

"I'm not worried about Brewster," John replied. "He's not going to harm me. And I won't let him harm you or Valerie."

"That's not what I mean," Jillian said. She flexed her hands with anxiety. "It's *more* than Brewster. *Worse* than Brewster. So much worse..." Jillian glanced up then turned away, briefly closing her eyes to stave off the tears. "I wanted to tell you this before, but I-I couldn't. You...you weren't ready. I wasn't ready. Maybe you're

still not ready, but you have to know...I mean...I-I just..."
Jillian winced, bringing a trembling hand to her mouth.

A moment of silence passed between them. John took a seat at her side, deeply concerned. Some women cry without shedding tears. Jillian did so now. He took her hand, felt it tremble against his own. Her lips parted as if she meant to finish her sentence. But all she managed to do was gaze at him with misty blue eyes.

"Don't be afraid to talk to me, Jillian."

"I was attacked by something. Something... something horrible."

He gently squeezed her hand. "I understand..."

"No," she said firmly. "The thing that attacked me...It's going to come back, John. It *always* comes back. And every night, every time I close my eyes, it's that much closer. There's nothing you can do to stop it. If you get in its way, it'll kill you. Just like it killed the others. And..."

Again, Jillian brought a trembling hand to her lips, unable to continue.

"What is it?" he asked, still grasping her hand. "Jillian, what attacked you?"

Her only response was a shake of the head.

"Jillian?"

"Mommy?

Jillian drew back her hand, clenched her jaw, and put on the best imitation of a smile he'd ever seen. Both brows raised simultaneously in an expression of maternal delight as Valerie approached. And although the woman didn't speak, the false message she relayed to the child was perfectly clear: I'm fine; everybody's fine; what is it that you want on this fine evening, honey?

"I'm all ready to be tucked in."

"Where is she sleeping?" Jillian asked, finally regaining her voice.

"My room. I'll sleep out here. It's easier to tend the fireplace that way."

Jill tucked a lock of hair behind her daughter's ear. "Go get into bed, honey. I'll be there in a few minutes to say goodnight."

"But I want to sleep with you!" Valerie said.

"No."

"But what if the monster comes?"

"You worry too much."

"Bu..."

"No buts."

Valerie went over to the piano, turned around briefly to throw a sullen pout in her mother's direction, and left the room. Bear, who had been curled up on the floor before the fireplace, trotted off after the girl, tail wagging.

John broke the silence. "Instead of telling her she worries too much, why not tell her that monsters don't exist?"

"My husband believed in honesty," Jillian began. "He said the problem with most children is that they have no trust in their parents. Valerie wasn't raised believing in Santa Claus, the Tooth Fairy, or the Easter Bunny. At first, I thought it was unfair. I wanted to give my child all the magic I had when I was little. But Jim was adamant about it. He said if you start lying to a child, you'll eventually kill the trust. Once they get old enough to question whether or not there really is a Santa Claus, they'll start questioning other things they've been told. They'll begin to doubt there's a God, or if He too, was just a convenient lie. They'll question the values they've been taught. I don't want that for my daughter. So, I try to be up-front with her about everything."

"I'm afraid you've lost me. It sounds as though you're saying monsters do exist."

Jillian unfastened the top button of her pajama top, exposing part of the wound he'd seen earlier. "If there are no monsters, John, then how do you explain this? It's not the first time I've found myself slashed to ribbons."

"You were attacked by a wild animal."

"A wild animal? And exactly what kind of wild animal is it that hunts during a blinding snow storm?"

He almost said, 'a hungry one.' But he saw her point. The human race depends upon weather forecasts. Animals do not. Any animal that wasn't already in hibernation would have instinctively sought refuge long before the storm hit. Even a polar bear – and there were none in this part of the world – wouldn't be out hunting prey during a blizzard. It was...illogical. Almost as illogical as monsters living in the twenty-first century.

The woman was visibly shaken when she continued: "Remember what I said earlier about acting out nightmares? What do you think would happen if those nightmares projected into reality? And when you woke up from the nightmare, it was still going on. And what if it was a recurring nightmare? One that you'd have to live with forever."

"The monster comes in your dream," he said then wondered why he'd think such a thing.

Jill nodded, lips pressed together. "And this is what it does," she said, once again exposing the slashes she'd shown him earlier. "This... This is what it always does."

Calm from numbness rather than apathy, John added: "And you make it become reality. Your dreams."

"My nightmares. That's why I can't allow Valerie to sleep with me. And why it takes so long to heal. If all my strength was used up making myself well, I'd have no way to fight back when...when it happens."

John inhaled deeply, exhaled slowly. In a roundabout way, the woman had just informed him that, sometime tonight, something very unpleasant might be visiting his home. He wished he could laugh and pass it all off as a joke of poor taste. But something inside him grated, churned. Fear was too mild a word. Sweat beaded above his brow. His palms were moist, cold. The only thing holding him in his seat right now was his inability to move. All along, she'd been telling the truth. He'd doubted her several times along the way. But not now, for the woman had no reason to lie. It was, in its own strange and unique way, beginning to make sense.

"Holy Mary, Mother of God," he whispered. "What have they done to you?"

"I'll understand if you feel threatened and want me to leave."

"No. You have...no place to go."

"Valerie is safe as long as she stays out of the room while I'm sleeping. You'll be safe, too. It's not like it happens every night. Just sometimes, and they are specific times. I thought I should warn you, just in case you should happen to hear me scream during the night. No matter how horrible it may sound, please, don't come in. I can take care of myself. I've been doing it for a few years, and I haven't died yet."

CHAPTER 10

John had no concrete evidence that it would make any difference, but when he looked at the cross he'd painted on the inside of the guest room door, he felt a little more at ease. He had a relaxed smile on his face at the time. He joked about it with the woman, as if it were a game. But it wasn't a game.

John pulled back a drape panel and stood at the window. The darkness of the still night had closed in around the house. It was as if a thick blanket of blackness had settled over the windows. There was no moon tonight, no stars, and no wind. The boundaries of the universe were the cold, stone walls of the house. Beyond that, nothing seemed to exist. He knew he could put an end to the problem. Brewster could be here within twenty minutes. But that would be like walking out on a four star movie halfway through. Or closing your eyes when Linda Blair's green infected head spun circles in *The Exorcist*. Or worse: Throwing a young woman and her child to the wolves.

He said goodnight to the woman then locked the door behind him as he left, pocketing the key. Sleep would not come easy tonight. Despite the battery meter being barely above sixty, he left the hall lights on and had the lamps glowing in the living room, where he was to sleep (or attempt to sleep).

He laid there, fingers laced behind his head, eyes wide open, listening to the seconds ticking away on the clock, waiting for the nightmare to begin. Twenty minutes later, he found himself in the kitchen boiling water for tea. From there, teacup in hand, he walked the length of the hall all the way around, coming out on the far side of the living room by the library. He glanced over his shoulder as Bear padded up from behind. The dog whined, tail wagging, as if looking for reassurance. John had none to give.

Only time would tell if the woman was lying. And John trusted she was not. Tertullian's ancient words entered his thoughts: *'Credo quia impossibile.'* Translation: I believe because it is impossible.

Every hour, John looked over at the clock to find that only a few minutes had elapsed. Each time he raised his head from the pillow or sat up, he sensed Bear's dark eyes boring into him. The dog's tail would begin to wag, tapping the floor. The whining would begin.

At half past three, John found it impossible to keep his promise. He bolted upright on the sofa bed, took the key from his right front pocket and headed for the guest room door, each step whispering that it was the late hour

– and nothing more – that had his nerves on edge. He was certain that if he could look in that room and find nothing abnormal, he'd finally be able to sleep.

She had extinguished the candle not long ago. The scent of hot wax hung in the air. And something else: the light scent of fresh soap. It was warm in there. And dark. John gave the door a gentle nudge and took another step into the room. The hall light cast his long shadow across the center of the bed. The quilt was folded back, leaving the woman with only a sheet. She was on her side, both knees slightly bent. Her head, centered on the pillow, eyes closed, lips parted. Her legs moved dreamily beneath the satin sheet while her hand slid beneath the pillow. He had almost forgotten the pleasure of watching a beautiful woman sleep. It was a pleasure he could stand not a moment longer.

John was about to turn around, when something caught the corner of his eye. Shadow moved against shadow along the wall by the window, as if a timid breeze had touched the velvet drapes.

He made it to the far side of the bed, when a voice from behind whispered into the night: "Oh...It's you."

Startled, John spun around quickly, losing purchase of his cane. His right leg took the brunt of his weight, screamed with pain all the way up then buckled beneath him. His hand made a quick sweep in the air, grabbing for the bedpost to soften the fall. The post, instead, popped him in the chin. The effect was similar to that of being hit in the head with a lead pipe. He was jolted, dazed. His body headed for the floor and there was absolutely nothing he could do to stop it. Dropping on his bad leg finished the trick. He experienced a brief but bright explosion of agony, and then passed out cold.

A moment of disorientation swept over him when he first opened his eyes. It was the view, he realized, which made everything seem odd. His head lay on a pillow – yes. But his back was to the floor, the guest room floor. He lay parallel to the bed. The woman knelt over him. The room was no longer dark.

A smile crossed her face when she saw his eyes open. "How are you feeling?"

He brought a hand to his jaw, which had been knocked out of whack. Fortunately, his leg wasn't throbbing, but ached only mildly. "Like a clumsy fool," he said with a smile. "I must have been out for an hour."

"No. Only a minute or two."

"My leg."

"I'm sorry. It must have hurt terribly. I didn't mean to spook you like that."

He sat up slowly, carefully, expecting his leg to send another agonizing message. It did not. He smiled with relief, flushed with humiliation. "I've got to admit, it's not every day I fall head over heels for a beautiful woman." What he'd meant to say as a way to lighten the mood had a very serious tone. The tone felt right. As did the way in which her glimmering eyes met his.

"Do you, by any chance, like classical music?"

"Very much."

"Spaghetti?"

She smiled. "My mother was Italian."

It was kooky. After all, she was his houseguest and had little choice. But he had to ask the question. "Will you have dinner with me, tonight?"

"I'd be delighted."

Using his cane, he picked himself up off the floor. He went to the window, found it secure and overlapped the drapes. "I guess this is the part where I'm supposed to explain my being here in this room."

She shook her head lightly. "You came looking for monsters."

"Guilty, as charged."

"You're lucky there were no monsters. Curiosity kills more than cats, you know. Two men are already dead because of my nightmares. Granted, they weren't the nicest men I've ever met. But I'm sure they had families who loved them and miss them still. The responsibility for their deaths is something I'll have to live with for the rest of my life, which may be a very long time. So be careful, John Mills. I don't know you very well, but I do consider you a friend."

"You have a tactful way of telling a man off and making him like it. Goodnight, Jillian. May all your dreams be pleasant ones."

Her nostrils flared as she sniffed the air. Then she stood perfectly still, listening for trouble.

"Something wrong?" John asked.

She smiled nervously. "No. For a moment there, I thought I heard something. I guess it was nothing. Goodnight."

CHAPTER 11

John spent the remaining predawn hours in the library, conducting a little research into the woman's problems. What he'd learned from the books was very disappointing. The average first-grader knows more about the planet Jupiter, than the entire medical community knows about dreams and their causes.

His encyclopedia set was only five years old. He had purchased every yearbook. So, it had been updated annually with the latest information. Almost everything he'd read on the subject of Dreams, however, was conjecture. It listed very few facts.

About the only insightful information was on "lucid" dreams. And, of course, half the medical community didn't believe in lucid dreams. But several of those who did claimed it was possible to control the topic of the dream through a type of autosuggestion. Topic could be controlled; content could not. In other words: Even if Jillian could make herself dream of a grassy meadow during the spring, she had no guarantee that her demon wouldn't show up uninvited.

He could always sit at her bedside and wake her the moment she showed signs of REM. However, the facts were clear on one issue: REM sleep is essential. Which meant, he was no closer to solving the problems now than a little more than three hours ago when he'd come in here.

Outside the window, the snow began to glimmer beneath the first rays of sunlight. Another night faded into morning. The lack of sleep showed on his face. His sore eyes were somewhere between open and shut. His back had gone stiff from sitting so long.

He felt old.

John folded the book closed on the table, lit a match and watched it burn, finding difficulty in keeping his eyes focused. His thoughts grew foggy. Yet, he was still able to draw a logical conclusion: His time in here had been wasted. A psychiatrist and a neurologist – with perhaps two-dozen years of medical school between them – had worked together, had searched for a way to stop the nightmare, and had ultimately failed. If an answer to the problem existed, it certainly wouldn't be listed in an encyclopedia.

Regardless, hope hadn't died completely. It would be several more days before he could get to a telephone. Even then, the person he wished to contact might have moved. A man with a reputation like Mel Talbot's wouldn't have his number published in a directory. And it had been four long years since he'd last seen Mel.

They had met many years ago at a book signing. John had bought the book, *Knowledge Unbridled*, for his wife, and asked the author, Mel Talbot, to autograph it. The man couldn't have been much more than twenty-two years old at the time. Talbot wore his hair long, pulled back with a rubber band. He sat there with his young wife, who passed out bookmarkers. After the book was signed and handed back, Mrs. Talbot asked John for his autograph. The mutual admiration society of three then convened for drinks at the pub down the street. By the time they'd emptied three pitchers of ale – Mrs. Talbot, who didn't look old enough to drink, was all smiles and giggles after her first glass – Mel had enlightened John as to the unlimited possibilities of the computer.

He remembered the way Mel tapped the long ash from his cigarette, leaned forward, and whispered: "Every system can be breached. You can bring an entire country to its knees with a computer, look into top-secret files, or transfer funds from Margaret Thatcher's bank account into yours. I'm not saying a person should do those things. Hell no! It's highly illegal, man. I'm just saying it's...well... possible...*if* you know a few tricks."

Top secret files. FBI medical files on Jillian Braedon, compliments of Dr. Carl Neas? There might be a way...

The woman's screams shattered the stillness. Every nerve in John's body jolted, coming alive at once. Though morning had arrived, it was obvious that the nightmare had just begun.

The dream was a familiar one:

Jill is alone in Jim's Volvo. She's driving down a dark street. No streetlights. To either side are trees. The headlights only work on low beam. The gas gauge is in the red. She's trying to find an open drugstore. Valerie needs Ora-jel. Or, perhaps Jim is the one who needs the medicine; Jill isn't sure. She can't even remember getting into the car. She knows it's summer. The night air is heavy, muggy, and laced with fog. The street is deserted.

A car comes out of nowhere, riding her tail. Its headlights are flashing between high- and low beam. She realizes the driver wants her to pull the car over. Yet, she doesn't slow down. She can't slow down. As the fear lurches into her mind, she's suddenly aware her life is in jeopardy.

Her eyes connect with the rearview mirror. She screams with stark terror. The incubus rises from behind her seat. Its huge, grotesque body is slick and shimmering as if covered with black oil. It hisses, blowing plugs of maggot infested snot from its pig-like snout. It snarls, revealing razor sharp teeth dripping saliva and blood. Large, pointed ears fold back against its hideously deformed head. It leans forward over the seat. Jill momentarily freezes as the demon's long, split tongue laps the side of her face. Its breath is tainted with putrid rot.

Her foot slams down on the brake pedal. With the car still rolling, she throws open the door. A twisted, talon-fingered hand swipes at her face. She ducks, but not before inch-long claws part the skin on her cheek. She fumbles with the seatbelt, shrieking with pain and terror as she jumps from the car...

...and fell to the hard stone floor of the bedroom. She lay wide-awake, but the nightmare had not ended. She rolled over on her back. In another world, a dog barked, a child screamed and cried. In this world, the foul smelling creature loomed over her, its massive chest plated with armor-hard scales. Talon-like claws swept through the air in a taunting fashion. Its reptilian tail smashed against the floor with a heavy thud, jarring the room, rattling the windows, knocking books from the shelves as it swept back and forth.

She scurried to her feet and turned to face the demon, heart jack-hammering beneath her breast. "You're not real!" she cried. "You're not real!"

Its demonic laughter thundered through the room, simmering down to a wicked cackle. It moved closer. Slowly. Closer. Jill retreated, body twitching with fear, matching its steps, backing into the wall. The smell was foul; she could taste the rot on her lips. The creature seemed to be grinning at her with purpose and intent. Its demented eyes expressing they had all the time in the world, that each moment would be spent in fear and in pain. Then it hunkered down, ears perked, tail whipping back and forth, hissing, as its orange eyes made a sweep of the room.

From deep within its scaly throat came a low-pitched growl. It flashed a set of razor-sharp teeth, dripping slime and saliva on the stone floor. The woman threw back her head and screamed bloody terror.

Jillian's battle in the guest room wasn't the only war being waged inside the house this morning. Bear continued barking, growling, racing up and down the hallway. Valerie cried for John to unlock the guest room door. Her eyes had gone wild with fear. Tears coursed down her face. Her little hands had balled into fists, which she used to batter John's legs. He refused to unlock the door and she threw herself against it, pounding, screaming, "Mommy! *Mommy! MOM-MEEE*!!"

A heavy thud came from within the room and the whole house seemed to tremble on its foundation. John tried to pull the little girl away. But she fought back and fought hard. Frantic, her arms flailed; her teeth bit into the soft tissue between his thumb and forefinger, drawing blood. John dropped his cane and sacked the screaming child over his shoulder. Leaning into the wall for support, the little girl kicked and screamed as he made his way down the hallway, into the master bedroom, where he dropped her on the bed and pointed a foreboding finger in her direction.

"Stay put!" he ordered.

"It's gonna kill her!" Valerie squealed, jumping to her feet, screaming, "You gotta help her. *Pleeeese*! You gotta make it go away!"

John limped to the closet – the pain in his leg not even registering – and took down his shotgun. He cracked it, slid two shells, one into each chamber and snapped it shut.

"Don't you *dare* leave this room!" he shouted. "You hear me?"

He didn't wait for a response. There wasn't time. The woman shrieked again. He knew that sound. It was the same sound his heart made five years ago, when he realized little Ryan had drawn his last breath. It meant madness loomed just beyond the threshold.

It stood only inches away, snout twitching and oozing, ears standing like membranous bat wings on its oily black head.

Jill tried to bring her thoughts into total focus. She feared the pain. And yes, feared dying. But she had to focus. She had to do the one thing that repulsed her most: make physical contact.

On the third attempt, John jammed in the key, turned it, and as he threw the door open, the floor trembled beneath his feet. Nothing could have prepared him for the repulsive abomination he saw. He brought the shotgun up, but failed to pull the trigger. His instinct for self-preservation demanded he shoot. He could not; the woman was in the line of fire.

"Out of the way!" he yelled.

The beast turned on him, venomous eyes of orange. It took a step towards him, cocking its demonic head from one side to the other, thick tail snapping through the air as if it were a separate entity. John leveled the double barrel at the demon's chest, repeating his command for the woman to move. John heard himself scream, "*NOOO!*" as she jumped the creature from behind, arms clinging around its neck, legs straddling its back.

It turned a full circle, throwing back its head, screeching, clawing at the woman who clung to it. John grabbed hold of the bedpost, working his way to the beast. He brought the gun up once again, only to have it knocked from his hands by a powerful blow. The demon spun around. Its tail caught him in the face, sending him sliding across the stone floor onto his back. John regained his footing, hair falling over his sweaty brow. He grabbed for the shotgun, brought it up for a third time and was knocked back down to the floor with a sweep of the monster's tail.

The pain was unbearable. His vision went blurry. His head swam in a sea of dizziness, throbbing where it had impacted the stone floor, stinging where it had connected with the long, whip-like tail.

He managed to get to his hands and knees, but for the moment, could summon neither the strength, nor the coordination to stand.

The woman's arms were locked about the creature's neck. She didn't appear to be trying to strangle it, but merely trying to hold fast as it clawed at her again and again. He glimpsed a gash open up on her shoulder. Blood ran, soaking into the silk pajama top she wore.

Using the wall as a brace, John got to his feet. His mind screamed that it wasn't real. His body was sheathed in cold sweat. The need for adrenaline had his heart thudding triple time. He swung a fist at the monster's chest and felt his body being lifted. He was a good eight feet off the floor, suspended above the creature's head, in its powerful talon grip. And now, he passed through the air on a collision course with the stone wall. His life did not flash before him. There simply wasn't enough time.

Every bone in his body reverberated with the crashing impact. It knocked him senseless. He could no longer hear the evil hissing. His eyes would not focus. He lay there upon the floor, immobilized, wondering where he was, and how he had come to be here. John closed his eyes, welcoming the darkness that promised to take away the pain.

CHAPTER 12

Valerie stood over John, tipping a glass. Water spilled onto his face, neck and chest. He shook his head, opened his eyes, sputtering.

"Mommy said to get you some water."

"Valerie, I didn't mean for you pour it on him!" Jill said from the doorway, both amused and appalled. She went to her knees, taking the empty glass from her daughter's hand. "John, are you all right?" She swept back his hair, pressed a cold compress to his forehead, and ordered Valerie to get a towel from the bathroom to mop up the water. "John?"

"You didn't...by any chance...see..." He shook his head again, eyes wild with awe, entire body trembling with the memory. "That was the...the meanest, ugliest sonavabitch that...that..."

"It's gone," she said with a heavy sigh. "John, you shouldn't have come in here. I am so sorry, so very sorry."

"Big ...*Huge*. Its eyes...they were orange. *Jesus*, did you see *its eyes*?"

Jill got up, went to the bed, and returned, slipping a pillow beneath his head. His eyes rested on the blood drying on her sleeve.

"I should be doctoring you," he said, lifting his head, and dropping it back to the pillow. "How bad is your shoulder?"

"Not half as bad as that welt on your forehead." Jill pulled at her torn sleeve. "It's just a scratch. I'll be fine."

"Where did it go?" he asked, suddenly realizing he had reason to panic. "Where?"

"Back where it came from."

"I got a towel," Valerie said. She looked down and frowned, seeing the pillow soaking up the water she'd poured.

"Honey," Jill said, "there's a bottle of peroxide on the nightstand. Get it for me."

John attempted to sit, but instead propped himself up on his elbow. "We've got to find a way to keep you from dreaming. I don't know how you can live with something like that sneaking out of your dreams."

"We all have our demons, John. And we all have to learn to live with them."

"No. We have to learn to defeat them."

"Mommy, I'm hungry."

John turned his wrist, noticing the smashed crystal on his watch. It was, however, still ticking. And, unbelievably, it was after ten o'clock in the morning. He had been knocked unconscious for nearly three hours.

"How are your legs?" Jill asked.

He moved his left leg – no problem there. He moved his right leg, smiling and gritting his teeth. Although his bad leg hurt, it only ached mildly. He'd been knocked around, thrown into a wall, and the only evidence he had to show for it were a few throbbing lumps on his head.

"I don't understand it at all. My leg should be screaming."

"You've had a few hours to recuperate," Jill replied.

Valerie gave her mother a sideways glance. And for several moments it appeared as if the two females were holding a silent conversation. Jill gave the child a slight nod. Valerie shook her head firmly. Jill smiled. Valerie did not. Jill winked at her daughter. Valerie crossed both arms at the chest in defiance. Jill got to her feet. And Valerie ran from the room, taking the peroxide with her.

"I don't understand," John confessed, shaking his head. "If it starts out as a dream…? I mean when? *How*? How does it end up..?"

"Real?" Jillian supplied, filling in the blank.

John nodded.

"Remember I told you that pain triggers the healing process? It attacked me in the dream. It always does."

John's eyes fell to the two-inch cut just below her right eye. He frowned, noting her face had already been washed and the wound beginning to heal. Following his gaze, Jillian brought a hand to her face. "It did that in your dream?" he asked. "Is that what started it? How is this possible? Where the hell did that thing come from?"

If the truth repulsed even her, how could she ever expect anyone else to accept it? Or accept her. Jillian glanced around the room, wishing to avoid the topic altogether. "We've been over this already. I thought you understood."

John inhaled deeply through his nose, letting it out slowly, trying to contain the outrage that caused his jaw to clench to the point of pain. He finally shook his head. "That *thing* is not a part of you," he stated firmly. "No matter what you say, no matter what *anyone* says, I refuse to believe it."

"John, think about it. Dreams are a product of the subconscious mind. A person is the sum total of the conscious and subconscious mind. If *I* didn't exist, then *it* wouldn't exist. And that makes it as much a part of me as my own two hands."

"So you say," John muttered. "But I don't buy it. Now, if you can find me my cane – it was left in the hallway – I think I can get up and fix breakfast before everyone starves."

When Jill returned with the cane, he was already on his feet, one hand leaning into the wall for support. She handed him the cane, then took a step back. "Why don't I fix breakfast," she suggested. "You look like you could use a soft pillow and a firm mattress for the next eight hours. I'll bring you in a tray when it's ready."

"What about your face and shoulder?" he asked, wondering if he'd ever be able to sleep again. "I think you need to take it easy for a bit."

"Don't worry about me. I heal quickly, or have you forgotten?"

As promised, Jill brought in a tray with one bowl of oatmeal and two cups of steaming tea. She had visited the master bedroom last night, in the dark. Now, for the first time, she saw it in the light of day. John hadn't fully closed the drapes and the sun was shining in all its glory. She noticed how neat and clean everything was in here. She took a moment to examine the books shelved near the doorway.

Pewter statuettes – a dragon, a wizard holding what appeared to be an amethyst orb, a miniature castle – were enclosed in a glass case by the bookshelf. A large mahogany desk stood before one of the many windows. A tablet of writing paper rested on the desk, a pen crossing it. She could picture John sitting there, leaning over the desk, pen in hand, drafting love letters to a girl he knew in England. The stone mantle over the fireplace served as a stand for several framed snapshots. She didn't need to ask; they were pictures of his wife and child. Christmas. Easter. Birthdays. The little boy with the blond hair was Ryan. He had his father's amazing eyes.

She went to the nightstand, pushed aside a candlestick, and replaced it with the breakfast tray. She didn't want to wake him. He rested so peacefully. She studied his features, which all fit together to form a handsome face, one that, despite reassuring herself they had never before met, was eerily familiar.

Jill turned away, embarrassed that she'd stared so long. Her eyes focused on the platinum albums that hung on the wall, encased in glass. There were five of them. Jill now understood why John could sound so much like the lead singer of Stretto.

She gave pause and her attention returned to the man in the four-poster bed. She'd once wondered what happened to all those Rock 'n' Roll legends that slipped off the charts years ago.

Now, she knew what happened to one of them.

Jill left the room quietly, leaving the breakfast tray behind, minus one cup of tea. Bear met up with Jill in the hallway and followed her into the kitchen where Valerie studied flashcards of the ABC's. Jill took a seat at the table, taking a sip of tea before setting it down.

Without looking up, Valerie said, "You made the monster mad, huh?"

"I had no choice."

"You didn't hafta do it."

"Yes, I did. John's gone out of his way to be nice to us. The favor had to be returned."

"Couldn't you have just said 'thank you' to him? You didn't hafta go and make the monster mad. Now, it's gonna come back and hurt you."

"Valerie, if you saw someone being hurt real badly, would you just stand there and watch? *Would* you? Or would you try to help?"

The child slapped the flashcards on the table, pouting. "It's just not fair!"

Jill took another sip of tea. "Honey, John tried to help me. Even when he knew he could be killed, he tried to fight the monster. How could I turn my back on him after what he did?"

"You really like him, huh?"

"I think he's a good man."

"You're gonna make the monster mad again, aren't you?"

"I haven't decided."

"But John wants you to, doesn't he?"

Jill shook her head slowly. "John doesn't know. I didn't tell him about it. I don't want you to tell him, either. At least, not until I've decided what to do."

Valerie picked up the flashcards, frowning. "I know it's good to help people, Mommy. And I like John, I really do. But it's just...not...*fair*!"

"Look at it this way: You might have been dead right now if it wasn't for John. He didn't have to send Brewster away, either. He could have told him we were here. John stands to lose a lot if the bad people find out he's been helping us. He could go to jail for that, or worse. We owe him our lives, honey. Isn't that worth the risk of making the monster mad?"

"You're gonna do it, huh?"

"Probably. But right now, I need to take a nap."

"No!"

"I have to be brave and so do you. I want you to go into the living room and take a nap, too."

Valerie stood up and Bear went to her. "It's coming, huh? You hear the bees buzzing, don't you?"

"Yes. But it's weak because I just fought it a few hours ago. It shouldn't be very bad this time."

"I know, Mommy. But I'm still ascared."

Jill walked the little girl into the living room. They prayed together, hugged each other. Then Jill went to the guest room, leaving Bear to guard her daughter. She found the key in the lock. And when she closed the door behind her, she secured it, putting the key in the nightstand drawer. Bees were buzzing. Rubber was burning. The air was charged with electricity. Her senses were aware that something terrible was about to happen. As many times as she'd been through the horror, her fear of it had not diminished. Instead, it grew stronger with each encounter. Angering the demon was much like placing a single bullet in a revolver, spinning the cylinder, and putting the barrel to her head for one pull of the trigger. The odds were in her favor. Yet the more she played the game, the more dangerous it became.

She slid between the cool sheets, thoroughly exhausted. It was possible to put off sleep for a few more hours. John had tea in the house, coffee in the house, and she wouldn't be at all surprised to find a few No-Doze pills in one of the medicine cabinets. Stalling, however, wasn't the answer. If she had learned nothing else about facing creatures of darkness, she had discovered that it was always better to do so in the light of day.

And so she did.

CHAPTER 13

The scream woke him from a sound sleep. He sat bolt upright in bed, listening to another sound, one that brought him into the hallway. Valerie stood before the guest room door, singing at the top of her lungs. Bear stayed beside her, barking, tail wagging.

"What's going on?" he asked.

She didn't respond, but kept right on singing as tears slipped down her cheeks.

"Valerie?"

"...played four.
He played knick-knack on my door..."

He tried the door, finding it locked. "What's going on? Is your mother in there?"

"With a knick-knack paddy whack..."

He turned the child around to face him. She didn't miss a note. "Is your mother in there?"

"This ole man came rol-ling home..."

"Jillian?" he yelled, rapping his knuckles against the door. "Jillian, are you in there?"

He went into the kitchen, calling the woman by name. From there, he passed through the dining room and entered the living room. He hurried into the laundry room, and opened the main supply cabinet where the duplicate keys to the house were kept. John pulled one from its post in the cabinet, checked its label then, key in hand, followed the hall around to the guest room.

The child continued her song. She appeared to be in some kind of trance. The tears had dried on her face. She had gone pale. Her eyes were vacant. John slid the key into the lock, turned the knob, and slowly opened the door. He told Valerie to stay in the hallway. The child seemed not to hear a word he said. Yet, he was sure she wouldn't follow him. She was too caught up in her song, seemingly oblivious to everything around her.

It was still daylight. The drapes had been left slightly parted. The woman lay quietly in bed. If there were any demons in here, they hid well. For the life of him, he couldn't understand how the woman could sleep with that racket going on in the hallway. Forgetting the child's loudness and intensity, the sour notes alone were enough to make anyone cringe. Jillian sighed and rolled to her side. John realized that for the past several seconds, he'd been holding his breath. He let it out slowly. Hers was not the face of a woman having a nightmare.

Regardless, he worried. Because the scream that woke him a few minutes ago had not been made by a child. And the child had evidently lost her mind.

He left the room, closing the door behind him.

"Valerie."

She didn't respond, but started the song over again for the third or fourth time.

"Valerie!"

He went into the kitchen, returning moments later with a glass of water. "Look at me," he said. When she failed to respond, he tipped the glass over her head, dumping its contents.

She gasped, shot a glance in every direction then began to cry. "My shirt!" she bellowed. "It's all wet! My shirt!"

"Valerie?"

"Where's Mommy?"

He couldn't help but smile. The water had done the trick. "She's sleeping."

Her eyes widened with alarm. "The monster!"

"I was just in there and am pleased to report there were no monsters."

She pulled at the large T-shirt, trying to keep the cold, wet spots from touching her skin. Her feet moved, high stepping, yet she wasn't going anywhere. "You sure?"

"Quite. Come on. Let's find something dry for you to wear."

As they passed through the hallway, Valerie stared at the empty glass in John's hand then lowered her gaze to the wet shirt. She looked up at him, lips pursed, a question in her eyes.

"Did you spill water on me?"

"Yes."

"How come?"

"For the same reason you spilled water on me. You wouldn't wake up."

Her eyes narrowed for a moment then she nodded. "I was sleepwalking again, huh?"

"That's a very big word for such a little girl. Yes. You were sleepwalking and singing."

"Mommy says I sleepwalk a lot. But she says it's okay, that a lot of people do that. She says once, just before we moved to California the last time, she woke up and couldn't find me, 'cause I was out on the porch. Most times, she says, I just get up and walk around for a while, saying funny things."

John went to the mahogany dresser in his bedroom, opened the second drawer from the top, and removed a fresh shirt. "Put this on. I'll get a towel from the bathroom to dry your hair."

She had already changed into the dry shirt and stood over by the fireplace when John returned with the towel.

"Who are in them pictures up there?" she asked, balancing on the balls of her feet, pointing to the stone slab of a mantle.

"My wife and my son." He draped the towel over her head, rubbing briskly, hoping it would keep her from asking more questions.

No such luck.

"Where are they? How come they don't live with you?"

"They died."

"Who killed them?"

"No one. It was an accident."

She pushed the towel back from her face. Suddenly, she looked gravely serious. "Was that the accident you hurt your leg in?"

"Yes."

"But it don't hurt real bad. Not *real* bad?"

"No. If it were real bad, I'd be in a wheelchair."

Her face brightened as she flashed a big smile. When John lifted the towel, she dashed out of the room like a child with a fist full of money on her way to the candy store, tangled black hair flying behind her.

John left the yeast to dissolve in some warm water then pulled the flour canister from the pantry shelf. While in there, he inventoried the onions, which hung from a length of twine just inside the doorway. There were three, all firm beneath the papery outer layers. One would be needed for tonight's spaghetti to give it that 'homemade' quality you can't find in a can. The rest would have to get him through until the Land Rover could make it into town. He picked the smallest onion, roughly the size of a tennis ball, and returned to the kitchen, setting it on the granite counter by the sink.

His mind had drifted to this morning's horror in the guest room, when Valerie disturbed the memory by walking into the kitchen with Bear at her heels. Thankful for her company, and the diversion that came with it, John found himself smiling.

She crinkled up her nose then wiggled her bare toes. Keeping socks on that girl was all but impossible. He didn't blame her, though. The snuggest socks he had in his drawer were nylon socks – that still fell down around her ankles – and she'd said they were 'itchy.' John agreed.

She stepped up behind him. "Whatcha doing?"

He turned, setting the bowl on the table. "Making bread."

"Can I help?"

"If you wash your hands."

When she returned from the bathroom displaying clean hands, John gave her a tablespoon then directed her to the sugar bowl. "Have you ever made bread, before?" He had learned over the past few days that it was better to ask if she'd done something before, rather than ask if she knew how. Better, because, he'd get a more accurate answer.

She shook her head lightly.

"Measure four spoonfuls of sugar into the large bowl there on the table. Then stir it slowly until it's all melted into the water."

John found two loaf pans in the storage bin beneath the oven. He rinsed them then placed them in the dish drainer. As he fetched a two-cup measure from the cupboard and set it by the flour, he envisioned those orange eyes. It was a picture that would haunt him for the rest of his life – however long or short that may be.

He watched the child for a moment, listening to the clinking of the metal spoon against the glass bowl. It seemed strange, after so many years of cooking alone, to have someone else in the kitchen. Strange, but nice. She was on her knees on a padded chair. The T-shirt covered her jeans and all but the chubby pink toes of the little feet that poked out behind her. Her chipmunk face hovered above the bowl, wide eyes gazing at the mixture with great interest.

"When you're done, bring the bowl over here and pull up a chair."

He told her to hop up on the chair then tied an apron around her waist. Her job was to pour the flour into the bowl. His job was to mix it. Minutes later, he turned the dough out on a floured cutting board. Two sets of hands went to work kneading. By the time it was placed in a greased bowl to rise, Valerie had flour in her hair, on her face, on the T-shirt, her jeans; even her bare feet were dusted with it. Some even managed to get on the apron.

John looked the little girl over then removed her apron, draping it over the chair. "Now, we boil some water."

"How come?"

He smiled, ruffling her dusty black hair. "For your bath."

While they stood by the stove, waiting for the water to boil, Jill came into the kitchen, dressed in a terrycloth robe that fell below the knee. The calves of her legs were perfect, shapely, without even a scar. She too, was barefoot, despite the slippers he'd left by her bed. Evidently, going without shoes was a habit passed on from mother to daughter. Or perhaps it was the other way around. John spared the woman a smile.

She took one look at her messy daughter, head shaking. "What have you two been up to?"

"I'm making bread, Mommy."

"Sleep well?" John asked.

"Yes, thank you. And you?"

"It was short but sweet."

"How's your head feeling?" Jill asked. She came closer to get a better look at the welt on his forehead then reached out as if to sweep back his hair. Reconsidering her action, she withdrew her hand, and in the same sweet motion, swept a lock of dark hair behind her own ear...as if that had been her intention all along.

"Fine," he replied. "And your shoulder?"

"It'll be all right. I'm afraid I can't say the same for the pajama top I was wearing."

"Pajamas can easily be replaced," he said, flashing a smile. "I'm afraid I can't say the same for the people who wear them."

He used a potholder to take the first of three steaming kettles from the stovetop. And as he walked towards the hall, he realized he'd been leaning into his cane a little less than normal. He felt better than he had in a long time. He felt alive and knew whom he had to thank: the company he was now keeping. As crazy as it all seemed, as confusing, frustrating, and even frightening as it was, having Jillian and Valerie Braedon in his home was also refreshing. For the past few years, he'd wanted nothing more than to be left alone. Now, however, as Valerie walked at his side, he realized just how empty his home had been, how empty his *life* had been. He looked down at the little waif then turned his attention to the child's mother. The hell these two females had been through was just now beginning to sink in.

Ever since he awoke from his short but sweet nap, he'd been wondering how to broach the subject of enlisting the help of Mel Talbot. Of course, it would have to be the woman's call. Because, he had no guarantee that Mel – or anyone else for that matter – could be trusted.

John stopped before reaching the entrance of the hallway. "Valerie, I believe this bath water is for you. Ask your mother to pick you out a clean shirt from my dresser. Second drawer down. And," he added, addressing Jill, "feel free to browse through the closet while you're in there. I'm sure the trousers will be a bit on the large side, but you can always take up the slack with a belt. Dinner's in seven hours."

CHAPTER 14

Dinner was spaghetti with a meatless tomato sauce; cold water straight from the faucet; and home-baked bread, hot from the oven. It was John's first meal in the dining room, the first time the fine china had graced this particular table. And, despite not having the greens for a salad, or butter for the bread, the meal went well. The pasta was cooked to perfection. The sauce, although it came from a can, had large chunks of tender onion and could have passed for homemade. A selection of chamber music played softly in the background. The battery meter was in the green, but the room was illuminated by yellow candlelight.

Jillian had chosen a white, French cut shirt. Instead of tucking it into the black trousers she wore, she simply let the tail hang free. Around her neck was a thin, black tie that John had forgotten he owned. The gold tie clip, which she had found in his jewelry chest, matched the cufflinks. He had to admit she looked better in his clothes than he ever had. From a man's closet, she had put together a look that was totally feminine. She was also totally barefoot, which only added to her appeal. The woman was stunning.

Beside her, sat little Valerie, tomato sauce on her chin and a stain or two on her shirt. Her shoulders were level with the top of the table. She seemed so petite for her age and that chipmunk face and voice of hers had already managed to capture his heart. Jillian had cut her daughter's spaghetti bite size, but the child still managed to slurp it. Every time she took a drink from her glass, John was sure she was going to spill it. For her little hands were slick with tomato sauce.

Looking at these two females, was like looking at a before and after picture. To the left, Jillian at the age of five, sweet and innocent and full of mischief. To the right, all grown up – still sweet, innocent, and he sensed full of mischief. They had the same straight black hair, the same porcelain white skin, and the same almond shaped eyes. Even some of their gestures were identical. The way they tipped their heads to take a bite of spaghetti; the way they used the bread to get the most of the tomato sauce; the way their noses crinkled up whenever they smiled. Valerie would break many a heart in the years ahead.

Jillian was breaking a heart now.

He guessed she was at least ten years his junior. The age difference, however, wasn't the problem. The problem was that she was beautiful, vibrant, personable, intelligent, and he had little to offer in return. She had immortality. He didn't even have two good legs. There are times, however, when a man has to try anyway. And John was giving that prospect a rather lengthy consideration.

When dinner ended, all three pitched in. The dishes were washed within minutes. The kitchen had returned to its usual immaculate condition. It was almost like having a family again. It felt good. It felt right. After Jillian went to tuck Valerie in for the night, John turned off the CD player and retired to the living room with a book he'd been reading. Although his eyes followed the print, his mind was preoccupied. After a minute or two passed, he marked his page and closed the book. His thoughts were restless, jumping from one topic to another.

The room he used for storage was actually another bedroom. He could clean it out in the morning, and when the road was clear, he could go into town and purchase a bed. The woman had nowhere else to go. She could stay here, she and the child, for as long as they wished.

Brewster would probably come back and pay another visit. But after a while – weeks, months, years? – the man would eventually give it up and find another more suitable prey to stalk.

As for the woman's living nightmare, well, there had to be a way to solve it. Mel Talbot wasn't a surgeon. But he might be able to get the information needed to reverse the process...if such information did, in fact, exist. The next step would be to find a doctor. Perhaps Dr. Neas was still alive. Maybe, just maybe. And then again, maybe not.

The question on John's mind right now was: *If it can't be reversed, can I live with it?* Screams during the night.

His house being torn apart. The little girl begging, crying for him to do something, when there was absolutely nothing that could be done. Night after night, waiting for his home to be invaded and the terror to start. Orange eyes boring straight into his soul. Sewing the woman's flesh together only to find her ripped apart the following day. Could he care enough for another human being to put himself through a lifetime of hell? Yes. Maybe. Yes. But there was more at risk than that.

Another kind of hell would follow, if he allowed himself to care too deeply.

He could picture himself decades from now, seventy or eighty years old: age spots on his wrinkled skin, hairline receding, dropping his dentures in a jar by the bed...and the woman just as young and beautiful as ever. The whole purpose behind falling in love is to find someone to share growing old with. It could not be that way with Jillian Braedon. The ten or so years difference in their ages, would become twenty years, twenty-five. Little by little, he'd lose her. Then one day, she'd look at him with a mixture of pity and disgust.

But if she could become normal again...

John got up, threw a log on the fire then returned to the couch. He seemed remarkably calm for someone who waited for the whole world to come crumbling down upon him. He watched the flames consume the wood within the fireplace with great interest, the same way a man might lose himself in a good book.

When Jill walked into the room, he didn't even notice her, until she said, "Valerie fell asleep the moment her head hit the pillow."

She sat down next to John, folding the shirttail beneath her, crossing her legs at the knee. He met her gaze. There was an exchange of polite smiles between two people who were sitting too closely to be at ease with one another.

Then John said, "I've been meaning to talk to you about something rather important."

"If you want us to leave, I'll understand."

John shook his head. "No. Nothing like that. You're welcome to stay. Seriously. For as long as you wish. What I want to talk about is a man who once was and probably still is the best friend I've ever had, someone who might be able to help."

He spent the next several minutes telling her what he knew about Mel Talbot. She asked a few questions, which he answered, evidently to her satisfaction.

"Mel's the kind of man who'd have nothing to gain by turning you in. He's well known. Perhaps not over here, but in the Kingdom and other parts of Europe. He isn't after fame or fortune, although he has both. He's anti-establishment, likes worthy causes. A man whose ideals are those of the sixties. Best of all, he likes a challenge.

"You'd said Dr. Neas was working on a way to stop the nightmares. Maybe he's found a cure by now. If this Neas person has given that information to the FBI, Mel's the man who can find out. If Neas is still alive, Mel can find that out, too."

"We can give it a try," Jill replied, all smiles. But there was something in her voice, a reluctance suggesting the smile was for his benefit, that she'd been this route before and was afraid of the disappointment that was sure to follow. "It's better than doing nothing."

"I think we should start by tracking down Neas."

"How much will all this cost?"

"I have no idea."

She folded her hands over her knee. Nothing of her earlier smile remained. "Take a guess."

"Your guess is as good as mine. It all depends upon how far Mel has to go, how much work is involved, how much risk. If we're lucky, tracking down Neas will be enough."

"That could take thousands of dollars."

"To begin with, perhaps. But it will be well worth every cent if something good comes of this."

She shook her head lightly, lips pressed firmly together with frustration. "Maybe it would be best to leave things as they are."

"Afraid of having your hopes dashed?" he asked.

She tried to smile; the smile faltered. "There's a bank in Fairshire, Massachusetts, with over two hundred-thousand dollars of my money. I can't touch it. Jim had two life insurance policies, worth half a million dollars each. I can't collect it. It's mine, but it isn't mine."

"I'll make you a loan."

"I'd never be able to pay it back."

He could sense her pulling away, which was the last thing he wanted to happen. Smiling, one brow raised, he said, "But you haven't even heard my terms, yet."

"It doesn't matter; I'm broke."

"Why don't we put this conversation off until after I've had a chance to talk to Mel. Who knows? Maybe he's up for the challenge for the sake of the challenge. As I've already said, Mel isn't interested in money. At least, not the Mel I knew a few years back."

He sat in an uncomfortable silence for a few moments, trying to rationalize what he'd just offered. He had offered hope – nothing more – and now the regrets began to surface. There was a good possibility he wouldn't be able to locate Mel Talbot, much less have Mel Talbot locate Dr. Neas. There was even a chance that Mel was dead or serving time in prison for hacking or some other information technology crime. Certainly, there were other gifted people out there like Mel Talbot. Finding one, however, would be next to impossible. It wasn't as if he could turn to the Yellow Pages under the heading of 'Computer Espionage' and choose a name at random. If the information that would help Jillian could be found, there was no guarantee that whoever found it wouldn't take advantage of the situation.

Maybe the woman was right; it was best to leave things as they were. Otherwise, immortality could be sold to the highest bidder. And everything the woman had been fighting to hide would come out in the open. On the other hand, by not helping her, he would lose her. There were too many 'ifs' involved. Too much left to blind chance. He could be subjecting the entire world to utter chaos, all for the sake of a woman and her five-year-old child.

It would be several more days before he could get to a telephone, but it wouldn't matter if he had the rest of his life to think things through. There were no clear-cut answers. Only God should have the right to make such decisions. And it seemed as if God already had. He'd made man in His own image, with one exception: Men were born to die.

"You're worried," Jill said knowingly. "Worried that something will go wrong." The softness seemed to melt from her face. Her eyes were no longer gentle, but glimmering with cold intensity. Bitterness creased her lips. The change took place within the blink of an eye. Yet it was the smugness in her voice that hit him hardest, when she said: "Sometimes, I think it would be better to put a gun to my head and pull the trigger. I'm not sure that would do the trick, though. Maybe some explosives. Or a guillotine. Or maybe a dive off a tall building. I guess if I had any guts at all, I could always find a vat of acid and fall in. Rightfully, I should be dead right now, anyway. And I guess that makes me a cheat. Richard was the strong one. When he made a mistake, he always faced up to it. That's the kind of guy he was: selfless. I guess that's why he killed himself, to protect me…and I'm still alive. I'm a coward. If..."

"Stop it!"

"If I died, everyone's problems would be solved. You know it. I know it. They would use or kill Valerie to get to me. But once I'm dead, they'll leave her alone. Sure, they might do whatever was necessary so she'd forget everything. But then, they'd find her a nice home, with two caring parents. She deserves that, you know? She should go to school. She should be able to live without fear." She sniffled; bottom lip quivering, yet the hardness in her eyes remained. "I've failed her. Damn, how I've failed her. Do you want to know how she spent this last Christmas Eve? I'll tell you. In a parking lot of a 76 Truck Stop, looking for a car to steal. Great way to be raising a five-year-old child, isn't it – stealing cars in the middle of the night. I found a van with the keys in the ignition and a snowmobile in the back. You want to know how many presents she had to open Christmas morning? None. If I don't do something to stop this, she'll never have a normal life."

John leaned a little closer, raising a questioning brow. "Are you through feeling sorry for yourself?" His tone was harsh and evidently stung. For she drew in a ragged breath and held it as if she'd just been slapped in the face. "Do you think you're the only person in this world with problems?" he continued. His cold smile was equal to the smugness she had just poured upon him. His face was flushed with anger. "If you want to take the coward's way out, I don't want to hear about it. I have no respect for anyone who would try to take her own life. *Especially* a woman who has a child. So, if you want to kill yourself, you'll get no sympathy from me. None whatsoever."

Her jaw dropped, quivering. She couldn't have looked more confused, more embarrassed and upset had she found herself standing naked in a public men's room.

"But if you want to fight this," he said, his voice taking on a gentle quality, "if you need a shoulder to lean on, mine is always available. It's all up to you."

"I...I don't want to die," she said, tears falling down her face. "It's just that...just that..."

He took the woman in his arms and held on tightly as her tears dampened his shirt. Her hands slipped around to his back. She was trembling. She tried to speak, but her voice remained caught behind the hard aching in her throat. When she pulled away, she did so slowly, head downcast as if ashamed of her behavior. She drew both hands into her lap, shoulders sagging.

He covered her hands with his own. "Jillian." He spoke her name softly, gently squeezing her hands. For several long moments, the only sound was that of the ticking grandfather clock and the flames crackling in the fireplace. "I won't tell you everything's going to be all right. About the only reassurance I can offer is that you're not alone in this. Not anymore. If there's an answer, we'll find it. If not, then no one can accuse us of not giving it one hell of a good try."

"You...you shouldn't get involved in this, John. If something goes wrong..."

"Too late," he said with a gentle smile. "I'm already involved. And if there's a way to stop the nightmares, we'll find it."

"About my nightmares. I won't be having one tonight. I just thought you should know, so you can rest easy."

"You're not planning on staying up all night?"

"No."

"Then how can you be sure?"

She glanced around the room with blue eyes that were faded with tears. She already loved this house and the quiet kept within its stone walls. It was the closest thing she'd had to a real home in a very long time. And she cared deeply for the man who made her feel safe here – deeply enough to hide the truth for a little while longer. The nightmares were intensified by a conscious decision. It was not possible to stop them altogether. Yet, she did have an element of control over them.

No, she wouldn't have any nightmares tonight, at least none that could project into reality. Because, Jill had done nothing to rile the monster. Eventually, however, she would. If not tomorrow, then perhaps the next day. Conscious decision or not, there were times when it was unavoidable – like the night John had found her all slashed to ribbons; it was either make the monster mad, or allow an innocent child to die. Sooner or later, he would figure it out for himself. He had a right to know, but now wasn't the time. To tell him now would hinder the decision she had already made.

"How can you be sure?" he asked again.

"Just trust me, okay?"

CHAPTER 15

Originally, they numbered eight. The Braedon woman had caused the death of two. Now, there were six of them. Five men, all tall, all with dark hair and dark eyes. One woman, a redhead who went by the name of Laurel. They worked in eight-hour shifts, two at a time, monitoring the goings-on at eleven desert homes in the vicinity, via eleven receivers – each tuned to a different frequency. Although Kevin Brewster sported a wedding band, none of them had ever been married. They had other things in common, as well: no mothers; no fathers; no sisters or brothers. They shared three basic needs: to eat, to sleep, and to kill Jillian Braedon.

A gas generator supplied electricity to the one room house. Unevenly distributed heat came from an old potbelly stove, left here by the previous occupant. The floor was made of hard packed dirt and lent a musty odor to the room now that the stove heater worked steadily. The walls were made of old wood that smelled of dry rot. Opaque sheets of plastic stapled to the otherwise vacant casings served as windows. The roof was a pitiful sight of galvanized sheeting, littered with small holes as if a barrage of bullets had hit it. During the day, sun filtered through the tiny holes, seeding the floor with light. During the night, it was just one more way for the cold air to find its way inside.

It was not really a home at all, just a shack with an outhouse out back that reeked of ammonia, among other things. And yes, the outhouse reeked, too.

Laurel sat in the only chair, legs crossed, feet propped on the table. She had a cigarette burning. But instead of sitting forward to reach the ashtray, she tapped the ashes on the dirt floor. She was tired, hungry, and her butt was sore from sitting in the chair. She grew impatient. Brewster and Andrews were scheduled to be here more than twenty minutes ago. Laurel was not one who liked to be kept waiting. She moved one size seven foot just enough to tap Barnes in the ass, then said, "Why don't you give them a call. I've had enough of this shit for one day."

Barnes, who had been pouring lukewarm coffee from a thermos, took his Styrofoam cup to the other side of the room and sat down on the floor. He didn't say anything to the redheaded bitch. If it were that important for her to find out what was taking Brewster and Andrews so long, she could get off her skinny ass and make the call herself.

Barnes hated women. He liked to look at women, pretty women. And Laurel, that redheaded bitch, was certainly pretty. He liked touching women. He liked hurting them, too. And as soon as this Braedon bullshit was over, Laurel was in for a whole lot of hurt.

"Hey, Barnes. Did you..." She stopped in mid sentence, ears picking up the familiar thump of a distant helicopter. Her feet dropped to the floor as her hand swept the table in search of a pen. The job they expected her to perform was a simple one, so simple that it was positively boring. She listened to the receiver and jotted down the time of day each receiver picked up voices, doing so on the corresponding tablet of paper. She didn't need to write down what was said, because the computer handled that. She really didn't need to write anything. Brewster liked to hand out as much busy work as possible. Even when there was not a single good reason. Boring.

Just the same, when Brewster and Andrews walked through the door, Laurel wanted to look busy. Not because she liked either of the two men. Not because she had any respect for them. It was only a matter of appearance.

Barnes greeted the relief team at the door, weary from having spent eight full hours listening to Laurel bitch and complain. It was always the same old song and dance with that woman. She trusted no one, hated everyone, and made her grievances known only to the poor sucker who was trapped into working on her shift. And the poor sucker always happened to be Barnes. He knew he ranked low on the totem pole, but he didn't know why. No one – not even Brewster – had a satisfactory answer for that. Brewster pretended to know, but he appeared just as much in the dark about the affair as the other five. The whole thing stunk like a bowl of rotten potatoes.

Who am I? He'd asked on at least a hundred occasions.

Brewster's reply was always the same: *You're FBI.*

I know that. But Who Am I?

It nagged him throughout the day, plagued him in haunting dreams at night. It was difficult to believe the fucking FBI could program a person to forget and to keep on forgetting more and more things. Events that had taken place as recently as two weeks ago were already lost to him. Yet, the facts remained firmly in his mind. He knew, for instance, that they'd been looking for the Braedon woman for the past three and a half years. How he knew such a thing, remained a mystery.

A man, thirty years old, remembers his ABC's – of course, he does. He cannot, however, remember who taught him. He knows he went to kindergarten, but cannot recall the teacher's name. Neither can he remember anything about the classroom, or the children with whom he had played. It's all been wiped away. And yet, the knowledge acquired during those years remains intact.

Yes, it was natural to forget something that happened twenty-five years ago. But two weeks ago? He knew two of the men he'd worked with were dead. The cause: Jillian Braedon. He could not, however, try as he may, remember their faces or anything else about those two men. They were dead; the woman was responsible – simple facts. Brewster had explained that it was done in such a way so they could focus more clearly on their jobs. That, and for security purposes. Take away a man's past, and he can't blab classified information to the public. Bullshit! Barnes wanted a better explanation than that. And he had the feeling the answer would only be found once the business with Jillian Braedon had been resolved.

Brewster slipped his sunglasses into the breast pocket of his silk lined jacket as he walked to the table where Laurel sat. "Anything?" he asked.

"No," she replied. "The Foremans and the Garcias have had their TV's on all day. I mean *all* day. I think, even being voice-activated, their batteries are going to go dead soon. Some kid at the Greck's house has been screaming off and on. The parents were talking about using the transponder to see if you might take them and their kid to the doctor. Oh, and the Kearneys are contemplating divorce. And then we've got several hours recorded of 'fuck yous' from the Detmer's house. Last but not least, Mr. and Mrs. Bain are thinking about growing a crop of marijuana in the spring to supplement their Social Security."

"Nothing from the other five?" Brewster asked.

"Not that amounts to anything."

Brewster stood over the area map on the table. He took a pen from his pocket, drawing a circle in red ink, and tapping the pen in the center. "We've located the snowmobile that belongs to the owner of the stolen van. It was right about here, about two miles from where we are now," he said, again tapping the pen on the map. "I think it's safe to rule out the Foremans, Koviches, Gutierrezes, and the Kearneys. And I doubt she and the child could have made it to the Detmer's before the blizzard blew in. We'll narrow our focus to the six remaining. If we could ascertain whether she and the child had continued in the direction they were travelling, it would narrow it down even more. We'd be left with the Garcias and John Mills."

Barnes walked over to the table, and studied the map with great interest. "We could save a lot of time and frustration by going into those houses and looking around."

"Can't without a warrant," Laurel reminded him. "To get a warrant, you'll need probable cause. Would you like to stand before a judge, Barnes, and explain what we've been doing for the past three and a half years?"

Barnes shook his head. "Fuck the warrant. We're FBI. Those people are so far out in the desert, we could blow them all away and months would pass before anyone found the bodies. Besides, we're running low on funds, as usual. You said so yourself, Brewster, just yesterday. We kill them, take any cash and valuables we find, and in the process get the Braedon woman. Sounds like an answer to all our problems."

Brewster dropped a hand on Barnes' shoulder. "You're forgetting something. One of those who you're talking about blowing away is a celebrity. We could deep-six the rest and it would be forgotten in a month. People are murdered every day. But when it comes to a celebrity, especially one as well known as Mills, there's apt to be one hell of a stink raised."

"I still think we should conduct a house by house search," Barnes said. The tips of his ears were burning red. He hated being low man on the totem pole. Hated it with a passion. Too many of his good ideas could go to waste because of it. He wasn't about to let it happen. Not when they were so close to finding the Braedon bitch. Not when he was so close to finding out why he couldn't remember who he really was. "Look, if anyone refuses to have their home searched, it'll point to their guilt. Then, we'll know. We'll know, damn it. It's better than sitting around here twiddling our thumbs."

"He's right," Andrews said, dipping both hands into his pants pockets. Andrews was a man of few words, which was why when he did speak, Brewster listened.

"We have to get to them before they have the opportunity to transport the woman into town. Otherwise, we'll lose her...*again*." He smiled lightly, confident they wouldn't find the woman. After all, she'd done a fairly good job of eluding them for the past three and a half years.

CHAPTER 16

John had to take a lengthy moment to consider his answer. He was exhausted, it was late, but the woman appeared more than mildly curious. It seemed important for her to know the truth, as if his response might somehow have an impact on her life. He'd realized that the question would be asked sooner or later. And now that it faced him, his mind seemed numb; the palms of his hands had turned moist. He knew the feeling well. Its name was apprehension.

Jillian had thanked him for his help, and now she wanted to know why. Why would he help her? He had reasons – several of them. Putting them into words, however, would be difficult. Because, as he'd learned a long time ago, the truth is usually a disappointment.

There was more to it than that, much more. Being in the music business was very much like being an actor. He would put on a show, never letting anyone know or get close to the real John Mills. The man seen on stage was little more than a fictitious character, an illusion he'd created to whet the appetites of potential record buyers. The real John Mills – a man who enjoyed doing sketches, listening to classical music, and quiet evenings alone with a good book – would have been a big disappointment to the thousands of screaming fans. Subsequently, he kept his private life to himself. Otherwise, comparisons would be made. Questions would be asked. Expectations would be dashed. Record sales would plummet.

Now, however, he had no screaming fans, no record or CD sales on the line. It was just he and the woman. Yet the apprehension remained. He worried what she might think once she learned the truth, that he was not the hero she believed, rather an ordinary, average guy with his own share of faults. The least of which was a bum leg.

First, he hadn't been able to turn his back on a badly frightened little girl. Of course, that all happened before he realized what he'd gotten himself into. So it had started out with something simple. His action wasn't heroic, only humane. He could take no credit for not turning away a freezing five-year-old child.

Second, he found himself in a position of responsibility. He had saved someone's life and didn't want Brewster to undo those laborious efforts. He wasn't some Good Samaritan out trying to win points with God. Not at all. What he felt for the human race was nothing short of contempt. He had dropped out of society because people, in general, are greedy sonsabitches who care only for themselves. If they would ask for an autograph from a critically injured man whose wife and son were laying dead less than ten feet away in the rubble of a helicopter crash, then nothing was beneath them. Regardless, John had to live with John. He was no Good Samaritan. He just had one hellava conscience to contend with, and he didn't want it eating at him for the rest of his life. Nothing heroic there.

Reasons three and four were not acts of heroism, either. He wanted to help the woman and her child because, in a strange kind of way, he was making up for the loss of his own family. A psychiatrist would have a good time analyzing that. And Jillian, having been the wife of one, probably understood the workings of the human mind better than most. More than likely, she'd be insulted. For it wasn't she who John had gone after during a blizzard and stitched up; rather, his deceased wife. And within a short time of saving Jillian – or the ghost of his wife – he had become aware of the potential danger should a small group of people own the secrets of eternal life. Again, selfishness. He didn't want to shoulder the blame for screwing up an already screwed-up world.

Reason five, was only semi-selfish. Jillian Braedon and her daughter had become the most important people in his life. He couldn't read more than a few moments without pausing to think of the woman. He couldn't walk the hallway at night without stopping by her room, resting a hand upon the door, and recalling her smile, her laughter, and her soft and feminine voice. Although he had already come to the conclusion that there was no future in it for him, he felt compelled to do anything within his means to ensure the safety of both mother and daughter. He'd never met anyone quite like Jillian. All preternatural abilities aside, she was still fascinating. He liked classical music. She liked classical music. She had complimented him on the details of his home. He'd failed to tell her so, but he had drawn up the blueprints himself. There was something about her that seemed positively medieval in nature: porcelain white skin contrasted by her jet black hair; subtle gestures that were also quite bold; glimmering blue eyes that spoke of a mystical intelligence. She belonged in this house, perhaps more than John himself did. It would have been a match made in Heaven, had the surrounding circumstances not come straight from the bowels of Hell.

Why would he help this woman? Simple, yet not so simple for him to put into words and come out a winner in her eyes. John Mills was powerless to do anything but. As frightening as it was to have so little control, just sitting here at her side – being the recipient of her warm and gentle smile – made it all worth his while.

"You're not going to tell me why, are you?" she prodded.

He smiled half a smile. Using her earlier words against her, he said, "Just trust me, okay?"

Her eyes glimmered as if she found his remark amusing. "My father once warned me about men who speak of blind trust."

"Ahh...But I'm not like all those other men," he quipped.

"How so?"

"I'm sincere." And the moment he spoke those two words, he did, in fact, appear quite sincere. He met her gaze, openly. Had it not been for the twitch at the corner of his mouth, he'd have carried the illusion off perfectly.

"And modest," she added with a smile.

"Quite."

Her smile broadened. "I'm serious about that. You've got to be the most modest man I've ever met. There are five platinum albums hanging on your bedroom wall – five! – and yet you act as though you're no different than anyone else. You haven't even mentioned it once."

"It's not as if I came up with a cure for cancer, or single-handedly conquered the problem of world hunger. I write songs. A lot of people write songs. I'm just one of the lucky ones; that's all."

She shook her head in disbelief. "But they're beautiful songs."

"You'd have written beautiful songs too, had the world been placed in your back pocket at the age of seventeen."

"See," she said. "Right there. That's just what I mean. The words you use. You're poetic by nature."

He had a strong passion for words, which was why he read so much, and why, when the mood struck, words became poetry and poetry was put to song. Nevertheless, he wanted to deny it because it was at exactly that point where the on-stage personality and the real John became the same person. And if they became the same in that one instance, then they could also be the same in everything else. It was difficult to believe that the man who lingered backstage with a bad case of nervous jitters and a glass of fizzling Alka-Seltzer, was the same carefree man who emerged on stage, in complete control before the masses. Very difficult indeed. Because the former was a private man who kept to himself, and the latter lived for the applause, for the cheering, for the women – young and old – who'd rush the stage in a crazed frenzy with only one thing in mind. And damn if he hadn't enjoyed the attention.

"If we do find Dr. Neas," he began, deliberately changing the subject, "if there is a way to reverse what's been done to you, you may have to make a very difficult decision. Getting rid of the nightmares may involve giving up something else. It's possible the only way to help you, is to make you like everyone else. No eternal life, no more being able to heal whatever ails you. You'd grow old."

Jillian was on the verge of explaining that she'd be giving up much more than that, when Bear went into another barking fit. She started with, "John, there's something I have to tell you," and ended with, "Oh God, it's them. They've come back."

"Damn," John whispered, getting to his feet. He listened carefully, at first hearing nothing but the dog's barking. "It can't be them. Surely they wouldn't come at such a late hour."

But then he heard it, a familiar sound that not only made him fear for the woman, but also brought back the painful memory of five years past:

The trip had started in St. Helens, about ten miles outside Liverpool. The intended destination was Whitehaven. John and Vickie planned to stay there one night – kind of a second honeymoon, or a third or fourth – he'd lost track. Then charter a ship to take them along the Solway Firth, and finally out across the Irish Sea to the Isle of Man, where they would meet up with Pete, the drummer, and Pete's new wife, for three days of relaxation.

Vickie was going to leave Ryan with her parents (now deceased; both parents went within a week of each other from what the doctor claimed to be natural causes; both died at the age of fifty-six, too young for natural causes), who lived on the outskirts of St. Helens. She was uncomfortable with the idea of taking such a young child on a helicopter ride, uncomfortable with the idea of being away from the boy for six whole days. It was a tough decision for her to make, but it had been made.

Then, on the day they were scheduled to leave, Vickie's mother called the hotel, saying that she was coming down with a virus. Chances were, it was just another allergy attack. The woman had them all the time. Vickie, however, wasn't inclined to take chances, especially where her only son was concerned, because Ryan had already suffered a bout with bronchitis once that year. A ride in a helicopter seemed much safer than exposing the boy to the flu.

There was a heavy fog that morning, which wasn't uncommon. The forecast called for cloudy skies and a twenty percent chance for rain. Rain was another thing that wasn't uncommon. Regardless, Vickie worried. A debate occurred in the hotel room, that morning. The debate stretched on past noon. Vickie wanted to travel to Whitehaven by car. John insisted the weather was fine and that they go ahead with their scheduled plans, which had been scheduled eight months in advance, so he could spend time with his wife before the North American tour kicked off.

He would always remember the afternoon Vickie stood there by the helicopter, holding Ryan by the hand. The way she looked up at the dark, overcast sky, frowning. The fear in her green eyes that she usually reserved for times when Ryan ran a temperature or had trouble sleeping during the night. Her golden hair dancing in the cold wind of the rotor. She was afraid. The deafening roar of the helicopter made it all too real. She didn't want to climb aboard.

At that moment, had she said, "John, I can't. I just can't do this," he would have relented, or so he had since come to believe. They would have gone on to Whitehaven by car, spent a wonderful three days on the

Isle of Man walking the rocky shores beneath a hazy
sun, and returned with happy memories of time well
spent. But a smile crossed her lips. It was an
adventurous smile. And off she went to her death, both
she and Ryan...

...Which was why John now had such a difficult time
with decisions. Make the wrong choice, and it's all over.
A man, who is choking to death on a piece of steak, is
wishing he'd gone with the fish. The man, who has a fish
bone lodged in his throat, dies wishing he had ordered
the steak. Too many choices to make. And no way to
determine the outcome. No way to go back and undo the
damage, should the unthinkable occur.

There was a good chance the unthinkable could occur
again. He could grasp no other reason for Brewster to
land that bloody helicopter in the yard at such a late
hour. According to the grandfather clock, it was nearly
eleven-thirty at night. Somehow, they had come to the
conclusion that Jillian was here. They would make her
talk then kill her.

While Jillian went to get Valerie, John went for his
shotgun, knowing there wasn't a minute to spare.

He went straight into the master bedroom and headed
for the closet when Jillian stepped into the room behind
him and suddenly cried out.

John turned, feeling her panic even before
understanding the nature of her fear. His first inclination
was to look for a face at the window. In so doing, he
almost overlooked the obvious: The empty bed. Little
Valerie was missing.

CHAPTER 17

Brewster and Andrews approached the house through the deep drifts of snow, while Barnes remained behind in the helicopter. Barnes was pissed off, to put it mildly, that he'd been ordered to stay so the other two men could take all the glory if it turned out well. He was glad, however, that Brewster had taken him seriously. And wouldn't it beat all if the Braedon woman were in that house. Wouldn't it be nice to stick in their faces that he, Tim Barnes, low man on the totem pole, was responsible for the plan that caught the woman? As much as he hated Andrews, he owed the guy a favor. If not for Andrews, they wouldn't be out here right now. But the guy had sided with Barnes. Even Laurel, who was in for a whole lot of hurt once this was all over, had decided to go with it. Brewster, on the other hand, showed his reluctance. And Barnes knew why. Mister Head Honcho was leery of any idea that came from a mere peon.

Regardless of his hostilities, Barnes decided to let bygones be bygones, at least for the time being. Because, either the woman was in one of the six houses outlined by Brewster, or she had died in the blizzard.

This was the fifth house they had stopped at tonight. And each time they stopped, Barnes told himself that this was it. This was where they would finally catch up with her. The four earlier disappointments didn't dissuade him from his belief that they'd find her tonight. If anything, each one had only psyched him up more. He couldn't remember the last time his heart had beat so fiercely. Or the last time his mouth had been so totally dry. Of course, that may have been as recently as two weeks ago. But none of that mattered now. Tonight, they would know whether she was dead or alive. And Barnes wanted very much to find her alive. He wanted to see her in pain and take revenge for what she'd done to his two good friends and coworkers (whose faces he could not remember), whose deaths she'd caused. And then he'd take revenge for the past three and a half years of 'living hell' he'd been through (but couldn't quite remember), on her account. Yes. Tonight was a good night. And after the Braedon fiasco came to an end, he and the redhead had some unfinished business of their own. Barnes felt so elated, he was afraid he might piss his pants.

The master bedroom was dark, but Jillian checked it nonetheless, looking through the closet, beneath the bed, having enough wits about her to understand the importance of not calling out for the child.

"She's not here," she said, rushing her way through the bedroom, one hand pressed to her knotted stomach. "The kitchen!"

"She said she sleepwalks," John said, following Jillian into the hallway.

"Yes."

"I'll check the guest room."

Brewster knocked on the door then stood back, breath turning to frost at each exhalation. He thought it odd that Mills hadn't been standing there waiting as he'd done during the last two visits. The helicopter screamed loud enough to wake anyone from a sound sleep. And that damn chow barked incessantly. Mills was aware he had guests. Yet Mills stalled. One reason came to mind. Only one. Mills was inside trying to hide any incriminating evidence, making sure no little girl's shoes could be found in the living room, making sure no woman's clothing hung on that rack by the fireplace. Was he stuffing comic books under the cushions of the chairs? Pulling dark hairs from his comb in the bathroom and flushing them down the toilet? Was he checking the dirty glasses in the sink for lipstick smudges?

Mills struck him as a thorough kind of guy. It might have been the man's British accent that made him seem that way, but Brewster thought it was more than that. A man like Mills probably had all kinds of tricks up his sleeves, was good at hiding things. Otherwise, he'd have been busted for possession of marijuana, cocaine, or whatever drug the Rock 'n' Roll junkies were into these days.

As Jillian raced for the kitchen, the worst-case scenario passed through her mind: they had Valerie; they had her little girl. The feeling became even stronger when she found the kitchen empty. It was a nightmare, worse than any monster, worse than anything she'd ever imagined, including the death of her own husband. A mother's purpose was to protect her young. Valerie was missing. Her baby. Her little girl wasn't in the bedroom. She wasn't in the kitchen. They had her. And Jillian grew even surer of this when she met up with John in the dining room. One look at his sober face and she knew: He hadn't found her.

"John," she said, tears slipping down her face. Someone pounded loudly on the front door. Bear barked repeatedly. "What'll we do?"

He grabbed her by the arm, leading her back into the kitchen, with the woman protesting all the way. "Jillian, listen to me. She's got to be in here some place. She's a very smart little girl. If she hears strange voices, she'll stay hidden. I'm sure of it."

"John, we've got to find her. We can't let them inside. Not until we *find* her."

"*We*?" he questioned. "You're going to hide in room off the pantry."

"Not without Valerie!" Jillian argued. Another loud series of bangs came from the front door.

John continued leading her through the kitchen. "We have no choice."

"They have her, John. What if they have her?"

He released her arm as they entered the pantry, knowing that if Jillian were right, the only chance they stood of getting the child back was the shotgun, which he kept in the bedroom closet.

"She couldn't have gotten outside without notice. She's in the house. Someplace safe. And that's where you need to be, someplace safe. If we stall any longer, they're going to be suspicious...if they're not suspicious already. You've got to hide. Now."

"I know," she replied, voice trembling, head shaking. "But I can't. I can't. John, I *can't*..."

John pushed aside the stack of canned tuna, pressed the button, and the opening into the triangular room appeared. "You can. And you *will*."

She stepped inside the small room. There was no time to argue. Even from where she stood, she could hear the relentless pounding on the front door. "Will you look one more time?" she pleaded, desperation leaving her eyes glassy, her heart aching. "*Please*?"

"I'll look," he promised, realizing there was no other answer he could give.

As soon as the small wall slid soundlessly in place, John started for the bedroom, peering into the guest room as he passed along the hallway. The child wasn't there. He went into the master bedroom, checking the bathroom one last time before retrieving his weapon, knowing that if they already had Valerie, he would have no choice but to kill them.

The outside light came on, illuminating a small patch of the porch and yard. He heard the deadbolt retract into the door. The doorknob turned. If Jillian Braedon were in there, Brewster would know within moments of seeing the face of John Mills. No man could hide that kind of guilt when faced with a search at such a late hour, especially with the stakes so high. And in the brief moment while the door swung inward, Brewster took the worst-case scenario into consideration. He might have to kill John Mills. Because, the only reason anyone would protect the woman from the FBI, was if she'd talked. Kevin Brewster had been given his orders only once. And although he couldn't recall the surrounding circumstances, although he wasn't sure if those orders had been given in person or had been sent in a message, he remembered word for word what those orders were: Terminate the Braedons and anyone else who has knowledge of this matter.

There were only two exceptions: a doctor by the name of Carl Neas, and another doctor by the name of Richard Manning. Neas, the man who'd performed the surgery to which Manning, brother of the patient, had assisted, was needed alive. Manning had taken his own life, quite neatly with a gun he'd grabbed from Barnes – that dumb bastard. And Neas, who had been taken into custody three times, was now either up in Heaven, or down in Hell – if either of those two places did, in fact, exist.

John un-tucked his shirt tail from his trousers; ruffled his blond hair so that it fell over his brow; unfastened, then refastened his shirt, so that the buttons were no longer mated with the proper button holes; then turned the collar of his shirt wrong.

The shotgun rested on the kitchen table, both barrels loaded. If needed in a hurry, he could get to it. If not, it wouldn't look overly suspicious to have a weapon within easy reach while a suspected murderess was supposedly on the prowl. When he opened the door and greeted his uninvited guests, he thought he had all bases covered, save the most important: the missing child.

Then, the interrogation began.

Brewster removed his hands from the pockets of his overcoat. "My friend Andrews and I were worried when you didn't come to the door."

John looked down at his miss-buttoned shirt as if mildly embarrassed. "I wasn't exactly dressed for company when you arrived. I thought it would be best to change into something more suitable."

Brewster asked, "Are you alone?"

"No. Bear's here."

"Are we interrupting anything?" Brewster asked.

John began buttoning his shirt properly. "Nothing that can't be put off until another time. I was just reading a book."

Andrews nodded, then asked. "Do you usually read so late at night?"

John stepped away from the door, inviting the two men into the foyer, neither of whom bothered to stomp the snow from their shoes.

CHAPTER 18

"I've been having a bit of insomnia lately, ever since you warned me about that crazed woman being on the loose in these parts," John said.

Andrews removed both hands from his coat pockets, and spoke again. "What book are you reading?"

John looked the two men over. He didn't like the feel of the conversation; what did it matter what book he read? He didn't like the fact that they both wore heavy coats, which probably concealed guns. He didn't like having them in his home. Most of all, he didn't like what these two men stood for. The government was supposed to protect its people, not chase them down and kill them. John thought about the shotgun in the kitchen and the whereabouts of Valerie; he wondered if Arizona carried The Death Penalty for murdering government officers. After a moment's pause, he replied: *The Scarlet Letter.* I'm halfway through it for the second time."

Brewster circled around him from the left, Andrews, from the right. John turned to face them, only they had continued forward. Brewster entered the living room, while Andrews decided to mosey around the dining room.

"If there's something I can do for you," John began, following Andrews, because Andrews headed in the direction to where the woman could be found, "don't hesitate to ask."

"Great," Brewster replied from the other room. "Then you won't mind us having a look around. We're checking all the homes in the area."

John felt as if he'd just been sucker-punched. A search. A search of his home, with Valerie being only God knew where. Regardless, he had no choice but to go along with whatever they requested. Anything less than complete cooperation on his part would alert them to the truth. And if Valerie were to stand a chance – any chance at all of staying a step or two ahead of these men – it was not only contingent upon the child keeping her wits, but upon John keeping his also.

As he passed into the dining room, he realized the mistake he'd made. By following Andrews, he gave them reason to be suspicious. He gave them reason to believe that Andrews was much warmer to finding the woman than Brewster. So, he went into the living room, heart in his throat and what he hoped to be a causal smile on his face.

"Actually," John began, "I do mind."

"Oh?" Brewster said, turning around. The front flaps of his overcoat were pushed back as he placed both hands on his hips. Still, John could see no weapon. That did not, however, mean the man wasn't carrying one. The man's jacket could easily conceal a weapon. And John suspected this to be the case.

"The average man doesn't like having his privacy invaded," John said bluntly. "Especially so late at night. I'm no different, Special Agent Brewster." To that, Brewster frowned. And John continued. "I'm not saying I'm without understanding of your position, which is why I'm not ordering you out of my home. There's a criminal on the loose. If you feel you must search every house in the vicinity, then you must have your reasons.

"However, since you haven't produced one, I'm assuming you have no search warrant. And, as you can see, since I am willing to cooperate, it's only fair that I set the ground rules of the search."

Brewster ran a hand down the length of his face, visibly perturbed. The man sighed heavily. "Which are?"

"Call your friend in here. I'll explain."

When Andrews came into the room, John offered both men a seat. John remained on his feet, leaning into his cane. His standing, while the other two men sat before him, gave him a psychological edge. It let them know exactly who was in authority here while he laid the ground rules.

"You have your interests to protect, gentlemen, and I have mine. You have no reason to trust me, because I am a stranger, and I feel the same way about the two of you. Your being here suggests that you aren't entirely sure of my integrity. Again, it goes both ways. And since I have many valuable antiques in my home, many small enough to fit into a coat pocket without my notice, I'm sure you'll understand why I must insist I be with you at all times during the search. It's nothing personal, just as I'm sure your desire to search the premises is not an intentional slam against my integrity. If you agree, you may look around. If not, then you'll have to leave and come back another time after a judge has issued a warrant."

John waited as the two men exchanged silent glances. It occurred to him that this was perhaps the best performance of his life. And certainly, it was the most important one. Standing here, before two men who were surely armed, insisting that they do things his way as if it were a perfectly acceptable thing to do, sweat trickling down the side of his face, knowing either of these two men could draw a gun at any moment...

At this moment, Valerie was his main concern. He didn't care about the antiques. There were candlestick holders that dated back to the sixteenth century. A more modern version would suit his needs just as well. There were pewter statuettes in a glass case in his bedroom, which had been handed down through six generations of Mills'. No, they couldn't be replaced. They were, however, just things. It would be disappointing to find one missing. Nevertheless, it would not send him into a depression; he'd had things turn up missing before. There was a small painted vase he'd picked up in a pawnshop during a brief stay in Wales. He believed it to be very valuable, but as yet, it had not been appraised. There were little trinkets all throughout the house. Some, worth tens of thousands of dollars. Others, he'd picked up at department stores. All his wife's jewelry was in a box in the room he used for storage. Aside from the monetary value of the diamonds, gold and emeralds – which had complimented her green eyes – he placed a great sentimental value on them as well. Regardless, that was not the basis of his insistence. Valerie's safety was his main concern. He had, however, a secondary issue.

He hadn't read many spy novels – westerns was another genre he usually tried to avoid with the exception of works written by Louis L'Amour and Zane Grey – yet he wasn't totally in the dark as to the many different gadgets used in surveillance. So John wanted to keep both men in sight at all times. He didn't want to give them the opportunity to bug his home. The effects would be disastrous. As it was now, he couldn't be entirely sure if the living room was safe. The same went for the dining room, and perhaps the kitchen...if Andrews had been in there.

"Sounds fair," Brewster finally replied. He got to his feet, hand held out as if to indicate John should lead the way, then said: "Let's get started."

The best place to start was also the last place John wanted to go. In the long run, he felt it wiser to get it over with, than to live with the dread a moment longer than necessary. Brewster walked at John's side as they passed through the living room.

As they turned into the dining room, John placed his cane. He started to take a step forward, when Brewster kicked the cane out from under him. John went down, and he went down hard, barely managing to shift his weight at the last second to land on his left side.

Fear and outrage sent the blood rushing to his face as he looked up into Brewster's dark eyes. The kick had been deliberate. No denying that. From his semi-sitting position on the floor, he groped for the cane that Brewster now straddled. Before taking a moment to consider the consequences, he brought the cane up quickly between Brewster's legs, dropping the man to his knees. John wielded the cane as one might a spear and turned on Andrews, who appeared to be suffering a mild case of shock.

Andrews held both hands up in plain sight, slack-jawed, eyes shifting from Brewster – who was now red-faced, gripping his balls in both hands – to John.

CHAPTER 19

"I'm armed," Andrews said. But he made no move for a gun. Neither did he sound as if he had any intentions of doing so. His remark was that of a young boy claiming to know karate while surrounded by a dozen vicious bullies who meant business. No, John didn't think the man bluffed about having a weapon. He simply believed Andrews preferred talk to violence.

It was now when the possible consequences began to sink in. The anger began to melt as the fear mounted. Getting up from the floor could be construed as a threatening move. He had assaulted an employee of the United States Government. Just cause or no, complications were sure to follow. And that wasn't the worst of it. John had no doubt that Brewster had intentionally taken him down and that they knew Jillian remained hidden somewhere in this house.

Had the shotgun been in his possession, he'd have used it, hoping that the two dead men hadn't left any associates behind in the helicopter. As it was, however, even though his cane had dropped one man and remained in his possession, John was defenseless.

"Fuck!" Brewster groaned for perhaps the twentieth time in five minutes. Twice, he'd said he was going to vomit. Both times, he'd been wrong. He got to his feet slowly, hunched over, one hand on his thigh, the other braced against the wall, knees bent and spread apart. His face had gone from a deep shade of red to a pale shade of ashen white. Sweat glistened above his brow. His teeth were clenched; yet his face hung loosely, making him look more like a cartoon character than the human being he pretended to be. From a hunched over position, he repeated what seemed to be his favorite word of the evening: "Fuck."

"Never underestimate a man with a cane," Andrews said as if humor could be found in the situation. And indeed, Andrews had a smile on his face.

With that having been said, John breathed a bit easier. He placed his cane, intending to use it to get to his feet, when Andrews extended a hand. John took the man up on the offer then brushed the wrinkles from his trousers once he regained a solid footing. Bear appeared at his side, curled tail wagging. John reached down, scratching the dog behind one ear. He didn't know whether to be relieved or upset that the dog had waited until now to put in an appearance. Had Bear been in here when Brewster attacked, the scene may have turned much uglier.

Brewster gave no explanation for his attack; neither did the man offer an apology. Brewster straightened out the best he could, shook his downcast head from side to side, then said through gritted teeth: "I guess that makes us even. Come on. Let's get this over with before I pass out."

"You all right?" Andrews asked.

"Do I look..." Brewster said then stopped. His dark eyes narrowed for a moment when he realized Andrews had directed the question to John.

"I'll be fine," John said.

Since the dining room offered no place to hide – you could see clearly under the cherry wood table, and the china hutch had glass doors – they passed straight through into the kitchen, where John flipped on the overhead lights. He watched, with great relief, how Andrews looked around as if it were all new to him, the way the man's eyes widened when he saw the shotgun on the kitchen table. It was safe to assume Andrews had not been in here earlier. But the question of Valerie's whereabouts – Valerie's safety – still plagued him, eating away at him like an accelerated cancer.

"Gun loaded?" Andrews asked.

"Yes."

Brewster went to the table, cracked the barrel, and removed both shells, dropping them into the pocket of his overcoat. "Not anymore."

Both men went around the room, opening top and bottom cabinets, carefully peering inside as if something horrible might jump out. John watched it all from the center of the room and would have been amused by the way they went about their job, had it not been for the surrounding circumstances. For all he knew, the child was hiding in one of those cabinets.

Aside from the one instance when Brewster had taken the shells, neither of the two men reached into their pockets. If they planted bugs, they used invisible ones.

Brewster inspected the sink. He found no dirty glasses to check for lipstick smudges. No butter knife or dish he could take to dust for fingerprints. No sign that the woman was here. Not even a dark hair on the counter.

John knew the pantry would be next. What he hadn't taken into consideration, however, was that Bear would wander in there. He started to call the dog, then thought better of it. Best not to arouse suspicion. Better to pretend everything was fine, than to draw attention to the dog. John felt his throat tighten; realizing Bear now stood only a few feet away from where the woman hid.

Then Bear began to whimper.

At first, it went unnoticed by everyone but John, whose heart had gone from beating double time, to triple. He cleared his throat, loudly. He accidentally on purpose bumped his cane against one wooden chair, loudly. And when that failed to bring Bear out of the pantry, John began to whistle *Fur Elise* while drumming his fingers on the table as if annoyed. Andrews pulled open the door of the broom closet and made a brief inspection. John's heart continued to race, even when he realized Valerie was not in there. Brewster ran a hand along the granite counter top, examining his fingertips, as if looking for a trace of dust he could identify as belonging to the woman. The closet door was then closed. Brewster and Andrews walked to the center of the room, where John stood with one hand, clammy and cold, resting on the table.

Bear's whimpering stopped and the dog issued one quick bark.

"Does your dog usually bark for no reason?" Brewster asked. Without waiting for a response, he started towards the pantry. Andrews followed.

As for John, he went slowly to the butcher block between the sink and the stove. The knife rack loomed before him. His heart pumped fiercely, dumping adrenaline through his system. He knew exactly what he was doing. He had no idea what he was doing. He withdrew a mincing knife. His eyes transfixed on its glinting, nine-inch, stainless steel blade. As his sweaty hand grasped the handle, he knew full well that once the deed was done he would be bound to it for the rest of his life – a life that might end within the next few minutes.

They were in his home. Searching at his invitation. While one person hid in a small, dark room. And the other, a five-year-old child, had to fend for herself. It was madness. Nothing like this was ever supposed to happen. His hand began to tremble; yet his fingers tightened around the wooden handle of the knife with complete resolve. There was more at stake than the life of a woman and her child. So much more, he dared not fail.

CHAPTER 20

As John turned to face the pantry, it occurred to him that killing those two men to protect Jillian was what he'd been born to do. And if more were in the helicopter, he would kill them too. Or better yet, hold one at gunpoint to pilot them away from here. He had no idea where they would go if he succeeded. But one thing he did know: after the killings, he'd be wanted by the U.S Government.

Jillian sat cross-legged on the carpeted floor. The room remained dark, cool. She thought about how small the room appeared when she'd first stepped inside. Now, in utter darkness, it seemed infinite. She could see no walls, not even a vague outline of her own trembling hand when she held it up before her eyes. As if to make up for the handicap, her hearing had intensified. Her heart beat loudly, the rapid *thud, thud, thud* so pronounced, she was sure it could be heard from any room in the house.

The muscles in both legs had already begun to cramp. One foot had been taken over by pins and needles from remaining in a prolonged awkward position. Yet she dared not move. She wished that, instead of sitting, she could stretch out on the floor. It was possible she might be trapped in here for hours. And Valerie. Her baby...

Light could not penetrate the walls. Sound, however, had a way of filtering through. Voices could be heard, but not clearly enough to understand or even grasp the topic of conversation. A pair of hard-sole shoes could be heard walking across the stone floor in the kitchen. And something else, a light clicking sound that drew nearer. Jill searched her mind for the interpretation of that sound. And now, it was only a few feet away. In the darkness, it seemed as if she could reach right out and touch it; it was that close, yet still unidentifiable...

...Until Bear began to whimper. If sheer will power could have sent the dog away, Bear would have been halfway around the world right now. GO! Her mind screamed. She closed her eyes as every muscle in her body tightened. And then Bear did the unthinkable: the dog barked.

Unaware of what she was doing, Jillian began to teeter back and forth restlessly, one hand pressed to her stomach, the other hand pressed to her own forehead. She could hear them coming, their shoes slapping against the floor. Even if she could make the monster mad, there was not enough time to summon it to her defense. They knew she was here; the dog had given her away. The moment she'd feared for the last three and a half years had arrived. If they found her, they'd find Valerie, too...if they hadn't already. A tear slipped down her cheek. Another soon followed. Jillian closed her eyes, lips quivering, and silently bid the missing child goodbye.

Brewster flipped on the light, allowing his eyes to make a sweep of the pantry before entering the narrow room. Andrews walked in behind him.

"Jeez," Brewster said through a sigh. "Is there any doubt as to Mills' favorite food? Grapefruit juice and tomato soup. I've seen less food in a bomb shelter. He's got enough tea here to last a lifetime. The English," he said and shook his head. "Strange sense of humor and even stranger appetites."

Brewster looked down at the dog that now stretched out on the floor, muzzle resting comfortably on his front paws, nose barely an inch from the end wall. "I wouldn't have a dog if I were deaf, dumb and blind. Lazy animals. All they want to do is eat and sleep. And better to sleep where the food is." He nudged the chow's hindquarter with the toe of his shoe. Bear's head lifted slightly as if annoyed, then dropped back down. "Come on, Andrews, let's get out of here. My stomach feels queasy enough without looking at all this food."

Andrews emerged first, stopping short when he saw the knife glinting in John's hand. A distance of perhaps ten feet stood between them. The stainless steel blade reflected the overhead light, like a mirror capturing the sun. For the second time tonight, Andrews issued a warning. "I'm armed." Unlike the first time, Andrews reached beneath his coat and now held a .38 caliber revolver in his hand.

John stared at the gun, looked down at the knife, and realizing the implications, he dropped it on the table. He held his free hand out at his side, palm out, backing steadily away from the table until the heel of his shoe struck the oven.

There had to be a sensible explanation – a good lie – out of this. John, however, had difficulty thinking of one right now, as he stared into the muzzle of a gun.

Valerie awoke to the sound of Bear's barking, not quite sure what room she occupied. She huddled in a corner, back to a wall, sitting on something bumpy. She scooted her back along the wall as she edged over, then reached down to pick up the object she'd been sitting upon: a shoe.

The last two times Bear had barked happened when the bad people came. She thought about Bear as she got to her feet and stepped out of the closet – finding herself in the room where her mommy was supposed to sleep. But Mommy wasn't in here now. The dog had barked only a few short moments ago. She listened, not for Bear, but for the sound of the helicopter. Instead, she heard muffled voices.

Valerie went to the door, reached under the large T-shirt she wore to scratch her belly, then rubbed the sore spot on her backside, which had been caused by sitting on that shoe.

"Mommy..? John...?" she said quietly, poking her head out into the hallway. She listened again. A voice. Not clear. A man's voice. Valerie moved into the hallway, eyes squinting in the light coming from the other end.

He'd been caught red-handed with a knife, a very large knife. Aside from killing, what was a knife like that used for? "Had I been aware that slicing bread was a capital offense, I'd have waited until after you'd left."

"Bread?" Andrews repeated, as if it were a foreign word. He took a few steps into the kitchen. Brewster did likewise.

"I've learned a long time ago not to take pain medication on an empty stomach. I assure you, the prescription is quite legal. There's no need to shoot."

Andrews regarded Brewster for a moment, while holstering his revolver. If eyes could talk, his said: See what you've done, Brewster? You knocked a cripple on the floor and now he's in pain.

"Go ahead and slice yourself some bread," Brewster said, and expelled a heavy sigh of disgust.

Valerie paused just before reaching the dining room. The voice she heard startled her. Someone was here. A man. John's voice was easy to tell. He had a funny way of sounding out his words that made him seem different. The man she heard now sounded different, too. But he wasn't *John.*

Valerie went back up the hallway, bare feet silently crossing the stone floor. She went to the doorway of the big bedroom, the room where she was supposed to sleep, and stood looking into the hallway with a handful of cotton T-shirt clutched in her fist. She had to hide. And she couldn't get to the secret room without being seen. She turned towards the bed, eyes momentarily glued to the crawl space between the frame and the floor. She spun back to face the hallway. Scared. Wondering where her mother was. Hoping the other man was a friend of John's and not one of the bad people.

From the kitchen, all three men passed through the dining room and into the guest bedroom. Though relieved the moment he flipped on the light, he failed to sigh or give his feelings away. The search was on. The closet. The bathroom. Behind the drapes. Under the bed.

Each man took a couple glances into the hallway bathroom. No shower. Just a sink and toilet. Brewster opened the hallway closet, moved a few linen sheets and blankets, frowned, then started for the next room.

"The master suite," John said as he stepped inside. He paused for a second or two before flipping on the light. He'd fully expected to see her there, but the bed stood empty. Valerie had to be someplace within his home, and he realized time worked steadily against him. It was like reliving the helicopter accident all over again. He still had hope that the two people he loved would make it through this alive. But it became more and more unlikely; he was sure they were closing in on the child. John could do little about it, as the shotgun remained in the kitchen, unloaded.

All three men were now in the master bedroom, Andrews sticking his head into the adjoining bathroom before walking to the shower and sliding back the glass door. Brewster started poking through the closet. John felt as if his heart was about to explode. And he thought about Jillian, a badly frightened woman sitting in a dark room, dying inside due to the uncertainty she now faced regarding her daughter.

Andrews knelt down at the edge of the bed, cocking his head to the side to get a good view of what might be hiding beneath. John could see the man reaching for something.

CHAPTER 21

Valerie stood behind the open library door, peering through the crack. She wasn't able to see anyone going into the big bedroom, but she'd heard their footfalls and knew their whereabouts. She stepped out from behind the door, poking her head into the hall, which was when Bear found her.

He padded up slowly then nuzzled her hand. She wanted to throw her arms around Bear's neck, but instead took a couple small steps into the hallway, staring in the direction of the big bedroom. No voices were heard. Not a whisper. Valerie stepped softly, feeling the urge to pee. But other than the one in the big bedroom, there were no bathrooms at this end of the hallway. She'd have to go through the living room, and make her way back around to the other end of the hall. The bathroom, though, wasn't safe. Neither was going all the way through the living room, through the dining room, kitchen, and pantry to the secret room. She had a choice to make. She didn't like it at all. But she couldn't stay here, or they might find her. She edged along the wall, moving closer to the big bedroom, wanting to get a peek of the men inside.

John stepped into the hallway first, saw the child standing less than two feet away, and he quickly turned around in the doorway, feeling sick in the pit of his stomach. "How many homes are you searching, tonight?" he asked the two men, knowing the child couldn't help but overhear.

"Six," Brewster replied. "Just one more after yours."

"If you find the woman, I'd be interested in knowing, as it would put my mind at ease."

Brewster pushed right past him, stepping into the hall. "No problem," Brewster replied. "We'll let you know."

The library required little more than a few quick glances, as the shelves were lined up against the walls. Brewster lifted the lace from the small table then went on to the next room, the laundry room. The inspection in there was brief. Andrews opened a door, a bit surprised to see several rows of black batteries. Other than that, he found nothing of interest.

Brewster's face remained flushed. The pain had eased, but the humiliation hadn't. Now, anger began to add color to his face. They were almost through with the search. More and more, it looked liked Barnes' plan was a complete waste of time. After this, they had only one more house to investigate. And it didn't look promising.

One last room. Brewster entered it at a brisk pace, more determined than ever.

There were cardboard boxes and a complete set of luggage, all of which they pulled out of the closet and inspected. They'd found two wooden crates, each large enough to hold three or four tightly squeezed people. And two large cardboard boxes. John fetched a hammer from the laundry room and dismantled the crates one by one, stacking the contents – hundreds upon hundreds of paperback books – on and beneath the weight bench. Removing every book seemed senseless. And yet he complied without complaint, not wanting to heighten the agents' suspicion. They took longer in the storage room than in the kitchen and pantry. Half an hour must have passed before Brewster finally came straight out and admitted they had wasted valuable time.

All three men then went into the living room. Brewster went to the fireplace. The transponder he had given John stood centered on the sculptured mantle, between two miniature brass cannons, exactly where John had set it just before he had gone to the door.

"I'd like to check the garage. When was the last time you were out there?"

Despite the fact that they'd yet to find Valerie's latest hiding place, John felt little relief. He wouldn't feel safe until Andrews and Brewster were gone, and Valerie was found...in that order.

"Yesterday," John replied. "That's where I store the firewood."

Brewster cocked his head to one side, smiling smugly. "Do you have any valuable antiques in there?"

"A garage is hardly the proper storage facility for precious valuables."

"Is it locked?"

"No."

Brewster threw a glance at his watch then placed the two shotgun shells on the mantle. "Andrews and I will check the garage on our way out. Hope we didn't inconvenience you too much."

Andrews walked over to John, extending a hand. "It was a pleasure to meet you, Mr. Mills. Sorry it couldn't have been under different circumstances."

John shook the man's hand and walked the men to the door. He stood there in the foyer, watching Brewster and Andrews trudge their way through the snow. Seeing them leave, John closed his eyes and whispered a "thank-you" to the Man upstairs. But the night wasn't over yet. Though he'd seen the child earlier, she was loose somewhere on the property, unaccounted for, and the men still had the garage to check. Unless the child had gone to the garage, they wouldn't find any incriminating evidence in there. One of them, however, might try to stay behind. So John stood in the doorway, chilled to the bone, making sure that when the helicopter took off, both men went with it.

When John finally closed the door, he leaned his back to it, sighing at the ceiling. Warrant or no, Brewster had been bent on searching the premises. He could think of only five reasons a man like Brewster had agreed to the stipulation John had set forth. Those five reasons were hanging on his bedroom wall, encased in glass. They equaled clout, respectability, and intimidation. If a man with five platinum albums went to the media over the abuse he'd endured at the hands of the FBI, the story would be nationwide. Never before had being a celebrity been more beneficial. And still, it bothered him: Despite the intimidation, Brewster, for reasons John could not fathom, had kicked the cane out from under him as if it were every day's business.

"Bear," John called. When the old chow appeared, tail wagging, John said, "Where's Valerie?"

Bear looked towards the dining room, whining. And John's shoulders felt much lighter. All throughout the horrible ordeal, he'd been thinking of Valerie as if she were a normal five-year-old child, instead of the resourceful munchkin that circumstances and fear had obviously created.

Although it seemed unlikely that bugs had been planted in his home, John didn't want to take any chances. He hurried through the dining room, knowing it and the living room would be off limits to Jillian and Valerie. Conversation, even in other parts of the house, would have to done quietly. Valerie wasn't what he'd consider a loud child. She was, however, something of a chatterbox. She couldn't go outside and play like other children her age. Now, making matters worse, she would have to be confined to the bedroom. Having no toys, nothing to keep her occupied except learning to read, the child would grow antsy within a few hours, stir-crazy by the end of the first full day.

John went into the pantry, pushed the six high stack of canned tuna aside, and hit the button beneath the shelf. The door slid open, and both mother and daughter brought a hand up to shield their squinting eyes. John found himself smiling as he lifted a finger to his lips, indicating that maintaining silence was still important.

Awkwardly, he hunkered down, relieving Jill of the child. Valerie's legs wrapped around his waist, her arms around his neck, her head dropped on his shoulder. He held on tightly, trying to convince himself it was finally over and the little girl was safe. John had the feeling he had just wakened the child from a nap. He hadn't a clue as to how long the child had been in there, but it was obviously long enough for her to get sleepy. Still sitting, Jill stretched her legs, knees popping, first one then the other. She straightened her back, rolling the discomfort from her shoulders, and dropped her head forward then back.

He nodded as if to say: Let's go. But Jill just sat there. Her predicament was obvious. Certain key parts of her anatomy had fallen asleep. While Jill let the flow of blood revive her legs, John went down the hallway to put the child to bed.

He had a question or two to ask of the child. And yet, they were questions that could wait until morning. "The bad people are gone," John whispered as he pulled the covers up to her neck. "But we have to be quiet."

She regarded him with half hooded eyes and spoke in a whisper. "That was a good hiding place. But it was so dark, I couldn't see."

"I'll put a flashlight in there in case they come back. All right?"

"All right. But how come we hafta talk in whispers?"

"Those men may have left something behind, a tiny listening device. There may be one in the living room, perhaps in the dining room, too, which means they'll be able to hear everything we say in those rooms. So, when you wake up in the morning, stay in here. Either your mother or I will bring you breakfast."

"Do I hafta stay in here all day?"

"Yes."

Valerie's eyes opened wide. "*All* day?"

"Shh," he said, laying a gentle finger across her lips. "As soon as I can get to town, I'll hire someone to come out here and check for listening devices. After that, you'll have a free run of the house again."

He started for the door, when Valerie whispered, "John?"

"Yes?"

There was a brief hesitation on her part. Then: "That sure was a good hiding place."

He smiled half a smile, trying to remember what it was like to be so young and so resilient. "Yes. It was at that."

It was nearly one o'clock in the morning, when he walked Jillian to the guest room. They both went inside, John last, quietly closing the door behind him. A large white moon stood behind the window, casting a pale light into an otherwise dark room. When he reached out to turn on the nightstand lamp, she stayed his hand with a lingering touch.

"John...you don't have to sleep in the living room." She smiled tensely, rolling her eyes up. "God that sounded cheap. I'm not very good at this. I'm not even sure what I'm doing."

"You're tense."

"Yes."

"And vulnerable."

"You say that as if it were a disease."

"It is. One of the main symptoms is saying things you'll regret later." He dropped his gaze, unable to spend another moment looking at her wounded expression.

Her eyes glimmered in the darkness. "I've met a lot of people in my lifetime, but never have I met a man as attractive as you."

"Attractive?" he repeated, raising a brow.

"*Very* attractive."

He unbuttoned his shirt and let it fall to the floor, with no intentions of seduction. If anything, he thought the scars would make her turn away with disgust. Her eyes fell to the silvery scar tissue that started just beneath his ribs and slashed downward, disappearing under the waistband of his trousers. Another scar, this one jagged, ran across his upper arm. Another one, curved, was directly over his heart.

Self-conscious of his own imperfections, he dropped his gaze and said: "Not a pretty sight."

"'What is beautiful is good and who is good will soon also be beautiful.'"

"You're quoting Sappho," he said with mild surprise.

"It seemed appropriate. I said I find you attractive."

"*Very* attractive."

"*Very* attractive," she agreed and smiled. "Even more so now."

He did what seemed to be the right thing at the moment, but knew he'd regret it later. He lightly caressed the side of her face. And when she closed her eyes, he brushed a kiss against her forehead and bid her goodnight.

CHAPTER 22

In the living room, the grandfather clock struck the hour. Outside, the crusted snow glistened beneath a nearly full moon. And three miles away, in what was once an abandoned shack, two men sat listening to utter silence, sipping black coffee from Styrofoam cups, fighting sleep.

Brewster read and reread Laurel's notes. Foreman, Greck and Garcia were practically tied for having the most entries. The Grecks had the sick kid. Their son, the one-year-old, screamed the entire time Brewster and Andrews searched the house. The mother said she thought it was an ear infection. Brewster had it figured different. He'd seen the bottle half filled with coagulated milk that the kid was sucking on. He'd seen the filth in that house, a week's worth of dirty dishes strewn about the kitchen, the stench of urine combined with cigarette smoke. If that kid was sick of anything, he was sick of being in that nasty house.

It appeared as though all the transmitters were in working order. Even those from the five homes they had not visited tonight had picked up bits and pieces of conversation, television broadcasts, and music. He ran a finger down the listings on each tablet, until he got to tablet number eleven, which corresponded with house number eleven, the Mills' residence.

"Andrews."

"Yeah?"

"Come here a minute, will you?"

Andrews, who'd been sitting on the floor in the corner of the room, got up and brushed off the seat of his pants. He went to the table, Styrofoam cup in hand. "Yeah?"

Brewster dropped tablet number eleven on the table and said: "What do you make of that?"

Andrews read: "Eleven twenty-five. Eleven thirty. Eleven forty-two. Eleven forty-four. Twelve-twenty."

"Doesn't it strike you as odd that the only logs we have on Mills, are the ones just prior to and during our visit?"

"He's single. He has no one to talk to."

"He has a dog. Dogs go outside. And how does a dog let the master know it needs to go outside?"

"It barks," Andrews replied.

"Exactly. So why is it that we've heard nothing until these five entries?"

"What you're implying is ludicrous. Mills has no way of knowing the transmitter you gave him is a bug. He's a musician, not a detective."

"Maybe the woman told him."

"Yeah. And maybe his dog only barks when strangers show up on the doorstep. Mills struck me as the kind of guy who'd keep to a regular routine. He gets up in the morning, lets the dog out. Before lunch, he lets the dog out again. Just before going to bed, the dog goes out, does its business. And the next day it starts all over again."

"Maybe."

Andrews pushed the writing tablet aside and took a seat on the edge of the table. "Kevin, only a drowning man grasps at straws. We're not drowning yet. That woman leaves an easy trail to follow everywhere she goes. Now that we know exactly what to look for, she'll give herself away. All we have to do is keep an ear tuned."

"Yeah," Brewster said and sighed. He was still angry. "She'll do one trick too many then we'll have her."

Andrews got up, took a sip of lukewarm coffee then headed off to one corner of the room. He knew Brewster was right. They had every reason to be suspicious of the quiet at the Mills' residence. The man was a musician. Andrews believed it wasn't uncommon for Mills to sit down at the piano and play a tune or two. Also, the part about the dog disturbed him. Yes, dogs bark. But something else was missing.

Andrews couldn't remember whether or not he himself had ever owned a pet, although, under the circumstances, he thought it highly unlikely. When it came right down to it, he couldn't remember much of anything. Regardless, when a person lives alone with a dog, there is conversation. One sided – yes. But people do talk to animals. So, there was reason to believe Mills had known about the "transponder" being voice-activated. And, reason for Mills to worry about it.

Andrews wouldn't have been at all surprised to learn that the transponder had been kept in a locked room up until the moment Mills first heard the helicopter landing in the yard. And maybe, had they gone there in broad daylight, they'd have found the woman. Chances were, she and the little girl ran out the back door and hid outside in the darkness while the house was searched.

It was the answer to the question that had driven him all but insane, ever since the blizzard: Yes, Jillian Braedon was still alive.

"Kevin?"

"Yeah?"

"Our shift ends in a couple of hours, and they'll be here with the chopper. I know it's been a long night, but I think one of us should pay Mills another visit."

"Why just one of us?"

"We don't want to intimidate the man. We have a bad enough reputation as it is without pushing around a celebrity. He'd be more relaxed if one man, instead of two, shows up on his doorstep. And...if he feels confident, he's more apt to slip up. You know, just drop by, pay a friendly visit, and see if he needs anything from town."

"You think I'm right about him, don't you?"

"Let's just say I don't like leaving anything to chance."

"Fine. You go. I'm sure Mills would rather see you than me."

Andrews nodded then downed the rest of his cooling coffee. That was exactly what he'd thought Brewster would say. Besides, Brewster couldn't pilot the chopper.

Time has a way of becoming distorted during the passage of night. Minutes are like hours; hours, like minutes. Tonight, the latter held true. The moon remained hidden and only a scattering of stars could be seen from the window. The night passed quickly, too quickly.

John left his makeshift bed in the living room to check on the sleeping woman. Slowly, silently, he opened the door. There she lay on her side – the woman who had quoted Sappho – resting between the cool satin sheets, her face a shadow against the pillow.

The hall held on to the hour's darkness, but John felt no need to turn on the light. He took the long way around the hall, so he could check in on Valerie. The child slept soundly on her side, both hands balled into loose fists beneath her chin, knees drawn toward her stomach. Although no one could take the special place in his heart reserved for his son, he had come to the conclusion that there were other special places. And Valerie, the little chatterbox chipmunk, had filled one of them quite neatly. She seemed to have stolen Bear's heart, as well. Bear got up from the rug at the foot of the bed and padded slowly to the door, following John into the living room.

The transponder Brewster had given him rested on the mantle, positioned between the two brass cannons. John picked it up, turning the object in hand. He looked down at Bear and then shook his head. "I'm a fool; you know that, Bear? The man says: 'Look before you leap.' Well, I'm looking. What I see in the distance is heartache, but I'm about to leap anyway. Does that make any sense to you, boy?"

Bear padded off and John returned the transponder to the mantle. He used the poker to stir the coals and then added a few sticks of firewood. As he headed towards the library, the grandfather clock disturbed the silence by chiming three times. Physically, he felt exhausted. Artistically, he was in rare form. Many years had passed since he'd written anything other than the occasional letter he sent to his uncle in Dover. And now, a haunting melody came together in his mind, complete with lyrics. As he had always done in the past, he took a moment to mentally examine the composition in the making, to be sure that it was an original and not something he had heard before. Once convinced that the music belonged to him alone, he searched his pocket for the box of matches he usually kept there, lit the candle, and took a seat at the small table.

By the yellow flame of the candle, John scratched the notes, one by one, down on the pad. The composition came so swiftly, flowed so evenly from mind to hand to paper, it seemed as if he were merely a tool of delivery, enabling the music to give birth to itself. Nearly two hours passed before he bit down on the end of his pen, going over what he'd written. After several moments of tedious deliberation, John set the pen down, rested back in the chair and gazed at the transparent ghost of the room that reflected off the window. It was finished. The grandfather clock chimed five times, reminding him that daylight was only a few hours away, and he had yet to get any sleep.

He reached for his cane and suddenly stopped. His attention returned to the window. Something moved just beyond the glass. He blinked. He blinked again, attempting to focus his weary eyes on the dark outside, only to realize what he'd seen in the glass was his own reflection.

CHAPTER 23

It gave him an odd feeling to think his home might be bugged, which added another good reason to not wait until the roads were clear to make his trip into town. One slip-up, one more visit from the creature that lived in Jillian's nightmares, one sleepwalking venture of a singing child – and everything could fall apart. He knew the woman's snowmobile couldn't have been left too far away. But even if he could find it and managed to repair the damn thing, using the stolen snowmobile to get into town could turn out to be a dangerous mistake. Twenty miles stood between here and Sandstone. Twenty miles of open space to cross without being caught by Brewster. A simple check on the vehicle identification number would prove who owned the snowmobile and lead them straight back here to Jillian.

John had something else to consider as well. The trip would take hours, and in that time, Jillian and Valerie would be here alone. Anything could go wrong. Brewster could show up and have the entire house either bugged or torn apart before John returned. Jillian might have another nightmare and – God forbid – Valerie would be alone to deal with her mother's screams and possibly alone to deal with the beast itself.

More and more, this house felt like a prison. He couldn't leave. It wasn't safe to stay. He had to deal with this situation and he needed to deal with it now.

John ran a hand down the length of his face and considered taking a much-needed rest, when inspiration struck. He had a way to get a message out to Mel Talbot, and it could be accomplished without leaving the house. If Mel were alive, and if he were at the same address, he could be here within four or five days. And if Mel could get here, then Mel could find a way into town and get things rolling.

John returned to the library and lit the candle. He took a seat, flipped the writing tablet to a clean sheet of paper, and took up a pen in his left hand.

Dear Mr. Talbot:
This is in reference to the equipment we discussed during our first meeting at the pub. I have given it a great deal of thought and am enclosing a cheque for the full amount.

You will also find a little extra to cover the cost of your trip here, in the event you decide to bring it in person. And I do hope that will be the case, since I am most certainly in need of instruction.

John paused for a moment. In the event someone else first read this letter – someone gainfully employed by the FBI – it was important that this seem like an ordinary, innocent letter. Which meant there had to be some reasonable basis for his request. He drummed his fingers lightly on the table, grinned, and wrote down the following:

I am in the middle of striking a new deal with a recording company. But it's on the hush, not presently meant for public consumption. I'm sure the programs and equipment we discussed will be most beneficial in that venture. Anything that can give life to my music and further my career will be well worth the expense.

Unfortunately, this part of the world has been hit by one snowstorm after another. There is no guarantee that it won't snow again just before your arrival. And since I am without a telephone, there is no way for you to contact me with your flight information. Consequently, I won't be able to meet you at the airport. Time, however, is of the essence.

If you fly in to the Phoenix airport, I'm sure you'll have no difficulty finding a helicopter to bring you here. Yes, I'm still in Sandstone, Arizona, U.S.A. To save on delays, please bring everything we discussed during our first meeting. The recording deal is to be decided within a month, and I need time to refine my presentation.

Looking forward to seeing you within the next few days.

Give my regards to the Iron Lady and her bank account.
Sincerely,
John E. Mills

He read it once, twice, then set down the pen and left to get his checkbook, address book, and an envelope from his desk in the master bedroom. If curiosity over the letter didn't bring Mel here, the amount of the check – thirty thousand American dollars – would do the trick. No, Mel wasn't interested in money, at least not the Mel John had known a few years ago. The check, however, should help insure the letter would be taken seriously.

After addressing the envelope and drawing a map of the area, John left the library and went to his safe. He slid the six high stack of canned tuna out of the way, pressed the button beneath the shelf, and the door slid soundlessly into the wall. He stepped inside the triangular shaped room and eased himself down on his knees. His fingers slid beneath the edge of the carpet, pulling back to expose a concrete floor that was home to a rectangular metal plate roughly the size of a shoebox lid: the cover of his safe. He removed the cover and withdrew a strongbox. He brought the strongbox into the pantry, took the key that was hidden between two boxes of Earl Grey tea, and slipped it into the lock. A moment later, he shuffled through the hundreds until he came to the smallest denomination in his possession, a twenty dollar bill – and pealed three of them off the pile, more than enough for expedited overseas delivery.

Now, the time had come to hide Jillian and Valerie so he could summon the delivery boy.

If the house was bugged, it only seemed appropriate to use it for his benefit. John took an old T-shirt from the rag cabinet in the laundry room and tied it in three knots. Next, he went into the kitchen and set the table with one bowl, one glass, one napkin and one spoon. He set a small kettle of water on the stovetop and pulled the oatmeal canister from the cupboard. From there, he went into the pantry and opened the door to what Valerie referred to as 'the secret room,' and what John referred to as 'the vault.'

"Comfortable, ladies?" he asked.

Jillian shone the flashlight into his eyes. "Like two peas in a pod. What about Bear?" she asked.

"Don't worry. Bear will be outside."

Valerie dropped her head onto one of the two pillows on the floor and huddled beneath the blanket. Jillian scooted down beside her and John closed the door.

He found Bear in the living room, stretched out by the fireplace, black fur highlighted blue by the flames.

"Something wrong, boy?" he asked. He took the knotted T-shirt and playfully shook it in front of the dog's muzzle. Bear reacted as expected. The dog snapped at the shirt just as John pulled it away. Again, he shook the shirt in front of Bear. As the dog snapped for it, John pulled back.

Barking, the dog got up. "What's wrong, boy?" John asked, using the shirt to lead the dog towards the foyer. "Is someone out there?" This time, when John teased the dog with the shirt, he let the dog get hold of it. Bear tugged, growling playfully.

John tugged, pulled to the left, to the right, and backed his way to the large oak door, which wasn't easy considering that he had only one good leg and Bear had four. When he opened the door, Bear barked. And goading the dog even more, John made as if to throw the shirt outside while yelling, "Go, boy!"

Bear darted out into the crusted over snow and John looked up, shielding his eyes from the glare of sunlight as a helicopter came into view. Even if his house were bugged, John didn't believe they could get here this quickly. He closed the front door to keep Bear outside then went into the laundry room to deposit the shirt in the washing machine, first untying the knots. Next, he went into the kitchen, turning on the gas burner beneath the kettle. He filled the glass from the table with water and before replacing it on the table John took a satisfying gulp. Outside, the helicopter whined as it descended to the ground.

As he headed to the front door, he went over the mental list he'd created earlier. The beds were made. The extra toothbrushes were wrapped in plastic and hidden in the linen closet. The shotgun was once again loaded. The hairbrush had been checked for dark hairs. The letter he had drafted earlier was in the library. And his two favorite people in the whole world were safe and sound in the vault. Everything seemed to be in order. Yet John's stomach needed an Alka-Seltzer.

And now with the stage set, his stomach tied in knots, and the audience waiting at the door, the time had come for the show to begin.

"This is a coincidence," John said, as Andrews stood before the doorway.

Andrews slipped his dark sunglasses neatly into his inside breast pocket, looking as if he'd not slept in days. His face was unshaven. The bags beneath his eyes sagged like small bruised water balloons. "Coincidence?" Andrews repeated.

"Yes. Just before you arrived, my dog started barking. He doesn't bark that often. I thought, perhaps, the woman you were looking for might be nearby, and I was about to use the transponder Agent Brewster had given me. Please, come in."

Andrews stepped inside, snow clinging to his hard-soled shoes. "Your dog probably heard the chopper."

"Yes. I'm sure that's what it was. Any news on the woman?"

"No," Andrews replied, as they walked into the living room.

John wanted to make small talk, hoping to set his visitor at ease. "Would you care for a cup of tea?"

"Thank you. A cup of coffee might hit the spot."

"Instant?"

"Instant's fine. Thank you." Andrews slipped out of his overcoat and draped it over the arm of the chair. "No cream. No sugar," he said, pulling at the knot in his tie.

"Make yourself comfortable. The kettle should already be boiling. I'll be right back."

The kettle wasn't boiling, but it was close enough, considering he didn't wish to leave Andrews alone for very long. When John returned to the living room with the coffee, he found Andrews standing over the Steinway, staring down at the keys. "This is quite a piano."

"It is. I had it shipped here from London when I moved. Couldn't bear to leave her behind. Do you play?"

"Me?" Andrews said, smiling. "No. But I admire those who do. Tell me, Mr. Mills...I've always wondered... What's it like to be on stage before thousands of adoring fans?"

John passed Andrews a steaming cup of black coffee. The question was one he'd been asked countless times in the past; so his answer, casual in delivery, was well rehearsed. "It's like being on the wildest roller coaster ride of your life. It's scary as hell, and the fear is fuel to the excitement. I miss those days."

"I bet you do."

"Which is why I'm planning a comeback." He dropped his gaze to the polished ivory and ebony. A melancholy smile briefed his lips. "It may not happen quite the way I plan. So, I would appreciate it if you don't mention it to anyone else." He shook his head lightly, as if to say: Where are my manners? Then said,

"I'm sure you didn't come here to discuss my music career, Special Agent Andrews. How may I help you?"

"Actually, I dropped by to see how you were doing. I'll be heading into town soon and was wondering, since you're snowed in, if you'd like me to bring you back anything."

"No," John replied. "I'm all set here. But I'd like to thank you for...Wait," he said as if an idea just occurred. "There is something you could do for me, if you don't mind. I have a letter that needs mailing. It's very important. You might say my career hinges upon its timely delivery. Is there any chance you'll be going near a post office or Fed-Ex any time soon?"

"I'll make sure it gets mailed today. It's no trouble at all."

CHAPTER 24

Andrews and Brewster walked down the quiet, snow-lined sidewalk, side by side in their three-piece suits and overcoats, looking very much out of place in this small high-desert town. They passed a young boy on the sidewalk who wore oversized rubber boots and a tattered bleach-stained denim jacket. The boy's brown hair was disheveled; smeared chocolate added a little more color to his lightly freckled face and hands. He appeared to be waiting for someone to come out of Sandstone Pipe & Supply. They passed a toothless, elderly woman who sat on a bench, gumming a peanut butter and jelly sandwich while waiting for the bus. Two teenage boys, dressed as if they'd just stepped off the cover of a lumberjack magazine, cut across the street with a basket of clothes each, and went into The Washateria.

Cars went by. A sixty-seven Mustang labored up the street with a faulty muffler, motor rumbling, wheels spinning in the dirty slush. An old Pontiac with the words: "WASH ME," written boldly in the filth of the rear window, pulled in front of Eileen's Diner, choking and sputtering even after the owner had pocketed the key.

Andrews and Brewster stepped into the diner. It was a small restaurant with booths lining one glass-paneled wall, round tables towards the center of the room that could comfortably seat four, and stools set along the length of the counter.

They spotted Laurel immediately, an easy discovery with her red hair and pale complexion.

"Need a favor," Brewster said as he slid into the booth seat across from the woman.

Laurel looked up at Andrews then scooted over to make room. Andrews, however, remained standing. She turned to Brewster, smiling. "What's up?"

"I want you to run a check on a guy named Melvin Talbot from Hammersmith, London."

"England?"

"That's the place," Brewster replied. He reached into his breast pocket and threw a sealed envelope on the table. "I need the info right away. We have a letter that needs to be mailed; but first, I want to know if it's safe to send the damn thing."

She eyed the return address on the envelope, observed no stamp, and said, "Where did you get it?"

"Mills gave it to Andrews to mail for him."

Laurel tucked a lock of red hair behind her ear, while dunking a French fry into a puddle of ketchup on her plate. "John Mills just handed it to you? Wouldn't it be simpler if you just opened the letter and read it?"

"I already have," Brewster said. He helped himself to her fries after smothering them with salt. "From what I've gathered, this Talbot guy sells or writes programs – computer programs, apparently – for musicians."

"Well, isn't Mills a musician?" Laurel asked, eyes glowing with sarcasm.

"Yes." Brewster pulled the plastic coated menu from its holder, speaking as his eyes hungrily passed over the print. "But that doesn't mean Talbot is a computer programmer. I mean, why send all the way to London for a computer or programs, when you can get top of the line everything right here?" He dropped the menu on the table, helping himself to a few more fries, while adding, "Either Mills can afford to simply blow a lot of money buying overseas what he could have bought cheaper here, or he's trying to pull something over on us. Considering his timing, I think he's up to something. And I don't believe in coincidences."

While Brewster busied himself feeding his face, Laurel looked up at Andrews, who stood there with both hands in his pants pockets. Silently, she mouthed the word "Paranoia," and Andrews smiled.

"Okay," she said. "I left my tablet at the shack. Give me an hour or two so I can get back to my computer, and I'll give you a history on Melvin Talbot."

"You going to eat those fries?" Brewster asked.

"No, I'm going to have them bronzed for posterity." She pushed the plate across the table and slid out from the booth. Her eyes glimmered as they rested upon Andrews. "You're looking handsome today, Paul." She flashed a catty smile, turned on her spiked heels, and waltzed through the restaurant on a pair of long shapely legs.

Andrews stood pleasantly stunned. Although his memory was far from perfect, he couldn't recall a single instance when Laurel had complimented anyone. Neither could he remember the woman ever using his first name.

While Laurel met with Brewster in Sandstone giving her report on Melvin Talbot – who turned out not to be a computer salesman, but a computer genius who wrote custom software, and step-by-step manuals for the computer illiterate – Valerie was over twenty miles away. The child sat in the guest room with her mother and John, finishing up on today's phonics lesson. She had graduated from flash cards, and had stammered her way through the opening paragraph of *Treasure Island*, with no help from either of the adults.

It was a sunny afternoon. And according to the radio announcer, the forecast for the next few days called for clear skies and temperatures ranging from the low thirties at night to the high forties during the day. Valerie closed the book on her lap and gazed out the window with a pensive smile. She didn't have to say what was on her mind, for it was written on her face. She wanted to go outside and play in the snow. She wanted to run, to build a snowman, to experience life as a normal five-year-old.

It was unlikely that would happen any time soon.

John left the room for a moment and returned with a writing tablet and an assortment of colored, felt tipped pens. "Have you ever played with paper dolls?" he asked the child.

"No."

He uncapped the black pen and positioned himself at the edge of the bed, so that Valerie sat between him and her mother. "Would you like to?"

Valerie nodded and John began to draw. Within a few minutes, he had a picture of a dark headed child on paper.

He flipped to a fresh sheet and before he finished the next picture, Valerie said, "That's Mommy!"

Minutes later, he flipped that sheet over and drew a man with blond hair. He placed the tablet on the bed, opened the nightstand drawer, and withdrew a pair of scissors, which he handed to Valerie.

"Am I apposed to cut them out?" she asked.

"You don't expect John to do all the work, do you?" her mother asked and smiled.

It took a while for Valerie to get the hang of using the scissors, but she seemed to enjoy the task. It didn't faze her at all that the mommy-doll's head had a V cut into it, and that one hand was lopped off the man-doll. She simply did the best she could. And when she finished, she collected the new paper dolls and went to the master bedroom to play.

"That was a very nice thing you just did," Jillian said. "Valerie's such a sweet little girl. She really is. I hate putting her through all this. Sometimes, I worry about the impact I'm making on her life. She's had to grow up too quickly. All I want is for her to have a normal childhood."

John shook his head and moaned. "God forbid."

"Why do you say that?"

"Next time you get the chance, take a look at what you call 'the normal child.' They have TV's in their rooms, with satellite piped in, video games, and top of the line computers, Internet. Half of them have their own cell phone by the time they're ten years old and for many of them, that means a *smart* phone with texting and Web browsing. They have dolls that not only talk, but also walk and tell stories. And they have absolutely no imagination. It eats up their creativity. They want hundred dollar tennis shoes that are outgrown in three months and jeans with designer labels. And for what? Most of those children don't even clean up their own rooms. They don't know how. Parents, these days, are smothering their children with gifts. And more times than not, the child is miserable because of it. They have too much and appreciate nothing.

"Did you see the expression on your daughter's face while she cut out the paper dolls?"

"She seemed very happy."

"Yes. And a happy child grows up to be a happy adult. When I was growing up, spoiling a child meant ruining a child. If something was spoiled, it either went down the drain or was tossed into the rubbish. These days, however, parents pat themselves on the back because their children want for nothing. Wanting is good. If you want for nothing, then you have no goals. And if you have no goals, you have no life, no drive, and no ambitions. Chances are, if today's children don't inherit a lot of money from their parents, they'll grow up and live off the welfare system."

Jillian raised a challenging brow. "I see. And what was *your* childhood like, John Mills?"

He smiled. "You don't really want to hear this."

"Oh, but I do."

"Well, before my parents passed away, I was a pampered little monster. I had a maid to clean my room, a nanny to wipe my nose and take me to the park, a mother who rushed me to the doctor if I scraped a knee, and a father who handed me money every time the wind blew. Then, I went to live with my Uncle George. The man was quite a character." John smiled, grinned with remembrance. "He always said, 'Why tell the truth, when a lie is ever so much more interesting.' And he lived by those words – believe me. Uncle George lost a leg from the knee down, during the war. The first time he told me that story, a grenade was responsible. And every time he told it thereafter, the story changed. Once, he even said a shark took his leg when he fell overboard during a storm at sea.

"When I went to live with him, it was I who had to wait on *him*. Nine years old and he had me scrubbing floors, cooking, doing the laundry. The house we lived in had rats, if you can believe it. All the money from my parents' estate had been held in a trust. And while it gained interest in the bank, I either went barefoot or wore shoes two sizes too small, and stood on the corner selling the paper every morning before school with my toes all squished.

"I loved my parents dearly. But if it hadn't been for Uncle George, I would never have learned to appreciate anything. He changed my life for the better, and I hated every minute of it. It's funny," John said, staring off. "At the time, I hated living with that old man. It was horrifying to lose my parents at such a young age. And an added measure of horror when Uncle George tugged me by the ear, stared down at my face, and told me I'd be going home to live with *him*. Dreadful. I remember it so clearly – how I thought to myself, 'I'm most surely in hell.' But now, looking back, some of my fondest memories are of the times he and I spent together."

"You have a way of making poverty sound appealing."

John took her by the hand. "Valerie is going to grow up just fine. She has too much of her mother in her to grow up any other way."

"Do you really think the man you sent the letter to will be able to help?"

"Mel Talbot? At the very least, he could get you and your daughter the documents that can allow you to leave the country. New names, passports, visas, whatever it takes. Doubtful Brewster will alert the CIA if he has no reason to believe you've left the country."

"Europe," she whispered. Her expression went bleak. She withdrew her hand. "I-I don't know. It's not like I'd be leaving any family behind, but...but Europe? I'd be completely lost over there. I mean...the customs are so different. The people are so different. I've been there before, several times – briefly – as a child. Even with Brewster on my back, at least here in the good ole U.S. of A. I know what to expect. To start over in a foreign country, knowing absolutely no one...well, I..." She shrugged lightly and began to fidget with her fingers. "I suppose I don't have much of a choice. Valerie will go to school. Make some friends. Europe," she said and forced a smile. "Life's just one big adventure after another."

"Speaking of adventures...Do you know if you'll be having one of those nightmares, tonight?"

Jillian bit down on her bottom lip, eyes making a sweep of the room. Until she felt sure that the house wasn't bugged, she couldn't afford to provoke the nightmare. Yet, she wanted to. She wanted to do it for John, because he had already done so much for her and Valerie. And she had a suspicion the nightmare wouldn't be as powerful as it had been in the past, because her outlook had changed. She now had hope and hope was a powerful weapon. Still, Jillian wondered what he'd say if the decision were left up to him. And for a brief moment, she considered telling him everything. Either way, however, she was sure to face disappointment. If he were to say yes, provoke the nightmare, then she would know that he didn't really care for her. And if he said no, she'd be bound by that decision.

"Jillian?"

She met his gaze, overwhelmed by the concern she saw in his clear blue eyes, taken aback by the voice in her head, a child's voice, Valerie, pleading in desperation: *Mommy, don't. Please don't. You've got to promise not to make the monster mad ever again.*

If he only knew...

CHAPTER 25

Laurel and Brewster met for coffee at Eileen's Diner at one o'clock that afternoon. It didn't bother her that she was already an hour late for her shift at that desert shack, for it meant one less hour she would have to spend with Barnes. She lacked any concern over the information she'd dug up on Melvin Talbot, despite the man's reputation.

About the only thing bothering Laurel this afternoon was that Andrews didn't show up with Brewster. That boyish smile he had given her when she lipped her opinion about Brewster was nothing short of a turn-on. The two of them had made a connection. And Laurel seldom connected with anyone. She found most people to be either too stupid or too boring for her taste. Andrews possessed a quietness – yes. But she had a feeling that a storm brewed behind those serene brown eyes of his.

"So," she said and sighed. "Do we mail the letter, or what?"

"Let me give it a little thought. I'll let you know."

"Before I go, I'd like to talk to you about having Barnes reassigned to someone else. He's really getting on my nerves."

"Barnes gets on everyone's nerves. If you want him reassigned, you'll have to come up with something better than that."

"How about harassment."

"Really?" Brewster said and grinned.

"Yesterday, I was telling him that someone ought to overlay that dirt floor. I told him it was a good thing that it's winter, or we'd have bugs crawling all over the place. And you want to know what he asked me?"

Brewster rolled his eyes. "What?"

"He asked if I knew how to get a pound of meat out of a fly."

"Well, how do you get a pound of meat out of a fly?"

She eyed him coldly while tucking a lock of red hair behind her ear. "You unzip it."

Brewster dropped back his head and laughed, hand slapping the table hard enough for the spoon to clatter against the saucer.

Her face flushed with anger as she clicked her long, polished fingernails on the tabletop. "That may sound amusing to you, but I call it sexual harassment."

"Okay. Okay. Simmer down. I'll have a talk with Barnes and see if that won't straighten him out."

"I'd rather you assigned him to someone else."

"Do you think you could get along with Carney?"

"Actually," she said, flashing a coy smile, "I was thinking of someone else: Andrews."

A waitress came by to refill their coffee, but Brewster waved her off. "I'll think about it. Seriously."

As Laurel walked off with the letter to Talbot in hand, she heard Brewster chuckling behind her. "Unzip it," he said, and laughed some more. God, she hated that man! Brewster and Barnes deserved each other.

Valerie amused herself with the paper dolls right up until bedtime. The following morning, after reading the first full page of *Treasure Island*, she asked John to draw some more paper dolls. That evening, he'd gone into the storage room and made a doll house from one of the cardboard boxes that had been used to store some of his belongings, cutting out doors and windows, using up his blue marker to shade in the house. Valerie loved it. The following day, December thirty-first, John and Jillian met the New Year with a glass of Remy Martin each. John sipped his slowly, while Jillian surprised him by sitting at the piano and playing Chopin's *Fantasie Impromptu*. He built a fire in the guest room fireplace. For the first time, she opened up and talked about her childhood.

She too, had started out as a pampered child. Unlike John, however, she remained a pampered child until she was old enough to be classified as a pampered adult. Some children thought themselves lucky to have a tree house in the back yard. Jillian's doting father had hired contractors to build his two children a playhouse when she was only two. Theirs had a cement foundation, two bedrooms, a spacious living room, a functional kitchen complete with stove and refrigerator, and wall-to-wall carpet – even in the bathroom.

Of course, they had a swimming pool. And of course, every summer vacation was spent abroad. For the most part, both Jillian and her brother had been straight 'A' students. And those 'A's' on their report cards hadn't gone without reward. Which was why she and her brother had horses, and why she and her brother each received a new car upon graduation. She had wanted to be a doctor, until, at the age of fourteen, her father took her to the science museum in Boston. One look at the lung half eaten with cancer she'd seen beneath the glass in the museum, and she realized she hadn't the stomach to become a physician. Instead, she decided to become a teacher. She'd finished four years of college when she'd learned of her pregnancy.

"I didn't want my daughter to be raised by babysitters," she said. "The first time I held her in my arms, I knew I wouldn't be going back to school for a very long time."

Two days after Valerie had read the first page of *Treasure Island*, John brought her into the library. There was one shelf filled with nothing but children's books, most of which had been purchased shortly before Ryan's birth. Valerie searched through the titles and pulled *Black Beauty* from the shelf. John allowed her to take it to her room, for she already knew to always use a bookmark, and always read with clean hands.

For the past few nights in a row, Jillian waited until after Valerie was tucked in bed before telling John she would have no nightmares. And for the past few nights in a row, John had gone to the guest room door and watched her as she slept, wanting to be there in case a nightmare materialized. She did have nightmares, several of them.

Sometimes she'd sit up, sheathed in cold sweat, gasping for breath. Other times, she'd moan softly.

Yesterday morning, she awoke with a small scratch on the palm of her hand. None of those nightmares, however, materialized into the room. At least, not that John was aware of.

He knew it was only a matter of time before the creature returned. And, he couldn't shake the feeling that someone would die as a result of the next encounter. He was correct on both counts.

CHAPTER 26

John realized his mistake in calculating the time it would take for Mel to get here from London. By figuring in the weekend and last Monday (New Years holiday), he now estimated it would be at least Thursday before Mel received the letter, and possibly not until the following Monday. The four or five days he'd previously estimated had turned into ten days. And on Monday evening, January eighth, when Mel still hadn't arrived, John knew he had no alternative but to drive into town and place an overseas call.

John went to his makeshift bed that night, wondering if Brewster and his men were somewhere close. Ten days had passed since he'd had any contact with

Brewster or his men. Instead of being relieved by their absence, it worried him all the more. Most of the snow had melted; the road was now suitable for a four-wheel-drive vehicle, which meant Brewster and his men now had access to the property without the helicopter giving them away. For all he knew, they now camped about a quarter of a mile away, behind the nearest mesa, waiting...

That wasn't the only situation bothering him. Every evening when Jillian informed him that she would not be having a nightmare, he'd ask her how she knew. Not once had she given a satisfactory answer. She'd say: "I just do," or, "Just trust me." Tonight, when he'd pressed her for a clearer explanation, she clamed up. He wanted to trust her. And, in fact, did. It was the idea that she kept such an important secret that bothered him most. Because, that secret could turn out to be the key to ending the nightmares. It only seemed logical that if she knew in advance, then she might also be aware of what caused them. Did she have some kind of warning, a premonition? John usually knew a day or two before it rained. His leg acted up, ached terribly. He wondered if Jillian experienced a similar warning, or if it were something deeper than that. And if she was aware of what caused them, couldn't it also be taken a step further? Couldn't it also mean she might be able to prevent them from happening? The fact that she'd had no nightmares since learning the house could be bugged supported that theory. And yet, it was difficult to fathom. Because, that would suggest the woman had control over it.

If anyone were to ask Mel Talbot his opinion as to who was the most stable, most law-abiding citizen he'd ever met, he wouldn't have thought twice before answering:

"John Mills." And if anyone were to suggest that John was in trouble with the law, Mel would look that person straight in the eye and call him a liar – even if that person were a she, and turned out to be Her Majesty, The Queen of England. Mel wasn't the kind of guy who beat around the bush. If he had something to say, he said it. And if you didn't like what he had to say, he would take a moment to explain how and why you were a fool. And if you still didn't agree, he'd simply tell you to fuck off.

Ignorance was okay. Ignorance could be cured. Bold stupidity, however, was something he never put up with. There were a few other quirks Mel Talbot had that most people found offensive. How he kept his house, was one of them. His mind remained totally organized. Pick a subject – any subject – and Mel could give a dissertation at least an hour long, citing passages from reference books, going into great detail and improvising with any last minute theories he'd cook up. As for his home, it looked about as organized as a dumpster. His reason for not hiring a maid was that he didn't want anyone snooping through his personal belongings and messing them up. He didn't have a laundry hamper; he didn't need one. The floor suited him just fine as a dumping ground for all his dirty clothes.

You were apt to find a half eaten, moldy sandwich in the bathroom sink, or on the nightstand next to his bed. The inside of his refrigerator looked like a lab experiment gone awry. He had two file cabinets in the study, both filled with not files, but junk he'd accumulated over the years. Precious junk, like a dead car battery; two or three watches that no longer worked; yellowed newspaper clippings – that sort of thing. When he dressed, he was lucky to find matching socks and equally lucky if he didn't have to wear mismatched shoes.

The only reason his home wasn't infested with bugs was that the exterminators came monthly. Until last fall when he hired an accountant, his bills were never paid on time. Such things he found to be trivial, meaningless. Which was why he found himself single only three years after he'd married. Julie had informed him that she couldn't spend another moment in such a filthy house, talking to the walls. And Mel, taking a moment to remove his reading glasses as he'd looked up from his computer monitor, said: "Goodbye."

Now, in a helicopter with the Phoenix airport miles behind him, he reflected back to those days when he and Julie had first married. Not because he was still in love with the woman. Opposites do attract, and Julie had turned out to be a hopeless airhead. He'd been ready for her to leave long before she had decided to go. He thought about those days, because it was then when he'd first met John Mills. John was one of the few people Mel respected and truly admired, which made it even more important for Mel to determine what manner of chaos had developed in the man's life to prompt such a bizarre letter. The letter John had sent was perhaps the most curious Mel had ever read, and stranger still because it had been written by the most stable, most law-abiding citizen he'd ever met. Either John had gone completely mad, or he was in deep trouble. Trouble so deep that he feared to spell it out in a letter for fear of reprisal. The question was: Reprisal from whom?

Mel strongly believed that genius is controlled madness. John, in his own right, was a genius in the field of music. Living alone in the middle of nowhere could have done something to that control. The closing line of John's letter put an end to that theory. The Iron

Lady's bank account. Yes. They had gone to the pub for drinks, and Mel, who couldn't resist any opportunity to brag, mentioned how Margaret Thatcher's bank account could be tampered with. But that was only part of the conversation. They had touched upon the subject of computer espionage. Adding up the important details of John's letter: the amount of the check; the mention of their first meeting; the Iron Lady's bank account; time being of the essence; and the request that Mel come in person – yes, John was knee-deep in something that didn't smell very sweet. The most important part had been written between the lines. The letter was formal, businesslike, not the kind of letter you'd send to a good friend. Had they discussed programs to help John's music career during that first meeting at the pub? Fuck no. So, Mel could safely deduce that John believed someone else might get hold of the letter first. And that was perhaps the most disturbing part of all.

The FBI, the CIA, the police? Mel had no doubt that he wanted to help John, regardless of the circumstances. But, even his imagination couldn't seize an explanation as to what a man like John Mills was doing under investigation.

The vagueness of the letter had him troubled, which was why – instead of leaving Friday, the day he received the letter – Mel had opted to take a full day to do a little shopping. He'd gotten the equipment through customs with no problem. And on the transcontinental flight over here, he'd thought of a few necessities he lacked. So, after arriving in Phoenix, he'd paid a little visit to the mall, where he found a sizable electronics store.

The pilot tapped Mel on the shoulder and pointed down to a pool of light which shown on a rather large house. Mel didn't bother to take out his map; like everything else he'd either seen or heard, he had it memorized. He gave a nod and the pilot took the helicopter down. Having slept off and on during the transcontinental flight, Mel felt perfectly rested. It may have been only two o'clock in the morning as far as the people of Arizona were concerned, but to him, it was ten a.m., time to start a new day.

CHAPTER 27

Mel stood at the door, annoyed. Not a single light came on in the house and yet a dog barked from inside. He knew he had found the right place. No one else would have been crazy enough to build a single story castle in the middle of a fucking desert. Ahh, but crazy wasn't the right word. No. The word that described Mills best was eccentric – a nice way of categorizing someone who suffered from obsessive-compulsive behavior. Mel remembered the first time he'd visited John's home in Dover. Had a microscope been available, Mel doubted he could have found enough dust for an adequate slide sample. And he was sure this house would be the same way.

Everything he'd brought with him was now piled up on the porch: one suitcase, three wooden crates, and one plastic sack filled with electronic goodies. The helicopter pilot waited for Mel to give the signal before taking off. Mel pounded on the door for the third time, and then crossed his arms as he leaned casually against the wall. He was tall, lanky. His face was mottled with two day's worth of black whiskers. And if his dark hair hadn't been buzzed so short, he would have looked as if he'd just stepped out of an early Def Leppard video. There wasn't enough good material left of his jeans to sew patches to. He wore a leather bomber jacket with the British flag stitched on the back. Sewn on the front of the jacket was a small patch with the words: "Designated Drinker." He wore a black T-shirt; its pocket partially ripped along the seam and flapped over. The boots he wore were scuffed so badly, not even a bottle of black shoe polish could help. Mel rolled up his eyes, sighing with impatience. He lifted a hand to knock one more time, and then he heard the deadbolt retracting.

When the door finally opened, Mel dropped his eyes to his watch and said quite seriously, "You know, I've been waiting out here for three minutes and twenty-two seconds." He grinned wildly as he looked at John for the first time in four and a half years. "You look like shit, man."

John stepped outside, closing the door behind him. "I see you still do your shopping at the same dumpster." He flashed a crooked smile and they clapped each other on the back, grinning like fools. "Damn, it's good to see you again. Glad you could come."

While John eyed the crates on the porch, Mel waved an arm, signaling the pilot to leave.

"It's freezing out here," Mel said. "I didn't travel halfway round the world to catch my death of cold."

"Before we go inside, I think you should know my house may be bugged."

Mel shook his head, still grinning. "Please tell me this is all one big joke. I'm dying to laugh, and I'd hate to do so at your expense."

"I wish it were something to laugh about," John replied.

Mel's expression sobered as he shifted from one foot to the other. "You're the last person I'd expect to find in trouble, John. What the fuck is going on?"

"Let's go inside. There's someone I want you to meet. Just be careful what you say in the living room and in the dining room. As you've probably already gathered from my letter, you're supposed to be here selling computer software. The rest of the house, I believe, is safe. Otherwise, they would have heard something and returned."

"Who is the 'they' you're referring to?"

"The FBI."

Mel rolled up his eyes and moaned.

After a brief talk, John left Mel in the guest room and returned a few minutes later with Jillian. Mel, who sat on the edge of the bed, got to his feet when Jillian entered the room. He'd had no idea that the someone whom John wanted him to meet was a woman. And a handsome woman at that. Once the introductions ended, Mel reseated himself on the edge of the bed and John went to the bathroom vanity for a chair.

"Are you the reason I'm here?" Mel asked in John's absence.

"I'm afraid so," Jillian replied.

John positioned the chair in front of the bed and Jillian took a seat.

"So," Mel said. He laced his fingers together and, bending his fingers backwards, cracked his knuckles. "The house might be bugged. The FBI is breathing down your backs. You all but drag me across the planet with your cloak and dagger letter, which, by the way, arrived with postage due. Would someone like to tell me what the fuck is going on around here?" He grinned as he gazed at Jillian. "You'll have to forgive my language. I may have been raised a polite English gentleman, but I was corrupted by your great American educational system."

John leaned his cane against the wall and took a seat on the bed. "She's been forewarned. I've already told Jillian all about you."

"Then I suppose it's time I hear all about Jillian."

Jill crossed her legs at the knee. "It's a long story."

Mel waved a hand in the air. "I've all the time in the world."

"It may be difficult to believe, but around five years ago, I was given less than six months to live."

"Not difficult at all," Mel said, fumbling with the drooping pocket of his shirt. His presentation of being preoccupied was just one more behavior most people found offensive.

"About a year before that, I noticed some swelling in my throat. Just one side. I experienced no pain, though, so I figured it was nothing. Then the other side started swelling. At the time, I was pregnant, under doctor's care. So I figured if there was anything wrong, of course my doctor would tell me. I didn't give it much thought, because, being pregnant, the rest of me was, well, swelling too." She smiled, tensely. "A few months before the birth of my daughter, I noticed a problem with my tonsils. They had enlarged enough so that swallowing became difficult. Still, like a fool, I ignored it. I ignored it right up until my birthday, which was a couple months after I had my daughter, Valerie.

"My husband threw a surprise party for me that evening. Until that night, I hadn't touched any kind of alcoholic beverage for over a year. Jim fixed me a whiskey sour. Twenty, maybe thirty minutes later, I was in agony. I went to my doctor the following morning, thinking I must have had an ulcer or something. I've heard that an ulcer is usually aggravated by alcohol and that sometimes the pain isn't confined to the stomach area. And mine certainly wasn't."

"Hodgkin's disease?" Mel inquired.

She looked at John for a moment, as if to convey a silent message that he'd been right about Mel. The man hadn't appeared to be listening at all. And yet, he seemed right on top of everything. "Yes. The last stages. It had already spread to my spleen. It was everywhere. If I had gone to the doctor when the symptoms first started, I would have had an excellent chance of recovery. Hodgkin's disease is one of the most curable types of cancer...or so the doctor tried to convince me. But I'd waited too long. The drugs and radium treatments only made me sicker. When it got too bad, I was hospitalized. And I knew the only way I was going to leave there was by way of the morgue.

"That's how my problems started. But that's not the beginning. Sometimes, it difficult to know where the beginning is."

"Take your time," Mel said. He placed his hands on the bed behind him, leaning back into them while stretching his legs. "John already told me you're wanted by the FBI, and every detail you can give me as to why they want you will be helpful."

"My brother was a doctor," she said. Her hands had been folded over her knee, and now she drew them into her lap, studying them meticulously. "My brother, Richard, worked under a Dr. Carl Neas at a medical research facility called Bio-Tox in Fairshire, Massachusetts. I didn't know exactly what kind of work they were doing. I knew that Neas had been into stem cell research. But he'd stumbled upon something else during that time. Richard kept pretty closed lipped about it. My husband knew some of the details. He and Richard were very close. Every Saturday night they'd get together for what they called 'brainstorming.' Anyway, I'll never forget that day in the hospital room. Richard and Jim had come in to visit me that day. It was on a Sunday. Richard came every Sunday right after church let out. Jim lowered the rail and took a seat at my side. And Richard...

...gripped his sister's hand. His blue eyes sparkled as his free hand brushed against her puffy face. He looked over at Jim. "You're right. I don't have a choice, do I?" He bit down on his bottom lip hard, as if the physical pain could make him forget the mental anguish. "Jill, Jim and I are going to take you out of here. We're going to get you some real *help."*

Jim, whose face was nearly as pale as the white shirt he wore, exhaled with relief. During the last two months, he'd dropped twenty pounds. Instead of going out and buying new clothes, he simply took in the slack with his belt. It was not the expected look of a prominent psychiatrist.

Jim nodded. "You're doing the right thing, Rick."

"Where are we going?" Jillian asked. She knew it was foolish to be vain at a time like this, but that didn't make it any easier to leave the hospital now that most of her

hair had fallen out. She didn't want anyone to see her this way. No one. Her body had bloated. Her coloring had turned ashen. She was weak, tired. The worst part was her hair, her beautiful black hair, now baby fine, and all but gone. She shook her head against the pillow. If she had to die, at least she could do it with dignity. "Ricky, please don't make me leave. I don't want anyone to see me like this."

"No one's going to see you," Jim assured her.

Richard pressed a cotton ball to her wrist, over where the I.V. needle went in. With his thumb in place, he pulled out the plastic needle, applying pressure until he was sure there would be no bleeding. "I'm taking you home, kiddo."

"What about Neas?" Jim asked Richard. "Have you discussed this with him?"

"I'll take care of Neas. He owes me, and he owes me big. If he refuses, we go it without him. But I think he'll go along with it. You take Jill to my house. It's too dangerous to try it at Bio-Tox. Security's tight. I'll get what I need and meet you at my house in three hours."

Four hours later, Richard arrived with Dr. Neas and a pickup truck load of equipment. Their first concern was for sterility. The guest room was completely emptied. They ripped the carpet up from the floor. The walls and floor were then washed down with disinfectant. Jim and Richard brought the table in from the dining room, overlaying it with freshly washed linen. All of this was accomplished in silence, as if by not speaking of it, they broke no rules.

The surgery itself was accomplished without anesthesia. As Jillian rested on the linen covered table, her head locked in a frame, Jim stood above her. A clean sheet draped over her body.

"I want you to relax," he said soothingly. "Now, close your eyes."

She did.

"Take a deep breath and let it out slowly."

She complied. She knew the routine well, perhaps as well as Jim. He would tell her to pretend that her eyes were too heavy to open. She would repeat each word he said over and over until it was embedded firmly in her mind and became fact. He would then suggest other things, such as: "Let that relaxing feeling pass over your body, all the way to your toes."

And then he said: "Your body is getting numb. All you feel is a light tingling sensation, nothing more."

"Nothing more," she repeated.

"While Dr. Neas does a little testing, I'm going to ask you a few questions and you'll answer them. What do you feel?"

"A light tingling sensation."

"Very good."

"Now, in a moment, I'll want you to open your eyes. When you open your eyes, you'll keep them open until I tell you to close them. And when you close them again, you'll be at peace, a wonderful peace that will take you deeper and deeper. Again, I'll ask you to open your eyes and the peaceful sensation will magnify tenfold. Jillian, open your eyes."

She did.

"Close your eyes." He waited a moment, and then said, "Open your eyes."

In a dreamlike state, she could see Dr. Neas standing over her at the head of the table. He had a hypodermic needle in his latex-gloved hand, which he set on the table by a tray filled with surgical instruments. He continued to work on an area of her head, doing something that made it tingle. And she felt wonderful, peaceful, totally relaxed.

"Now, I'm going to hold your hand. When I let go, the date of your birth will disappear from your mind. The more you try to remember that date, the further it will be pushed away until it's completely lost to you." Jim released her hand. "Try to find your birthday and it's gone. Allow it to go. Now it's gone, isn't it?"

"Yes."

Jim looked over at Dr. Neas. "It's done. Somnambulism. She's ready." He then took a sterile scalpel and slowly sliced into the meaty part of her left hand. "What do you feel?" he asked.

"A light tingling sensation."

Jim nodded and Richard began handing Neas the instruments as he called for them. About an hour into the surgery, she watched Neas pick up the hypodermic and Richard immediately filled another from a sealed vial.

"What do you feel?" Jim asked.

"A light tingling sensation."

Richard stepped around the table and took hold of Jill's hand. Using a fresh scalpel, he repeated the procedure Jim had done just before the surgery began, slicing into the meaty part of her hand. "What do you feel?"

Her response remained the same as before.

After wiping her hand with a cotton ball soaked in Betadine, Richard took a straight scalpel from the tray. He looked at Jim, at Dr. Neas. "You'll feel a light tingling sensation," he said softly.

"Yes."

"You can't bleed."

"Can't bleed," she responded.

"You're completely relaxed. Nothing can change that until I say so." He then brought the scalpel down, slicing into his sister's hand once again. There was blood, but only a minute amount. Richard held her hand up before her eyes. "What do you feel?"

She gave the suggested response.

Jim stepped up and took over. "In a moment, I'm going to ask you to make the tingling sensation go away. But the only way you can do that is to make the cut go away. Do you understand?"

"I understand. I make the cut go away."

"Okay," Jim said. He took in a deep breath, his eyes locked on the gash in her hand. "Jill, I want you to make the tingling sensation go away."

Her eyes narrowed, then widened – the whites had gone a pale shade of pink. Her eyelids fluttered. "Can't."

"Try."

Her nostrils flared, her eyes went out of focus. "Can't."

Neas, who had been at the head of the table for the past hour, bustled his way to where Jill could see him. He pulled the surgical mask from his narrow face and leaned down until his warm, sour breath played against her cheek. "For every second that passes, the tingling sensation is going to become more and more painful. Within a minute, it'll be absolutely unbearable. The only way to stop it is to heal the incision."

He took an alcohol solution and poured it directly into the cut on her hand.

"No," she said weakly. "No!" Her teeth clenched against the pain. Her expression twisted into a grimace. Eyes closed, she shuddered uncontrollably. Her shoulders started flinching, and the muscles tightened. Her blue eyes, which brimmed with tears, rolled back in her head. She had lost the state of hypnosis and fought

to get it back, fought to believe the pain wasn't there. Lip snarling, saliva dribbling from the corners of her mouth, she screamed violently, writhing on the table. Richard tried to steady her, his gloved hands grasping her knees, but he couldn't hold her. Her legs started thrashing, bucking on the table.

"Stop it!" Jim yelled. "My God, stop it! You never handle a patient under hypnosis this way. Never!"

"It's getting worse, Jill," Neas said coldly. "You're the only person capable of putting an end to the pain. It's getting much worse!"

Her arm swept through the air. Her hand grasped wildly for anything to cling to, grabbing Neas by the shoulder, fingers digging into the old doctor's muscle until he let out a scream and yanked back.

Then all at once, she stopped. Jill went into a state of total relaxation. Her breathing slowed to normal. Richard watched in amazement as the heart monitor dropped from two hundred ten to seventy-four beats per minute in the blink of an eye. Likewise, her blood pressure stabilized: One-ten over seventy.

"Jill," Jim said, dropping a hand on her shoulder. "Honey, how do you feel?"

"Warm."

He picked up her hand, turning it to examine the gash from the scalpel. A small trace of blood had smeared across her palm. All three of the scalpel cuts, however, were gone. He quickly grabbed her other hand, just to make sure he'd not somehow mixed them up. Both hands were free of injury.

"We did it," he whispered, jaw dropping. "We did it," he said again, a smile sweeping across his face. "By God, we actually did it!"

"We're not through yet," Neas reminded him. "Or have you forgotten the reason for this procedure? The

suggestion of pain worked for her hand. Let's see if it'll work equally well in fighting the disease that's taken over her lymph glands."

"You can't do that," Jim stated. "It won't work. All you'll manage to do is wake her."

"Stop the negative suggestions and watch me," Neas said. He turned to Richard. "Ready the EEG. I want a printout on this."

CHAPTER 28

Mel looked at her, grinning. "Please, do go on. Haven't heard such a whopper since last I'd seen John's dear ole uncle. You're an excellent liar."

Jillian held her tongue for several lengthy moments, eyes narrowed, mouth agape, simply staring in Mel's direction in disbelief of his rudeness. The man was goading her. She turned briefly, watched John nod as if prompting her to continue, then put on a smile of her own as Mel's grin turned to laughter.

Jillian said, "Pain receptacles became triggers, stimulating a normally sluggish area of the brain that is literally capable of miracles. When injured, I can greatly speed up an already accelerated healing, by focusing on the pain. Or, I can create a sense of pain through self-hypnosis."

"So," Mel said, sitting forward, "now you're claiming that the FBI is trying to put a lid on it. The FBI – are you sure?"

"They're trying to kill me. At least two of the three doctors involved are dead. I've been running ever since."

Mel scratched the whiskers on his chin as he turned to John. "John, this is ludicrous. I can't believe you'd drag me out here with a story like this. How long have you known this woman?"

"They've been here, Mel, looking for her."

Mel shook his head as if to clear the confusion. "You're fucking with me, right?"

"I think you know me better than that."

Mel hesitated as he examined the serious expressions on John's and then Jillian's faces. "Okay, let's just say you're *not* putting me on. Let's assume everyone here has a good grasp on his or her own sanity. How exactly do you propose for me to help?"

John and Jillian exchanged worried glances. Then John said: "We need you to locate Dr. Neas. He may still be alive. And he's probably the only person capable of understanding what's actually going on inside Jillian, and reversing the procedure."

"What do you mean by 'reversing the procedure?' If your friend here wants to die from cancer, she can get all the cigarettes she needs from the fucking store."

Again, a worried exchange of glances. This time, Jillian spoke: "Whatever it was that they did to me...it's still going on."

"Elucidate."

Jillian stood up and, seeing the skeptical glimmer in Mel's dark eyes, she went into the bathroom, returning a moment later holding a thin razor blade between a thumb and forefinger. She set the blade on the nightstand long enough to roll up her sleeve. After showing Mel the inside of her wrist, she brought the razor down, cutting deeply enough to slice an artery and draw a steady pumping of blood. Mel jumped back, and shot a desperate look at the doorway as if contemplating a quick dash back to England, while Jillian dropped the blade on the nightstand and pressed her hand over the wound for all of ten seconds before letting go.

Grabbing a tissue from the dispenser on the nightstand, she wiped away the blood and held her unmarred wrist out for Mel's inspection.

Mel stepped closer, carefully, his eyes first lighting on the blood-stained razor blade resting on the nightstand. He moved even closer, eyes widening then focusing on the woman's wrist. The moment of realization stuck hard, and sent him pacing back and forth, scratching his head, dropping his head back to stare up at the ceiling, scratching his chin, scowling, grinning, cheek twitching. He stopped, facing John, who now held the woman's hand. "This. Is. Not. Fucking. Possible."

John found himself smiling. Two weeks ago, he'd been in the same position as Mel was in now. "Are you not the same man who once said nothing is impossible?" he goaded. "Seems to me, you are. I do remember you using those words, Mel."

"But not in this day and age, John. It's not possible. Fifty years from now – perhaps. I'd sooner believe there's a god, than this. But I've seen it with my own eyes. I've got to be dreaming. I have never been more impressed in my life." He hiked up the legs of his jeans, hunkering down on the floor at Jillian's side until he sat on the heels of his scuffed boots. Grinning, he said: "Marry me, dear lady and together we'll rule the world."

"There's more," John said. He then told Mel about the nightmares.

The three of them sat in silence for a good five minutes. Mel, fidgeting with his pocket again. John, staring down at his hands. Jillian, shaking her head lightly from time to time. John got up and asked if anyone cared for a drink. Mel wanted whiskey, but John had none. The only alcohol in the house not lethal in moderation was the cognac left over from New Year's Eve. Half a bottle at best. And that was exactly what John brought into the room on a tray with three glasses.

Mel did the honors, first pouring for the lady, then John, not bothering to pour a glass for himself, but claiming what remained in the bottle.

After taking a hardy swig from the bottle and wiping his chin with the back of his hand, Mel said: "If you want my advice, forget about finding Neas and go where they're least likely to expect. Let's broaden the canvas a bit, shall we? Leave the country."

John set his glass on the nightstand, empty. "Mel, would you care to live for a thousand years, dreading what may happen in your sleep each and every night?"

"To live a thousand years...damn straight, I would. I'd walk a mile barefoot every day on a bed of broken glass, if it guaranteed my immortality." He eyed Jillian, lips smacking as he rubbed the dark whiskers on his chin. "You don't know how fortunate you are. You're living every man's dream. Count your blessings and leave the country. There's no way to find Neas. If the FBI hasn't found him, we can't find him. Chances are, he's dead, anyway. I can get you out of the country in a week, perhaps sooner. Before the FBI alerts the CIA of a possible move to the other side of the Atlantic, you'll be a completely different person. Even with new identification, though, it would be wise for you and your daughter to travel separately."

"No," Jill said. "Valerie and I won't be separated. Not even for an hour. Anything could happen."

"Jillian," John said. He reached for her hand; it felt cold, clammy. "He's right. They'll be looking for a woman travelling with a young girl."

"No."

John said, "Mel, is there any way for you to access FBI files by computer? If nothing else, perhaps they'll give us some insight. Neas may have given them information that could help Jillian."

"Listen, John, peeking into classified files isn't as easy as it once was. Times have changed and I haven't kept up with them. Even with the proper password, they have technology – and have had it for some years now – that would shut me out. There's a program that, once the site is entered – not logged into, mind you, but by just *bringing* on the site – immediately traces the IP, giving a complete history of whomever is at that address. Log in, and satellite photos of the location are taken, vehicle registrations run, etc. In other words, in order to access their computers, I'd need much more than a password and username. Who knows what else. Even then, it would be a tricky deed. Security is becoming more and more sophisticated. Especially in this country. It's different here in The States. I'm sure they have equipment and programs I've never heard of. We're talking about the FBI, not a fucking database at a bank. I'd have to wing it. If I were lucky enough to be invisible and call up the right file, but failed to enter the proper clearance code, I'd be locked out. They'd know something was wrong, they'd know exactly where to find me, and I'd be fucked."

"But can you do it?" John persisted.

Jillian sat on the edge of her seat.

Mel fidgeted with his pocket. Then all at once, he ripped it clean off. A scattering of rolled lint fell to his lap. "Will you look at that?" he said, holding up the black square of material that was once a pocket. "Damn, I hate these cheap clothes."

"Mel?"

"It'll take some time. No promises." Mel frowned, looking more like a boy than a man. The color had drained from his whisker-mottled face. John had never seen the man look more sober, more worried. And as Mel raised one arched brow he added: "I'll expect you to pay my funeral expenses, though. You will do that for me, John, won't you?"

Jillian shook her head – no. Enough people had died already.

John's eyes narrowed considerably. He nodded, but not in acknowledgment of anything that had been said. No. He acknowledged defeat. And as he gazed into Jillian's eyes, he knew she too would not expect Mel to lay down his life. He shook his head, clearly frustrated, which was when Mel cut loose and bellowed laughter.

"Got you," Mel said, grinning wildly. "Oh, don't look so bloody serious. It was only a joke. You fell right into it." He shook his head. "I'll tap a few sites, scan the headlines until I find a piece on the FBI. There's sure to be names of some of the top brass. I'll run a few of those names up, get a little background information on them, a few addresses, and *voila*, I'm as good as in – if you don't mind a little B and E. Better yet, to expedite this, I know a man who can do that for me in half the time. Sure is going to be fun. Haven't broken into a house or office in a good many years. It ought to be interesting. I will, however, expect you to pay all expenses. Airline tickets, lodging, camcorders, auto rental, solicitor fees should it come to that, hospital bills, that sort of thing. I'll deduct it from the thirty American K you sent, and give back the rest."

"I'll pay you for your time and effort," John offered.

"Fuck no," Mel replied. He swallowed hard, scared shitless, still grinning. "Just call it my contribution to the world. Who knows, a virus here, a virus there, a few bogus directives, and all the files and hard copies containing info on Jillian could be destroyed." He hoped. "Certainly beats sitting at home, watching it rain."

He took another swig of Remy Martin, and then positioned the bottle between his thighs. "Of course, Jillian, you'll still need to leave the country, regardless of what I find. Computer files can be erased, but the memories of those who've been chasing after you can't. Your Agent Brewster will still be after you. We need to make it as difficult as possible for anyone to find you, so it's time we broaden the playing field by adding another continent. I suggest you allow Valerie to accompany me back to Hammersmith. Should John attempt to leave the country, t'would be like waving a red flag in front of Brewster's face, which means you'll have no escort when it's time for you to leave.

"If you love your little girl, and I suspect you do, you'll make the right decision; she'll be much safer travelling without you. There's no time to mince words, here, Jillian. If you're too much of an over-protective, selfishly doting and smothering parent to do this, I must know now. I'm not about to put my neck on the chopping block only to have you back out at the last minute."

The part that bothered her most was the separation from Valerie. But Mel had made a point, a very valid point. Brewster wanted her, and anyone caught with her was as good as dead. "I appreciate your position and your candor. As much as I hate it, you're right. I'll do it."

"Good girl. A couple more questions. Are you absolutely, one hundred percent sure that it's the FBI who are after you, and not the police or some other government organization?"

"I saw Brewster's credentials," John said. "He's FBI."

"Last question. And then I'll want you to write down some personal information. How, exactly, does this nightmare become real?"

Jillian turned to John, anxiety etched on her face. The question in her eyes was: How much should I tell Mel? She watched John nod, as if to prod her for a full account, despite John's prior denial of the truth.

Jillian returned her attention to Mel, heart pounding in her throat. "It's my fault. I cause it. Dr. Neas realized that in a hypnotic state, the healing process could be speeded up to an even more astounding rate."

"Healing process?" Mel repeated, his tone reflecting the glimmer in his eyes. "I'd hardly call that talent of yours a 'healing process.' It's not cell renewal; it's freaking creation. But point taken."

Jillian continued. "The deeper the trance, the more powerful and possibly even unlimited the ability becomes. Being in a hypnotic state is basically the same as being asleep…with one major exception: The hypnotic state is a controlled state. And so, with REM being a very deep state, and with the pain in the nightmare triggering this ability for creation, and with my subconscious mind basically running amok…I create that…that *thing*. It's a part of me."

"No," John argued. "That's where you're wrong. It's not a part of you. It's a dream. A nightmare. The misfiring of synaptic nerves."

"Okay, okay," Mel said, holding up his hand. "I get the picture. But I have one more question. Do you have any idea what drug Neas used during the surgery? What I'm getting at is this: drugs eventually wear off. So I'm thinking it has to be more like a vaccine – something that desensitizes you to certain organisms. Or, perhaps even a toxin. Or perhaps even a retrovirus."

"I don't know if it was a drug or a vaccine. I really have no idea," she replied. "Neas discovered that several small areas of the brain worked together in a counter-productive way. He told me – jokingly – that God, as an after-thought, must have made it that way when He realized humans didn't deserve immortality. Carl didn't go into the details, which I probably wouldn't have understood anyway. He basically put those areas out of commission, saying that the brain would then reroute itself, which brought about this...ability."

She watched as Mel opened his mouth to speak, only to pause, as if considering what she'd just said. His eyes shifted away from hers, and an uncomfortable silence fell between them.

CHAPTER 29

Mel decided it was best to put a reasonable distance between himself and John in order to protect John from further suspicion that might be aroused by certain activities. As it turned out, John's house had been bugged. The good news was that the technology was much more limited than an Internet bug, and John had thought clearly enough to keep the transmitter in the closet. After staging a little chat in the living room on customizing music programs that could further John's career (which included the mention of going to Phoenix to a specialized electronics store), the pocket sized transmitter Brewster had left behind was returned to the linen closet between a few blankets.

While John stood at the kitchen stove making oatmeal, Mel took several snapshots of Jillian and Valerie with his cell phone. After breakfast, Mel took the Land Rover and made the four-hour trip to Phoenix, where he rented a box at a mail station, did a little shopping, and then finally rented a motel room on Van Buren. He'd had one run-in with two of Brewster's men – actually, one was a woman – stationed at the turnoff to the main highway leading to Sandstone. Thanks in part to the earlier staged conversation between himself and John, Brewster's men had let him pass without much ado.

According to the information Jillian had given him, she was twenty-nine years old. He needed to obtain a birth certificate for the woman and one for the child. They would also require passports. Visas were not necessary to enter the U.K. Without a visa, they could remain in England for up to six months. And sometime before the six months ended, Mel would see to it that the woman and child got new identification, which would make them 'citizens,' and nullify the need for visas. The process was simple, and one that a dear old friend, Arthur Billings, could handle quickly. With a birth certificate, he could get a Social Security Number. With a Social Security Number he could get a driver's license. And with a driver's license, he could get a passport. All of which could be sent to Mel's mailbox within a week. The documents would look and feel like the real thing. The best part about it: they'd all check out, as well. If all went well, as soon as his business with the FBI was complete, Jillian and Valerie would have everything needed to leave the country.

One of the many problems he could foresee was getting Jillian and the child out of John's house. He'd met Valerie this morning. She was a small tyke, small

enough to squeeze into one of the crates he'd brought
and definitely light enough to carry. But Jillian...

Jillian could not be smuggled out in a crate. Getting
her out of that house would be next to impossible. That,
however, would be John's concern.

Now that he had partially absorbed the biggest shock
of his life – Jillian's uncanny ability to heal herself –
Mel was able to sit back and dissect her story piece by
piece. He had a few more questions that needed to be
asked. Of the many things that puzzled him about her
situation, two concerned him the most. First: How did
she know that her brother had committed suicide? She
evidently wasn't there to see it happen. And if there had
been a write-up about it in the paper, how could she be
so certain that the FBI didn't fabricate the story. So, was
it possible that her brother was still alive?

Which led to the second part: It was important to
know how the FBI had repeatedly tracked her down.
According to her story, she'd been all over the country,
never staying in a single town for more than a couple of
months at a time before they'd get wind of her.

If she'd been doing something foolish, such as letting
her mouth run to one of her temporary neighbors;
allowing herself to be seen in too many public places;
performing one of her 'mighty miracles' where someone
might see; or more likely: contacting old friends and
relatives whose phones might be tapped, Mel had to put
a stop to it now. Otherwise, getting her off the continent
wouldn't be enough. Because, if the habit continued,
making it possible for them to trace her to the U.K., then
it was just as feasible that he might be implicated in her
flee from the country. In other words: He'd have the
fucking CIA breathing down his back. Jillian struck him
as a rational woman, and yet, she had to be doing

something wrong, something to keep drawing attention to herself.

Something...

The last nine miles of road leading Mel back to John's desert dwelling was a mixture of slush and mud, which would explain the filthy condition of the Land Rover. Climbing the hills required nerves of steel. And one hill in particular that half-looped up and around a mesa in a way that had his heart stuck in his throat even after that hill stood a quarter mile or so behind. The nine miles of roads between the main highway and John's house weren't really roads at all, just a seemingly endless series of bumps and ruts, making it impossible to drive faster than twenty miles per hour without having his teeth rattle. What he found most interesting were the trees. Pinyon pine, scrub pine, juniper. They looked lifeless and stale, reminiscent of something you might find in the yard of a haunted mansion. He supposed, in its own bland way, the desert country possessed a certain beauty. It offered quiet, solitude, which was a plus if you were into that sort of thing.

But Mel, although he valued his time alone more than he valued the company of a willing woman, preferred the city. He felt a certain kind of security in knowing he could throw open any window of his house and scream for help, even though chances were no one would answer the call. Although his answering machine picked up every voice call placed to his residence, it was nice to know he had a phone there if it were needed. If ever forced to live in a nothing wasteland like this, he would survive, but that would be the extent of it.

It made him wonder about John, worry about John. The man had shut out the world shortly after he'd lost his family. It wasn't healthy. Neither did it seem fair. It was, nonetheless, John's way. So Mel had refrained from interfering, hoping the guy would come around. Now, because of what seemed to be the worst crises to hit the planet since organized religion, John was more alive than he'd been during the past five years. Was it blessing or curse, Mel wondered.

The only way to decide that was to play it out to the end. Mel's determination held firm. Not just for the sake of friendship (although that was a great part of it), not because he felt obligated to Jillian (although she was quite a beautiful woman), but because his curiosity rose to all time high. The thought of never dying. The concept of infinity and what it may bring. To be living through one era after another and seeing all there is to see...and more. No, immortality should *not* be sold to the highest bidder. And yet, it could have its place in society.

Had Shakespeare been allowed to live for all eternity, if men like Galileo and Isaac Newton possessed immortality, the world would be a better planet. Now, it was possible. Those who would dedicate their lives to The Sciences and The Arts could receive the ultimate reward. Instead of striving for the Nobel Prize, those deserving few could opt for eternity without death.

"The cleverest minds," he stated. "The gifted men of vision. The elite. The peacemakers." He grinned at his reflection in the rearview mirror. "Me."

Two days after Barnes' reassignment, Laurel decided she didn't care for Andrews very much. She went from working an eight-hour day, to working a sixteen-hour day. Someone had to maintain a post at the cutoff to San Pablo Road to check the desert dwellers who wanted to drive into town. Being stuck with the same person sixteen hours a day, seven days a week, was like having a bad rash. She couldn't really complain about Andrews' behavior towards her, unless lack of interest could be categorized as a crime. He behaved as a gentleman. He didn't tell uncomely jokes or sit in a corner mumbling to himself.

She had, however, misinterpreted the storm she'd noticed behind his dark eyes. Yes, a storm brewed there, one that made her perfectly uncomfortable. He knew things the rest of them didn't know. And Andrews didn't seem inclined to share his insight with anyone. He'd let that English guy, Talbot, through the roadblock without even bothering to check the back end of the vehicle. Had he been so easy on everyone else he'd encountered, she might have viewed him as a pushover. But when the Kearneys stopped for the inspection, Andrews had gone through their van, opening up Mrs. Kearney's suitcases (it seemed as if the Kearneys were through talking about divorce and had decided to do something about it), checking the compartment for the spare tire, looking under the hood for the smallest piece of incriminating evidence, while the two detainees stood idly by on the side of the road.

The same went for the Detmers. And Mr. Bain. And the Foremans. Now that they were stuck in that damn shack with the dirt floor again, Laurel decided to press her luck and ask a few questions. No, Andrews wasn't the type to get violent if someone tried to invade his thoughts. He was, however, quite capable of giving her a cold and determined stare that she'd just as soon never see again.

Laurel got up from the chair and poured herself a cup of coffee from the thermos. Casually, she strolled over to the plastic that posed as a window to where Andrews stood with his hands stuffed deeply into his pants pockets.

"Do you really think she's still alive?"

Andrews didn't have to ask whom Laurel referred to. The woman had a one-track mind – obsessed, way beyond the call of duty, with Jillian Braedon. He shook his head, not bothering to turn around. "Could be."

"Brewster still thinks something's going on at the Mills' residence."

"Yeah?" he said, glancing at Laurel over his shoulder. "Then why hasn't he done something about it?"

"I guess he's waiting Mills out. The guy has celebrity status. That puts a lot of pressure on Brewster."

"Pressure?" he said, turning around. He shook his downcast head, lips held firmly together. "The only pressure he's under is staying alive. And he's going about it the wrong way."

"What's that supposed to mean?"

"You just don't get it. Nobody does. No one knows the real reason we're here."

Laurel took a smooth sip from the Styrofoam cup, and then said, "I suppose *you* do?"

He turned back towards the window, standing in silence. He had no doubts: The Braedon woman was very much alive. Since the night of the storm, she'd stayed with John Mills. As for Talbot, he'd flown in not to instruct Mills on computer software, but to help the woman escape the FBI. No. Correction: Talbot wasn't helping her to escape the FBI, for that particular agency couldn't care one way or another if the woman lived or died or took a cruise to Hawaii. Undoubtedly, if they had knowledge of the special talent the woman possessed, they'd come after her.

But the way Andrews had it figured, the only people who knew about the Braedon woman, were the five people he worked with, and two others: John Mills and Melvin Talbot. The facts spoke for themselves.

The FBI doesn't resort to stealing in order to fund a project. That, however, was how this particular project had subsisted. They had no contacts. No one to whom to report, save Brewster. The order to terminate the woman gave another reason for doubting. And it wasn't just the woman they wanted destroyed, but the child, as well – and anyone else who happened upon the secret. Does a Federal agency conduct business that way? Killing innocent American children? Andrews didn't think so. Not deliberately, anyway.

The part that concerned him most, however, remained much more personal than that. *The problem with his memory.* Facts, he could remember, but the way in which he came by much of his factual knowledge eluded him. He couldn't remember ever going to school. He couldn't recollect the faces of his own parents. He had a driver's license, but couldn't recall taking the test.

Neither could he remember ever making a decision to join the FBI.

He couldn't remember having friends, except the five people with whom he worked, and that didn't count, because he didn't consider them friends, just coworkers. It seemed as if everything he knew had been programmed into his brain. The only difference he could find between his mind and a computer was that he often asked the question: *What am I?*

The most frightening part: he knew the answer to that question.

And, although Brewster did his best to pretend otherwise, Brewster knew, too...or at least suspected the truth. It was the only explanation as to why the man wouldn't make a move on Jillian Braedon.

Fact: two of his associates had been killed.

Fact: the creature that killed them was brought into this world through the imagination of a woman.

It scared Andrews. The implications of what he might soon have to face...if he followed orders. The handful of people he might soon have to kill...if he wanted to have any chance of survival.

CHAPTER 30

Because he thoroughly enjoyed every opportunity to brag, Mel didn't waste a moment telling Jillian that her new ID could be picked up within a week. He explained how he'd E-mailed the pictures he'd taken that morning to his friend Arthur Billings, for the driver's license (American, for the state of Arizona) and passports. He explained how Arthur would go about the task of setting her up with a 'borrowed' birth certificate. He rambled on about the beautiful countryside between Heber and Payson, which was mostly mountains and tall pines. Then went on to say how it paled beside the beauty of England. And when he finished, he flashed a smile and said: "Any questions?"

She had at least a dozen, and didn't know where to begin. The least of which was: Where do you get all your spunk and energy?

Mel, taking her silence as a 'no,' then said, "Good. I do, however, have a few questions for you." He smiled at Valerie, who'd just walked into the living room, then said, "Don't you have a few dolls to play with in the other room?" And as soon as Valerie left with a sulky scowl on her face, he returned his attention to the woman.

It turned out that Mel had been right. Jillian was smart enough to have realized the phones of friends and family could have been tapped. And he was right again; she'd been desperate enough to try it anyway. According to Jill, about a year and a half ago, she'd called her distant aunt, Betty, who in turn gave her a message she'd received six months back via the U.S. Postal system. The message read that her brother, Richard, had killed himself, and that Dr. Neas had been with Richard when it happened. Neas, in turn, used that opportunity to escape Brewster's men, and could be found the first Friday of every month, twelve o'clock noon, at the snake exhibit at the San Diego Zoo.

Jillian, who lived in Florida at the time, made the trip to California, eager for more information. She'd found Neas just where he'd said he would be, and she'd found much more: Six of Brewster's men, including Brewster himself, waiting for them. Neas, Jillian and Valerie were then taken into custody. During which, Neas had been shot in the arm.

"I had one of my nightmares, that night. Two of the men who guarded me were left dead. When that happened, I took their guns, ran from the room where they were keeping me, found Valerie, and forced them to let us go. I don't know what happened to Neas. They said he was gone. Maybe they were lying...I really don't know. If not for Valerie, I'd have forced the issue. But I couldn't stick around placing my daughter's life in more jeopardy. If he's dead, it's my fault. I shouldn't have let Betty give me that message over the phone."

"What about all the other times they found you, Jillian?" Mel asked. "What were the circumstances, then? Did you call your aunt again?"

John came into the living room and announced that dinner was served. Instead of turning around and going into the dining room, he stood there a few moments, bothered by what he saw. Mel and Jillian sat together on the couch, closely together. He was struck with, not quite jealousy, rather the need to protect her. The way Jillian fidgeted with her fingers concerned him. She bit down on her bottom lip, eyes seemingly focused on nothing. She was tense, uncomfortable. And Mel was either oblivious to her turmoil, or simply didn't give a damn.

With Mel capable of causing such a reaction here, John could only imagine the position Jillian would be in once she got to London, and had to rely solely upon Mel to lead her through until she could make it on her own.

"Is everything all right?" John asked.

"Fine," Mel replied.

"Jillian?" John said, raising a brow.

"We'll be there in just a minute, John," she said, and smiled. "Mel and I were just going over some of the details."

When John left the room, she turned to Mel and said, "If I can put an end to what causes the nightmares, Brewster won't be able to find me again...I hope."

The chess match between John and Mel started shortly after Jillian and Valerie went to bed. The marble board rested on the kitchen table. Mel, who had the side of red, made the first move, putting his king's knight into play.

"If things don't go according to plan, John, are you prepared to spend the rest of your life in an American prison?"

John cleared the way for his queen's bishop, and then folded his arms on the table, staring soberly at the board. "They won't put me in prison, Mel. I know too much."

"Scares the shit out of me," Mel said, pondering over his next move. "We're making history, here. History that won't go down in any books...if we're successful. When this is all over, I hope you won't mind too much if I knock the hell out of you for getting me involved."

"Not at all," John replied without batting an eye.

"Not that you had any choice," Mel said, putting his queen's bishop pawn into play. "I'd probably want to knock the hell out of you if you hadn't involved me in this mess. I mean, how many people can honestly say they are responsible for saving the world?"

"There may come a time in the very near future when you'll eat those words, Mel. Risking your life for your ideals and actually dying for them are two different things. You have a lot more at stake than I. I've already lived my life. But you...you have your whole life ahead of you. So if you want out, I'll understand."

"I'm in," Mel replied. "You know me. No one talks me into anything I don't want to do. And I want this. I want it badly."

John put his queen's bishop into play. He thought about tonight's dinner and how most of the table conversation had been between Jillian and Mel. The two of them seemed to have hit it off well.

"She's quite a woman, isn't she?" John asked.

Mel grinned. "I certainly wouldn't kick her out of bed, if that's what you mean."

John smiled wryly. "You hurt her in any way, and I'll know where to find you."

"I knew it. You've got a thing for her, don't you? Is it love, John? You know it's been a long time since you lost your..."

"Your move," John said, nodding towards the board. "Don't read anything more into this. I barely know the woman."

"That's not an answer to my question."

John leaned back in his chair, no longer interested in the chess match, for there were more important problems to dwell upon. "What I think and how I feel are absolutely irrelevant. Don't you understand? She'll be leaving soon. I doubt I'll see her again."

"And..?" Mel asked.

"For me, when she leaves, it's 'end of story,'" John replied. "You, however, seem to have a lot in common with Jillian, more so than you and your ex-wife. You're the only other person Jillian can talk to about her situation. And that puts you in a very unique position, Mel. And Mel, I'm not blind. I saw the way you looked at her during dinner tonight."

Mel's hand slapped the table. "I'm confused. Do you or do you not have a thing for her?"

"I'm counting on you to take good care of her and Valerie. You'll do that for me, won't you?"

"Of course. But..."

"Valerie's been through some rather tough times. She'll need a lot of love and understanding to get over her past. I know how you feel about children, but don't shut the child out. She's a very bright little girl. Do you know she learned to read in less than a week? She needs a father figure that'll set a proper example. I think you could be that father figure."

Mel held up a hand. "Let me get this straight, because I certainly don't want to do anything that could damage our friendship. You're in love with Jillian, but you're stepping back and asking that I step forward. I don't get it."

"I'm stuck here. You said so yourself. Just be good to her," John said. He gripped his cane and got to his feet, feeling sick, as if he'd just taken a blow to the stomach. He knew he'd lose Jillian sooner or later. And sometimes, sooner is best.

As he headed into the hallway, Mel called out to him. John, however, didn't feel much like talking, so he ignored him and took two sets of bedding down from the linen closet. He bowed his head as he stood there, the guest room door behind him. Jillian needed Mel. She trusted Mel. And a secret such as hers could bind two people together for eternity. As for Mel, John believed Jillian was just the woman to straighten him out and lure him away from the computer long enough to enjoy the finer things in life.

He turned around and went into the living room, one arm around the bedding. The only way to get through all this without any regrets was to convince himself that he'd made the only proper choice.

"John!" Mel called from the kitchen. "Are we going to finish our game, or what?"

"I'm ready to call it a night."

"Fine," Mel said.

John heard Mel's footfalls, and dropped one blanket and one pillow on the couch. "Are you still planning on leaving first thing in the morning?"

"The earlier, the better."

CHAPTER 31

In a town the size of Sandstone, renting a car meant travelling all the way to the nearest town of size, Show Low. John regretted having to leave Jillian and Valerie alone, and when Mel hopped out of the Land Rover, John was hit with more regret. Even now, he felt certain that he could talk Mel out of it. Yet, much in the same way as he'd allowed Victoria and Ryan to fly off to their deaths, he was on the verge of allowing Mel to drive off to his. And death seemed inevitable, unless he did something now to stop it.

John rolled down the window as Mel came around to the driver's side door. He cut off the engine. "Mel," he said, exhaling slowly. "Maybe this isn't..."

"Don't say it, man. The decision has already been made. If you try to talk me out of it now, it's only going to piss me off."

John nodded. "All right."

"You're the only true friend I've ever had, John. I haven't seen you for years, but that hasn't changed things. You're closer to me than my own brother. But I'm not doing this for you. I'm doing it for me. I've always loved a good challenge. I suppose this is the challenge I've been waiting for all my life. There's no turning back. I want this. Don't you see? I want this badly. I'm a selfish bastard and don't you ever forget it." He grinned. "So fuck your guilt." He slapped his hand against the door, while scuffing the soles of his boots on the asphalt. "See you in about a week."

Mel zipped up his jacket, and walked off, wearing the same ragged jeans he'd had on when he first arrived on John's doorstep. John turned the ignition key, staring off at the British flag stitched to the back of Mel's jacket, experiencing a surge of mixed emotions. His best friend was as good as dead. Regardless of what Mel had just said, John claimed full responsibility. He never should have sent that letter. *Never.* And yet, in his heart he understood it was the right decision.

Without any warning, he became suddenly homesick, more so than he had ever been in his life. He yearned to be in a place where the people didn't talk so strangely, where the rolling countryside was green from an abundance of misty rain. Homesick not only for a place, but for a special time, when the answers to life's problems were easily found, because nothing was too complicated that it couldn't be resolved during a quiet walk along the beach. Homesick. And like Mel, John wondered if either of them would live long enough see England again.

Mel's intended destination was Los Angeles. He never made it. After ten hours of driving, stopping twice along the way to grab a quick bite to eat and fill up the tank of his rental car, he left Interstate 10 and cruised into Palm Springs by way of Gene Autry Trail. He made a right hand turn on Highway 111, a.k.a. Palm Canyon Drive. The temperature here usually kept a good thirty or forty degrees warmer than the upper desert region of Arizona. He'd shed his jacket about an hour ago and now lowered the electric window for some fresh air.

He passed through the heart of this thriving oasis of manicured lawns and lush vegetation peppered with cacti – a peculiar yet interesting mixture of both tropical and desert climates. Tall palm trees lined the street. Stucco buildings with red clay tiled roofs, blended into the clean scenery. It seemed as if it had gone from winter to summer, all within a few short hours. As he drove through the quaint little city, he noticed mostly tourists walking the sidewalks, dressed in shorts and T-shirts, sun dresses, and only a few in long trousers, carrying bagged items. A group of long-legged women stood at the corner of Baristo and Palm Canyon, chatting up a storm while waiting for the street light to change. One of the women reminded him of Julie. She had the same shapely legs, well tanned and firm, and thick auburn hair that fell nearly to her waist. The woman looked stunning, as was Julie. But he hadn't driven all this way just to admire the scenery. So, he passed clear to the far side of town just to scope the place out, then doubled back to look for a motel with a vacancy.

An hour later, after taking a cool shower and shaving for the first time in several days, he stepped out of the bathroom with a towel wrapped around his scrawny waist and began to set up his equipment. His first inquiries were to obtain a little background information on the medical research facility where Jillian's brother had been employed. Mel sat down at the keyboard and accessed a database containing five-year-old newspaper articles from the Fairshire *Gazette* in Massachusetts. After an hour of tedious searching, he found no mention of a Dr. Neas, or of a research facility called Bio-Tox. He almost gave up to chase down a different avenue, when he came upon a third page headline dated three and a half years ago:

Authorities Seeking Prominent Immunologist For Questioning In Last Night's Blaze

FAIRSHIRE--One firefighter was killed, and three security guards were critically injured, in a series of gas explosions that rocked the Bio-Tox building late last night. Identification of the firefighter was being withheld.

"I thought an airplane had crashed," said Lynn Clarke, an eyewitness whose car was bombarded by flaming debris. "It [the Bio-Tox facility] just suddenly blew up, sending glass and brick all over the street and my car," Clarke said. Clarke was not injured.

According to Drew Phillips, a security guard at Bio-Tox, Dr. Carl Neas, 67, of Fairshire, was seen exiting the building minutes before the first explosion shook the research facility. No motive has been established. Investigators were unable to locate Dr. Neas for questioning.

The fire that swept through the Bio-Tox building wasn't the only fire to hit Fairshire that night. The second fire, the one in which Dr. James Braedon lost his life, occurred at one o'clock that morning, evidently after the paper had gone to the press, for it was covered briefly in the Fairshire *Gazette* on the following day – along with a lengthy article about a missing doctor by the name of Richard Manning who happened to be brother-in-law of the deceased and also an employee of Bio-Tox. According to the paper, Neas, Manning, and Jillian Braedon were being sought by the authorities – not as suspects, but as possible witnesses.

Mel was amazed. What should have been celebrated as a triumph over mortality had instead resulted in death. But what else could he expect of such a twisted world?

It was eight o'clock in the evening, four o'clock in the morning in the U.K. But time has a way of losing its relevance when faced with adversity. Mel realized he needed help from someone with a few connections, someone who had kept up on the times. Because sooner or later, his snooping around would arouse Brewster's suspicion, and it would all lead straight back to John. A third party was imperative. Someone he could trust to do the job right. And someone who wouldn't ask too many questions. So, if Arthur Billings didn't like having his phone ring at four o'clock in the morning, well, fuck him.

John watched the sunrise from the library window. He knew if he had reason to worry about Mel, then he also had reason to worry about Jillian. Even in Los Angeles, Mel's activities could lead Brewster straight to John's door. It was a simple matter of tying Mel's inquiries to John. There would be no warning. If they caught Mel, John wouldn't know until Brewster barged in with armed men to search the house.

He stared down at the pile of charred matches on the table, then struck another match and watched it burn. They had made a mistake, a big mistake. The first priority should have been to get Jillian and Valerie out of here and safely off the continent. She had already lived with the nightmares for more than a few years. Another week or two of wondering if they could be resolved wouldn't have hurt anything. Surely not.

As the match burned close to his fingers, he shook it out and slammed his hand down on the table. He couldn't remember the last time he'd been in such a foul mood.

"Good morning," Jillian said from the doorway.

John shot her a glance and mumbled, "Good morning."

She wore a pair of his dark trousers and a white T-shirt. Barefoot, she walked soundlessly into the library and smiled sadly down at the pile of charred matches on the table. "Been up all night?"

"Woke up around three. Couldn't go back to sleep."

"You should have knocked on my door. I've been awake since two."

"Any nightmares?" he asked, raising an inquisitive brow.

She shook her head.

"Will you be having any tonight?"

"I don't know."

He felt like smashing his fist against the table. If he couldn't get a straight answer from the very person he was trying to protect...

John met her gaze with a pair of stark eyes, nostrils flared. "*When* will you know?"

"It all depends," she replied. "It's different every time. Sometimes, I know hours in advance. Other times, I don't know until just before I fall asleep."

"*How* do you know?" he asked. He grabbed for his cane and got to his feet, tired of playing games. He wanted the truth and was determined to hear it. "Jillian, *how*?"

"Just trust me, okay?"

John shook his head in frustration, jaw clenched. "Trust you? Is that all you can say? Because of you, my best friend is out there, risking his life. At any moment, Brewster may come pounding on my door and kill us all. I've done everything within my means to accommodate both you and your daughter. All I'm asking in return is a simple question, which you refuse to answer. And damn it, woman, I want to know why! Trust *you*? How about *you* trust *me* and give me an answer!"

She took a step back, lips parted, confused. He advanced a step. She retreated another step, and he seized her by the arm. "Answer me!" he ordered.

"I can't!" she said and jerked her arm free.

"You can't or you *won't*?"

"I won't!" she snapped, eyes flashing with stubbornness.

He threw his head back, and growled at the ceiling:
"'If all the harm that women have done
Were put in a bundle and rolled into one,
Earth would not hold it,
The sky could not enfold it,
It could not be lighted nor warmed by the sun.'"

"Very cute," she remarked. "So, you've read James Kenneth Stephen," she said, wearing a plastic smile. Sarcasm brought a rush of color to her cheeks. Her shoulders became straight, rigid. She could hear Bear bark in another room, but misinterpreted the dog's message of alarm. "Since you're evidently into quoting the dead, how's this:
'But man, proud man,
Drest in a little brief authority,
Most *ignorant* of what he's most assur'd,
His glassy essence, like an angry ape,

Plays such fantastic tricks before high heaven,
As make the angles weep.'"

"I see you like Shakespeare," he retorted, both intrigued and in disgust. Her words stung like a slap to the face. He couldn't remember the last time anyone had dared to insult him this way. Bear's barking rose with the tension, but not enough to silence the heated voices that echoed throughout the house. John ignored the dog's warning and continued: "But was it not he who said:

'Freeze, freeze, thou bitter sky,
Thou dost not bite so nigh
As benefits forgot.'"

"Call me an ingrate, if you wish," she snapped right back. "But in pointing that out, you point a finger at yourself as well. Where is your modesty? Or was it false? As Donne so aptly put it:

'I have done one braver thing
Than all the Worthies did,
And yet a braver thence did spring,
Which is to keep that hid.'"

John felt as if he were fighting a Literary Battle of Wits. And although he was quite confident he would win, she proved herself a worthy opponent, one who had already won his respect, if not his heart. And yet he couldn't resist: "'Women are only children of a larger growth.'"

"Dryden," she said, crossing both arms beneath her breasts. "You sure like to quote the dead."

"Close, but wrong. It wasn't Dryden."

She took a defiant stance, chin held high. "Then who?"

The last of the anger left him as he glanced from one shelf of books to another in search of a clue. For the life of him, he couldn't recall whom he'd just quoted.

Unwilling to admit defeat, he gave the first name that entered his mind: "Sir Thomas Browne."

"Wrong. You're guessing," Jillian said. Her nose crinkled up as she smiled with cool smugness. The smile turned into a grin, but it wasn't an ordinary grin. She was using it to taunt him. "You don't know who said it, do you, Mr. Literary Genius?"

"Well, it certainly wasn't Dryden, Your Literary Highness."

"Would you care to make a bet?"

"You're wrong," he stated flatly.

"*You're* wrong," she shot right back.

"You're both wrong," came an amused voice from the doorway. "It was Lord Chesterfield."

CHAPTER 32

Jillian startled, then flushed with embarrassment as Mel stepped into the room with Bear at his heels. Mel dropped his jacket on the table, and then crossed his arms. "Valerie let me in. I didn't mean to interrupt. Please," he said with a nod, "continue."

"Why are you back so soon?" John asked.

Mel turned to Jillian. "The names you'd given me: Kevin Brewster, Paul Andrews, Timothy Barnes – they didn't check out."

"What?"

"I had an acquaintance of mine do a little snooping. Safer that way. Because, if I were implicated, you would be implicated. But don't worry. Arthur has no idea why I wanted the information."

"Well?" John asked.

"Those men who claim to be FBI, are not FBI, active or otherwise. Neither are they CIA, DSA, or any other known intelligence agency here in The States. Furthermore, aside from the interest of the Fairshire police department, the FBI is quite interested in meeting you. Not because of the special talent you have, but to question you regarding the fire that burned Bio-Tox to the ground and the fire in which your husband was killed. Oh, there was a Paul Andrews working for the FBI about ten years ago. That man, however, is now fifty-four years old, or would have been had he not died during surgery two years ago.

"Since I thought you'd be eager to know, I took the first flight from Palm Springs into Phoenix. I flew into Winslow and rented another vehicle, all at John's expense." He grinned. "Hope you don't mind."

"I don't get it," Jill said. "Then who are they?"

"I have a theory on that," Mel replied. "If I'm right…" He paused long enough to rub his chin, which now looked as smooth as a baby's bottom. "Hell, we can discuss this later. What's for breakfast? I'm starved."

Breakfast was the usual: Oatmeal without milk and hot tea served with Creamora and sugar. Throughout the entire meal, Jillian did her best to press Mel for his opinion as to who those men were. And Mel did his best to change the subject every time by inviting Valerie into a more meaningless conversation about cartoons.

Leaving his dirty bowl and empty teacup on the table, Mel rose to his feet. "John, care to go for a little walk, outside?"

"Now?"

"Now."

"Mel," Jillian said. "What about your theory?"

He tapped a finger against his temple and said, "I'm sure it'll still be here when we get back."

John dropped his linen napkin on the table, and stood with the aid of his cane. The two men headed for the door and met up with Bear in the foyer.

"What's this all about?" John asked.

"Outside," Mel said as he grabbed two jackets from the closet.

The hard packed dirt upon which they walked was a reddish brown and littered with a variety of dead weeds. Only a few patches of snow remained from the Christmas blizzard, yet the breeze whipped crisp with frost against their exposed skin. Mel stuffed both hands into his jacket pockets as he strolled out into the yard. With the toe of his boot he kicked up a loose rock, and turned to face John.

"I don't believe that the men who are after Jillian are American citizens."

"Then who are they?"

"Don't know. Could be Russians. Fuck, they could be from another planet, for all I know. It all fits in. They destroyed Bio-Tox and killed practically everyone with knowledge of this, thereby guaranteeing themselves sole possession of the secret."

"And?" John questioned.

"And that makes it rather difficult to find a safe place for your lady-friend to start her new life. It's my firm belief that those men are working under assumed names. Which means there's no way of finding out which country they're from, short of obtaining fingerprints and running them through a database. Even then, we could come up empty."

John shook his downcast head. And when he looked up, his face had gone pale with worry.

"John, what if they're *our* men? What if Jillian arrives in London, only to find out every member of British Intelligence has her picture engraved in his or her mind? Until we know who they are, there's no safe place to take her. Not one. I've been called 'insensitive' in the past. But even I can see how devastating this may be to Jillian. Which is why I wanted to talk to you in private."

"How is it a foreign government could get wind of this, while leaving the U.S. in the dark?"

Mel kicked the heel of his boot at the dirt. "You've just struck upon the one aspect that's bothering me most. Although it's not impossible, it is highly improbable. Had Brewster's organization been involved from the very beginning, and should this experimental drug and surgery be their baby, certainly they wouldn't have picked to do it on American soil. There was nothing in the Bio-Tox records that made any mention of the experiment or those involved. So how did they find out about it? Shit man, it's as if they plucked their information from thin air."

"Thin air," John repeated, absently stabbing his cane at the ground.

"It's crazy. And there's something else: Neas is dead. The only man possibly capable of reversing the surgery is dead. It's hopeless. Damn it all to hell, John. It's hopeless."

"Mel."

"I've thought and thought this through to the best of my ability. You know I don't give up easily. But we're at a dead end, John. We've done all we could."

"*Mel.*"

"We don't know who we can trust. We don't know where the woman will be safe. There's no way to reverse what's happening to Jillian. It's over, John. I'm sorry, but it's over."

"*Mel!*" he growled.

"What?"

John turned to face the wind. His blond hair danced in the light breeze. For several long moments, he said nothing. The thoughts that raced through his mind were absolutely incredible, almost too incredible to put into words. He opened his mouth to speak, but instead just stood there with his mouth agape, stunned into temporary silence by what could very well turn out to be The Explanation. And yet, it meant trouble. Terrible trouble. A tormenting anguish that could last a lifetime. Which, for Jillian Braedon, could mean eternity.

"I know that look," Mel said, cheeks flushed red from the winter air. "It means your brain is boiling. What is it?"

"She'll never be able to accept it," John muttered to himself. "It'll kill her." He inhaled deeply, exhaled slowly. "No. It can't be...but, God help us, I think it is."

"What can't be?" Mel asked.

"I know who those men are," John said. "And how they were able to find out about the experiment. What I'm about to say may sound crazy, yet it goes along with all the other craziness."

As John spoke, Mel didn't pick lint from his shirt; he didn't fiddle with any loose threads, play with the snaps on his jacket or kick his boot at the ground. He didn't glance around as if his mind was a thousand light-years away. Instead, he listened attentively. It was one of the few times when Mel's interest actually showed on his face.

"If you're right," Mel finally said, "the only logical thing to do, is find out how many of them there are, and kill them all."

"What good will that do if others replace them?" John asked. "There may be no end to this as long as Jillian lives."

"You'll have to tell her, John. She has a right to know. She must be made aware of what's going on. It's the only way, John. The only way."

CHAPTER 33

Jill worked in the kitchen, drying the last of the breakfast dishes when John came quietly into the room. He watched her for a moment as she stood on her toes to place a stack of clean bowls on the top shelf. The trouser legs were rolled up just above her ankles. And he now understood why Jillian wouldn't wear the slippers he'd provided, or even socks. She had the loveliest bare feet he'd ever seen.

He stood there watching, both hands shoved deeply in his trouser pockets. "We have to talk," he said flatly.

She turned around on the balls of her feet, lips parted, eyes wide and anxious and glassy, like two perfectly matched blue marbles. "Something's wrong," she said knowingly. "Something's very wrong, isn't it?"

He didn't actually hear her words, but felt them. The raw tension in her voice cut into his heart. He ached to cross the ten feet of floor separating them, take her in his arms and promise that everything would be all right. But that was not what he had come in here to do. With a stiff nod of acknowledgment, he said, "Yes."

Jillian grabbed up the dishcloth and started wiping down the counter top for the second time this morning. Halfway through, she gave up, abandoning the dishcloth on the stove. She found a can of Comet and a sponge in the cabinet beneath the sink, and sprinkled it until the stainless steel sink was hidden beneath the pale green powder. With tense muscle power, she scrubbed as if her very existence depended upon its cleanliness. Her eyes were sore and watery from not blinking. Her teeth clenched in determination. He called her name, but she kept scrubbing, stopping long enough to turn on the faucet. And when his hand fell upon her shoulder, her tense muscles became even more rigid and she dropped the sponge, fingers splayed and trembling, as if she'd just discovered that the sponge she'd been holding was infested with bugs.

"Mel is in the living room, amusing Valerie," John said softly. "No doubt teaching her algebra or computer programming." He tried to smile, yet couldn't bring the smile to erase the seriousness in his troubled eyes as he watched Jillian rinse her hands.

"It's bad, isn't it?" she asked, gazing downward at the sink.

"Come on," he said, and took her gently by the hand so that his fingers slipped between hers. "We can talk in my room."

They didn't pass through the living room where Mel and Valerie discussed cartoons, but took the long way around the hall. The bedroom door stood open, until John closed it behind him.

"Have a seat," he said, nodding towards the bed.

Jillian folded her arms beneath her breasts, smearing wet Comet on the white shirt, not moving from where she stood until John placed a hand to the small of her back and guided her to the bed. They sat down together, John positioning both hands, one on top of the other, over his cane.

"I'd like to ask a few questions," he said. "First, however, I want you to know that, no matter how things turn out, I am now, and will always be, on your side. You've been through over five years of hell that began with a death sentence. You're not responsible for the surgery and drugs they gave you. And you're not responsible for what it caused. You, Jillian, were used, much in the same way a guinea pig is used. The people who did that to you are the ones who are responsible. The blame is theirs. I can't and won't blame them for wanting to save your life. But they are still responsible for everything it caused – both the good and the bad. Remember that."

While biting down on her bottom lip, Jillian drew both hands into her lap, fidgeting with her fingers. "What are the questions?"

"Do you remember back to when you first realized the FBI was after you?"

She gave a stiff nod. "How could I forget. It was the night Jim … died."

"You told me that you left the house around midnight, and took Valerie with you. But you never told me why."

"Valerie was fussy that night. She was cutting teeth, again. Sometimes when she couldn't fall asleep, I'd take her for a drive. It usually calmed her down within a few minutes. I already told you this, John. What's going on?"

"But you were gone for several hours. Why?"

"I-I needed the time to think, to clear my head." Her bottom lip began to quiver. Both hands flexed then curled into fists, then flexed again. "I was scared. I-I wanted to get away. I wanted to just drive away and never go back."

"Why?" he asked.

"Because I knew...I-I knew they'd be coming after me. It was only a matter of time before someone made the connection between my getting well, and Bio-Tox."

John covered her hands with his own, squeezing gently as he watched the first of many tears spill down her cheek. "You had a dream that night, didn't you? You dreamt the FBI was after you. That's why you were so antsy and couldn't sleep anymore that night."

She withdrew one hand, covering her mouth with a loose fist. "Yes."

Calmly, softly, he said: "And just like the nightmares you have about that demon, the men from your dream became real. First they went to the Bio-Tox building and destroyed it. Then they came to your house. Only you weren't there. You'd run. And you've been running ever since. Not from the FBI, but from the men in your nightmare."

She shook her head fiercely, dark hair falling over her face, dragging in a hissing breath through clenched teeth, tears falling freely. "No," she whispered. "No!" she cried, burying her face in both hands. "That means...God, No. No. It's my fault. I killed them. My own brother. My own husband. Oh, my God. My God!"

He embraced her tightly. Her head tucked beneath his chin as she hitched uncontrollably in his arms and sobbed. It wasn't until this moment that he realized how deeply his feelings went for the woman. He would have given anything to take her pain away. Anything. Including his life. And so he held on, whispering comforting words while hating himself for the horror he had just made her face.

Before Jillian retired for the evening, the three adults sat around the kitchen table and decided to go ahead with the rest of the plans. Mel would take Valerie to Phoenix in the morning. And as soon as the new ID's arrived in his mailbox, the two of them would leave for London. Jillian would follow in a few days. She would be able to find her new ID and passport in Mel's mailbox, to which he'd already given her the spare key.

Wearily, still quite sober from this morning's revelation, Jillian bid both men a goodnight, then left them to discuss whatever men usually discuss in the absence of women. Which was when Mel reiterated an earlier question: "You love her, don't you?"

John did his best to dodge the topic. He was in no mood to be hounded. In fact, he'd come quite close to telling Mel to shut up. Mel, however, remained quite persistent...in a preoccupied sort of way. It was a habit of his to deliberately allow the conversation to take a one-eighty degree turn, only to bring it back around when it suited him.

"I think you should consider going home," Mel suggested.

"I am home."

"You don't belong here, John. This isn't your country. Wasting away in a barren desert isn't healthy. Neither is turning your back on a woman who obviously adores you."

John rested back in his chair, arms folded, staring at the stone wall that separated the kitchen from the dining room, bleakly, as if facing the dark chasm of oblivion. "I close my eyes and I see her face," he whispered, and swallowed hard. "Jillian's face. It used to be Victoria's face I saw. Life's strange, isn't it?"

"So, you do love her."

"As La Rochefouchauld once put it: 'There are many people who would never have been in love if they had never heard love spoken of.' Sorry to have to tell you this, Mel, but love is only a myth, induced by the power of suggestion. And as you surely did learn from your three-year marriage, that one suggestion clears the way for a whole lot of disappointment... Better to feel nothing."

"I can see I'm wasting my time trying to talk sense into the likes of you. Fuck it," Mel said with an annoyed sneer. He got up from the table, clearly agitated. Had John been anyone else, the conversation would have ended. But John was a friend. The best friend he'd ever had. And so he said: "A great man once wrote: 'Emotion, like the air, cannot be seen. And like the air, it fills the cup. Even more so when that cup is thought empty.'"

"A great man?" John questioned. "Sounds more like the inane ravings of an eighteen-year-old boy."

"Well, once he was great. Inane – yes. But still great. Or so half the people on the planet thought. Then one day, he decided to hide himself out in the middle of the fucking desert. There's a rumor going around that he's dead. Listening to you now, I do believe that rumor to be true. You're dead."

"Mel, that's enough."

"You know what your problem is, John?" he asked and grinned. "You're a chicken-shit asshole. You're warped in the head from living so long apart from society, and twist everything around to suit your warped and narrow mind. If you weren't a goddam cripple, I'd knock the shit out of you right now, just for the fun of it."

John slowly rose to his feet, jaw clenched.

"You know what else?" Mel continued. "You're a lily livered, white-washed, fuck-faced bastard."

"Mel," John growled.

"Oh, is he getting pissed off?" Mel taunted and grinned all the more.

"Is that what all this is about? Trying to piss me off?"

Mel walked around the table and cocked his head to one side. "You want to hit me, John? Go ahead," he said, pointing to his jaw. "Let me have it. For once in my life, I'd love to see you pissed off enough to actually hit someone. Come on, hit me, asshole!"

John pressed his lips firmly together, brows furrowed as if in deep consternation. He dropped his head slowly, inhaled deeply so that his nostrils flared, then he busted Mel in the face.

When Mel picked himself up off the floor, he rubbed his jaw, grinning. "There," he said with a slight nod. "Feel better?"

John shook the pain from his left hand. "Much," he replied, devoid of any readable emotion.

"Good," Mel stated. "That, my friend, is what life's all about. Feeling good. And if something pisses you off..." Mel made a fist and popped John square in the mouth. John's head snapped back, but thanks in part to his grip on the high-backed chair, he remained on his feet. He licked his lip, tasting blood as Mel finished his sentence.

"…you fight back. Because only then, can you truly be happy."

Before the smile made it to John's face, his bloody lip had swollen to twice its original size. "Okay," he said, then gently wiped his puffy mouth. "You've made your point."

"Good. Now tell me: You love her, don't you?"

CHAPTER 34

The morning Valerie left with Mel was the second morning in a row Jillian cried. She put on a wonderful *façade* in front of the child. All smiles, bubbling over with false excitement, telling Valerie they would soon all be where the bad men could never find them, telling her that she'd soon be able to go to school and make many friends, friends who she'd grow up with, friends who'd have slumber parties and play jump rope and jacks. Even when she went into the guest room with Valerie, you wouldn't have known by looking at her that she was nearly in tears.

Shortly before eight o'clock, John took the transmitter out from the linen closet and placed it on the mantle between the two brass cannons. His lower lip was still a bit swollen, making it slightly painful to speak.

"Mel, it's been a pleasure doing business with you. If the recording deal goes through, expect to find a bonus in the mail."

"The pleasure's been all mine," Mel said. "If you ever find yourself in London, give me a ring. We'll do lunch."

"You can count on it," John replied.

"If you find yourself needing more programs, or have any suggestions on how to further customize the programs you already have, you know who to call. Are you sure you don't want me to leave you the laptop? It might come in handy. A man can never have enough computers. I'll leave it if you want...at no extra cost."

"Doubtful I'll need it. Thanks anyway."

John picked up the transmitter and returned it to the linen closet. He then knocked on the guest room door, letting Jillian and Valerie know it was safe to come out.

Mel knelt on the stone floor by the smallest of the three crates he'd brought with him. He'd placed a pillow inside. When Valerie stepped into the crate and crouched down, Mel put the lid in place and used a hammer to sink the nails.

When John came into the living room, he was armed with a Smith & Wesson .357 with an inch and a half of barrel. He handed it to Mel, who in turn checked the cylinder and stuffed the revolver into the pocket of his bomber jacket.

"All set," Mel said, and smacked his lips.

Jillian knelt down beside the crate, laying a hand against the wood. "Honey, I'll see you within a week. Be a good girl."

"She'll be fine," Mel assured her. "We'll eat all kinds of junk food, stay up half the night watching the telly, and I won't make her brush her teeth or take baths. How's that?"

It started with a slight twitch at both corners of her mouth. And within a matter of seconds, Jillian broke. Tears streamed down her face. Her eyes turned a misty shade of blue. And yet, you'd have to be looking at her to know she cried, because she didn't make a sound other than a brief sniffle or two. "You take good care of my little girl."

"The best care," Mel replied sincerely. He lifted the crate, balancing it carefully so not to bruise or injure the precious cargo. By the time he reached the foyer, John had the front door open.

"See you in about a week," Mel said to Jillian. And shifting his attention to John, he said, "Wait about a month before you come. And you will come, or else..." In a terrible Arnold Schwarzenegger impersonation: "...I'll be back."

"We'll see," John replied, placing a crowbar on top of the crate. "Take care."

When Mel pulled up to the roadblock in his rented Ford Bronco, the redheaded woman waved him out of the vehicle. He applied the emergency brake and shifted into neutral, leaving the engine to idle. Not wanting to let his reluctance show, he hopped out quickly, stuffing both hands in the pockets of his jacket. During his first encounter with these two agents, he had used up the expected chitchat. He'd asked how dangerous the woman they were looking for might be. Asked if they had any new leads. He even offered his services. All innocent prattle.

Now, with that line of idle bullshit exhausted, he resorted to other tactics to take his mind off the threat he was under. Mel tipped back his head and gazed up at a darkening overcast sky. "Looks like rain," he said, while Andrews looked through the rear window of the vehicle. "I was under the impression that it seldom rains here. Must have picked a bad time to visit."

"Where are you headed?" Andrews asked.

"Home. Hammersmith, that is."

The redhead walked to the driver's door, reached in, lowered the rear window, killed the motor, and removed the key from the ignition. She came around to the rear of the vehicle, on a pair of spiked heels definitely not intended for desert hiking.

It was almost like being able to see into Jillian's mind. For these people were Jillian's interpretation of FBI. A woman in a power dress and sheer nylons, and a man who would look more at home riding the range than he did in the three piece suit he wore. Mel stepped back as the woman inserted the key into the back door lock. He retreated even further when she opened the door and picked up the crow bar from the carpeted floor by the crate.

"Sorry to have to put you through so much inconvenience, Mr. Talbot," Andrews said, stuffing both hands deeply into his overcoat pockets.

It had reached less than forty degrees outside, and Mel found himself sweating. His forehead glistened. His palms felt moist. He tried to swallow, finding it difficult. He wondered how fast he could draw the gun that was already in his sweaty grip, if the report from the gun could be heard by anyone else, and how quickly Brewster would arrive once the first shot had been fired.

The redhead positioned the crow bar between the slats of wood. Then Andrews stepped up. "Allow me."

The redhead passed Andrews the crow bar.

Andrews said, "Check the glove box and the suitcase in the front. Don't forget to look under the seat. I'll take care of this."

As the redhead went around to the passenger door, Mel walked right up to Andrews, sweat stinging his eyes. His breath caught in his throat. He was going to kill them both. He saw no other way. Neither would he have any regrets. Because they weren't real. They weren't human. They were the imagination of Jillian Braedon. Demons in human form. A side effect of an experiment that never should have been. Freaks. The question on his mind was: Could he kill them? Was it possible for a bullet to destroy imaginary beings manifested in the flesh? There was only one way to find out. Only one way. What he needed was to have them both lined up for an easy shot.

Mel wasn't quick to the draw, but Mel knew a bit about guns. And Mel knew if the people impersonators lined up just right, a single bullet from the .357, provided the load was correct, could down them both, and reduce the chances of getting shot himself. That, however, wouldn't happen if Andrews opened the crate and alarmed the redhead as to the contents.

Hidden from the woman's view, he edged up to Andrews, stuck the muzzle of the revolver into Andrew's ribs, and whispered, "Move and you're dead."

"Laurel will have your head blown off before my dead body hits the ground," Andrews whispered. Yet, he didn't move. He valued his life. Empty as his life was, forgetful as he was, tired as he was of taking orders from Brewster, Paul Andrews feared death. He feared it because he understood that, once his lights went out, neither God, nor Devil would greet him. For in a strange kind of way, Jillian Braedon was his god, his creator.

And her realm was here amongst the living, exactly where Andrews wanted to remain.

Which was why he said, "If Laurel doesn't hear the lid being pried off this crate, she'll be suspicious. Do you want that, Mr. Talbot?"

"Do it," Mel said. "But don't get too cocky. The person you're looking for is already out of the state."

While Andrews slid the crowbar beneath the lid of the crate, he said, "Do you believe in God, Mr. Talbot?"

"Not since I grew a brain."

"Well, if there is a God, and He suddenly died, don't you think all of creation might come undone?"

"Suitcase is clean," Laurel reported from the front of the vehicle.

"Check under the hood," Andrews ordered. He then returned his attention to Mel, who sweated nearly as much as he himself did. "How much do you know?" Andrews asked.

"More than I want to know. I know you're not one of us."

"Is that how you rationalize murdering me?"

Andrews pried off the lid and Mel leaned close enough so that Valerie could see the finger he laid across his lips. The blessed child didn't say a word. She just crouched down even further and buried her face.

"Mr. Talbot, I'm on your side. Why do you think I sent Laurel up front?"

"Fuck you," Mel retorted, jabbing the man with the muzzle.

"Think about it. You know where I came from," he said, using the crowbar to drive the nails back in place. "I came from nothing. And that's exactly where I'll go if anything happens to the woman. The only reason Brewster doesn't have her right now is because of me. Because I don't want to die. I'd kill Brewster before I'd let him get his hands on that woman. If you think about it, you'll know it's true. And you'll also know that if you kill me, Brewster will be down on you in a matter of minutes. You'll never get away. That little girl will die right along with you."

"Everything's fine up here," Laurel announced, slamming down the hood.

"Think about it. But don't take too long."

As Laurel started for the back of the Bronco, Mel hesitated only a moment before returning the revolver to his jacket pocket.

"Did you check him?" she asked Andrews.

"He's clean," Andrews replied.

"You're free to go," Laurel said, tucking a lock of red hair behind her ear. She stood by the vehicle while lighting up a cigarette. "And Mr. Talbot," she added, "we appreciate your cooperation. I hope this won't deter you from visiting our country in the future." With that, she flashed a white toothy smile. "We're only doing our job, which is to protect the people, here. You understand?"

Andrews closed the back door and dangled the key ring for Mel to take. "Have a pleasant trip, Mr. Talbot."

CHAPTER 35

In all his thirty-five years, Mel Talbot had never found himself in such a precarious situation. The decision he now faced was one of life and death, one that could change the world forever. If he were lucky enough to kill both agents without getting shot himself, Brewster would know. Even if the report from the revolver went unheard, the earlier conversation he and John had staged was evidence enough that Mel had been here at the approximate time of the shooting. And even if it took two or three hours before Brewster realized two of his agents had been murdered, it would be enough time for Brewster to locate Mel before he could catch a flight out of the country – especially since it might take two or three more days before Valerie's passport arrived in Mel's mailbox.

Brewster would come after him. Both he and Valerie would be killed. By identifying Mel as an accomplice, it would lead Brewster directly to John, who would also be killed. The woman, Jillian Braedon, would be taken into the custody of her own imagination. Once they got their hands on her secret...well, it could be as devastating as an all out nuclear war.

On the other hand, trusting Andrews could also mean death. Andrews could put a bullet through Mel's head the moment he turned his back on the man. Then, Valerie would die. John would die. Mel brought his left hand to his stomach, feeling as if he might vomit.

"Mr. Talbot?" Laurel said, crushing out her cigarette with the toe of her shoe. "You're free to go."

"You don't look well," Andrews said.

"Stomach virus," Mel replied. "I think I'm going to be ill. Very ill."

"You should see a doctor. You shouldn't be driving in this condition. If Laurel doesn't mind being deserted for half an hour or so, I could drive you into town," Andrews offered. "Or just ride with you, if you prefer. I'll hitch a ride back. No problem, really."

It may not have been a permanent solution, yet Mel welcomed the reprieve with an eager nod. "Ride with me? Appreciate it."

Andrews, known by his five coworkers as a quiet sort of guy, dispelled that assumption by talking up a storm during the twenty minutes it took to get to Sandstone. He gave Mel a brief run-down of the facts, most of which Mel either knew or suspected. Neas was dead. Brewster wanted the same for Jillian, but only after he obtained the needed information. No government plots existed to acquire the secrets of immortality, simply because the government remained completely unaware of the experimental surgery. Everyone who'd been involved in that area of the research, except Jillian, had died. Which meant the only threat under which Jillian remained was the threat of Brewster's men, minus one: Andrews. When Mel asked how many of Brewster's "FBI agents" were out there looking for the woman, Andrews explained there were only six. And when Mel asked how they'd been able to track Jillian all around the country, Andrews said:

"The woman has a soft heart. It's been getting her into trouble from day one."

"Care to elaborate?"

"Factual, yes. I'll give you a recent example: The day before Christmas, one of Jillian's neighbors, a little girl named Kimberly Shelter, was hit by a car. It was bad. Numerous broken bones, severe head trauma. The girl wasn't expected to live. Mrs. Braedon changed all that with one visit to the hospital emergency room. Kimberly was home in time to open her presents, Christmas morning."

Mel slammed on the brakes, simultaneously jerking the wheel. Tires screeched across asphalt, coming to a slanted rest on the dirt shoulder. Eyebrows raised and mouth gaped open, he faced Andrews, slinging his right arm up on the back of the seat. "Fuck," he whispered in awe. "She didn't tell me any of that. You're not shitting me, are you, man?"

"If I had a mother, I'd swear on her grave."

Mel shook his head, grinning wildly. "She never said a word about it. Not one. I don't believe this. Of course, I believe this...That's why Brewster kicked John's cane out from under him. He believed Jillian to have cured John's bad leg."

"Exactly, and was Brewster ever surprised. So was I. I mean, the way Mr. Mills acted. Never has anyone told us how to conduct a search. Most people are intimidated when government officials knock on their doors. They panic. They agree to most anything, disguising their fears in patriotism. Either that, or they get downright ugly." He shook his head, smiling with admiration. "Not Mr. Mills."

Mel pulled back onto the highway, rear tires spinning up sand and pebbles, only to chirp when they caught dry asphalt. Glancing over his shoulder, he yelled: "Valerie, you all right?"

Her muffled voice came back: "Yeah. But my foot's falling asleep."

"So," Mel said. "What's the deal with checking under the bonnet? You fellows actually believe someone might smuggle a woman out in the engine?"

"Intimidation," Andrews replied. "When a job is done thoroughly, it lets everyone know we mean business. Besides," he said and smiled half a smile, "it breaks up the monotony."

Up until lunchtime, John remained extremely tense, agitated. Within an hour of Mel's departure, John, wanting to leave no evidence behind for Brewster, had fed Valerie's cardboard dollhouse and paper dolls to the fire. Once completed, he attempted to sit down and finish *The Scarlet Letter*, but found himself pacing the floor, and sometimes gazing out one of the many windows overlooking the dirt road. The drive to Phoenix should take four hours. He wasn't about to breathe a sigh of relief until he knew Mel had reached the motel safely. And the only way to know such a thing was to wait it out. It was definitely a case of "no news is good news."

Jillian burnt off some, but not all, of her nervous energy by scrubbing the entire kitchen. She'd been amused to find no crumbs in the bottom tray of the toaster, yet she wiped the tray down anyway. It was the same way with all the cabinets. No dust. Even before she'd started, it was clean enough in here to eat off the floor. When the grandfather clock in the living room chimed twelve times, letting her know the four hours had ended, she headed for the living room, only to meet up with John in the dining room.

"Since the house is not surrounded by imitation FBI," John began, "Mel must have made it. I have a strong feeling it's all going to work out."

"Smuggling out a forty pound child is one thing," Jill said. "But a full grown woman won't fit inside a small crate."

"No need to fit you in a crate. You'll be riding up front with me."

"*What*?" she asked and immediately froze.

"I've spent the last few weeks trusting you, Jillian. Now, it's your turn to trust me. According to Mel, Brewster has a couple of men stationed at the end of San Pablo, checking all vehicles passing into town. I don't know how many men Brewster has, but we have the opportunity to lessen that number by two."

"I don't know, John. Sounds risky. Very risky."

He agreed. However, it was sounder to take on Brewster's men two by two, than having to face them all at once. Eventually, all Brewster's men had to be destroyed. As Mel had pointed out, getting Jillian out of the country wouldn't be enough. Even if they were unable to track her to the U.K., there would always be doubts, there would always be the threat hanging over her head that one day they'd find her – turning eternal life into an eternal hell of constant dread.

CHAPTER 36

Shortly before dusk, Tim Barnes made an important discovery, one that would lead them directly to Jillian Braedon. And the person he had to thank for it was Kevin Brewster, who had pissed him off royally.

Brewster, who had a constant craving for food, and a bigger appetite for making Barnes look like a fool, wanted something other than a cold baloney sandwich and lukewarm coffee for dinner. He sat in the only chair, leaving Barnes to either stand or sit on the dirt floor. Brewster removed the cellophane from one of the two sandwiches he'd packed, took one bite, and with a mouthful said, "Hey, Barnes, how would you like some take-out fried chicken from Eileen's Diner?"

"Sounds great," Barnes replied, his stomach grumbling in agreement.

"Good," Brewster said. "And while you're picking it up, get me some too."

Barnes cursed under his breath as he went to the door. When Brewster said, "Aren't you forgetting something?" Barnes turned around, expecting his boss to hand over some money.

Instead, Brewster threw him the keys to the Jeep. "And hurry back. I like my chicken hot. And white meat. That means breasts, not wings."

Barnes had no intentions of hurrying back. Neither did he specify white meat thirty or so minutes later when he stopped at Eileen's and placed the order. A part of him knew Brewster could make his life miserable if the man didn't get exactly what he wanted. But the biggest part of Barnes didn't give a flying shit. So instead of heading straight back to that rundown shack, Barnes went for an extended ride through the desert.

Night approached. The air had turned bitter cold. Regardless, Barnes rode with the windows down, delighting in every bump that bounced him out of his seat, in every torturous curve, including those of Disaster Hill. He came down the hill with the speedometer resting on thirty-five miles per hour, nearly overturning when the tires hit loose gravel in the wash below. He felt alive, exhilarated. And damn if that chicken didn't smell absolutely delicious. He drove on for perhaps another quarter mile before coming to a stop at the base of a rocky mesa. He felt no need to pull the Jeep off the road. It wasn't as if he'd be holding up traffic.

Barnes slapped his hands together, and then rubbed them briskly. Chicken, creamy mashed potatoes and coleslaw happened to be one of his favorite meals...only because he'd had Eileen's chicken dinner three days ago, and could still remember how it tasted.

He opened both Styrofoam take-out plates, choosing the one with the largest portions for himself, even though they were both fairly equal. And leaving the top to the other plate open so Brewster's food would get good and cold, Barnes dug in. The meat pulled right off the drumstick in large, juicy bites. The crust was cooked to perfection, good and crispy, nice and spicy. With greasy fingers, he tore into the cellophane wrapper and removed a plastic Spork. He crammed his mouth full of mashed potato and stuffed a spoonful of coleslaw right in on top of it. While nearly choking from making a pig of himself, Barnes opened a half-pint container of low-fat milk and washed it down.

After polishing off everything on his plate except the bones and cartilage, he tossed the mess out the window and wiped his greasy hands on the thighs of his pants. He looked out at the Styrofoam plate, at the milk carton he'd crushed before tossing out, and saw something else that didn't quite blend into the dusky desert scenery: a woman's shoe. Okay, so he'd seen a lot of garbage along the sides of these desert roads. Old tires with rusted rims; a refrigerator with the door missing; car parts; a discarded bicycle that looked to be a hundred years old. None of those things had seemed to matter, though. Sure, they didn't belong there, but somehow it seemed natural to see those old items discarded in such a manner. The shoe, however, bothered him. So he got out to take a better look.

It was a brown slip-on with a flat heel, old by no means. It had a scuffed sole, dusty with sand. But the rest of it seemed almost perfect. In fact, the lettering inside was clear. The shoe was a size six and had been made in the USA. Barnes walked a little ways with the shoe in hand, keeping his eyes to the ground. The sun settled below the peak of a distant mountain, turning the sky a mystic shade of orange. He walked alongside a narrow ravine, in and out of the mesa's shadow. Had his eyes not been glued to the ground, he might have stepped right on it: a woman's purse, brown, the same color as the shoe, and also fairly new.

He sifted through the contents and pulled out a leather wallet. What it revealed was an expired driver's license. Even without the name, he would have recognized the owner. The picture had long ago been burnt into what was otherwise a faulty memory. Goosebumps gathered on his arms. His head felt all prickly, as if his hair now stood on end.

He'd found Jillian Braedon's purse...and more.

The cut off to the Garcia's lay over a mile back, heading towards town. There was only one house up this particular road. The woman had to be there. One house. And it belonged to John Mills.

With Valerie out of the house, hopefully safe and sound in the great city of Phoenix, it was just her and John, alone. The decision had been made. The threat of the house being bugged was gone. So, if the up and coming nightmare got out of hand – and it definitely would – Brewster wouldn't be listening in. She would also have a few days to recuperate before she herself had to make the long journey to London. And taking time out for the recuperation process would be vital...if she survived. But she didn't want to think about that right now. Because she would survive. It was a simple matter of knowing her limitations. Or believing she knew them.

Even after putting Kimberly Shelter on the road to recovery (the worst case she'd ever dealt with), there had been enough strength in reserve more than twenty-four hours later to revive Valerie (who had passed out from exhaustion). Kimberly had been close to death. John was not. And, John's leg already showed improvement compared to when they'd first met just weeks ago. She'd seen to that herself, because she'd felt responsible for the pain he was in on two separate occasions: the night she'd spooked him and he'd fallen, and after his encounter with her living nightmare. Yet, those two incidents were mild in comparison to what Jillian now had in mind.

The timing was right. If she didn't owe John her life, she'd do it anyway. Because when someone you love is in pain, you do whatever it takes – what*ever* it takes – to put an end to that pain...even if that person doesn't love you in return. Yet, she suspected John did. And she was about to put that speculation to the test, not only for her sake, but for his as well.

"I heard Mel mention that you might be going to England," she said. "I hope you do. Otherwise, I'm going to miss you."

It was exactly what he'd been waiting to hear. And still, it had somehow taken him by complete surprise. "We've only known each other for a few weeks. I'm sure you'll have forgotten all about me by this time next year."

"Does this mean you're not going? Please reconsider. I cannot go without you." She hesitated briefly, searching his eyes for a sign that this was the right moment. "John, I think I've fallen in love with you."

"Jillian," he whispered and met her gaze. His hand went to the side of her face, the pad of his thumb stroking her cheek tenderly. They found themselves standing closer. The touch of her skin beneath his hand, the way in which she gazed into his eyes, caused an almost painful surge of desire. He wanted to pull her even closer, feel the warmth of her body pressed up against his own. For several long moments, he remained lost in her deep blue eyes, eyes that would forever remain just as young and beautiful as they were now. John withdrew his hand, clenching and unclenching it at his side. It would never work. He had the choice to either explore or end whatever possibilities might lie between them. The former brought with it a feeling he'd thought lost to him forever. But also a sense of what he would eventually lose if things between them became any more complicated. "A woman like you...You, Jillian, deserve so much more."

"More?" Jillian lowered her gaze, stepping back. "I'm sorry. I didn't mean to make you feel so uncomfortable. You're probably tired of women throwing themselves at you, and that wasn't my intention." The moment the last few words left her lips, she realized it was a lie. She *was* throwing herself at him. "On second thought, perhaps that is my intention."

Damn, how he'd thought this through. He had to make her understand that *he* was the problem, not she. *He* was the one who'd grow old. *He* would become the burden.

"Jillian, listen to me. Every day, I grow a day older. Days have a nasty habit of turning into years. Honestly, Jillian, if the situation were reversed, would you even consider being with someone who would stay perfectly young, while you turned into a wrinkled, decrepit bag of bones? It wouldn't be fair to either of us. Think about it. I'd always be waiting for that day when you look at me with pity and see nothing but an old man. And I will grow older. But you, you'll always be young and beautiful."

"It doesn't have to be that way."

John walked slowly to the window, staring out at the darkening sky. A large slice of white moon hung low over the horizon. He'd gazed upon this same hard, cold piece of rock as a child; the same lifeless orb Jillian would gaze upon for centuries to come. He could not expect her to give up her youth to grow old with him. Nevertheless, the sentiment touched his heart.

"Jillian," he said, turning from the window. He put on a casual smile, despite the aching in his heart, and stuffed both hands in his trouser pockets. "I have a strong feeling that you're going to be just fine without me."

"If you care about me, please rethink this," she said barely above a whisper.

"Because I care, I cannot."

"I wish you were going with me. I am going to miss you."

"I'm going to miss you, Jillian."

"If only I had something to remember you by."

His face brightened, despite having been let off the hook that he'd just as soon ensnare him for eternity. "Choose anything in the house, and it's yours. Anything."

She raised a spirited brow. "Anything?"

"Anything."

"You."

He couldn't help but laugh. God, she was beautiful. "You know what I mean."

"How about something from your bedroom? A little knick-knack. Something that, when you wake up each morning and see it missing, will make you think of me. And when I wake up each morning and see it by my bed, I'll think of you."

He followed her into the master bedroom, where she went directly to the glass case of pewter statuettes by the desk. After studying each little statue briefly in the dusky room, she went to the nightstand and looked down at the candlestick holders. When he came up behind her, she turned to face him.

"John," she said and paused. Her eyes closed for a brief moment as she inhaled deeply then exhaled through a tense shudder. "I'll be leaving in a few days"

He allowed his fingers to slip through her silky dark hair, and she stepped into his arms. She could feel his heart racing, his heavy exhalation as she breathed him in. He brought a hand to the side of her face, watching as she stared, lips parted, at his mouth.

A moment ago – although it wouldn't have been easy – he could have turned and walked away. But that moment had passed. He leaned his cane against the wall, in the narrow gap between the nightstand and the bed. Cupping her face between his hands, he kissed her softly on the mouth. He could see no further than this moment, now.

"No regrets," she whispered, trembling inside.

"No regrets."

He kissed her deeply, her body responding, melding to his own. He unbuttoned her shirt, slowly, as he caressed her throat with soft kisses. She reached up to unbutton his shirt. Their lips met again, more urgent this time, desire laying its claim to one another. Her shirt hit the floor.

"You're so beautiful," he whispered. There wasn't a hint of a scar on her exposed flesh. He stroked her throat up and down where the wound had once been, and then traced a finger along the curves of her full breasts. Although he didn't say as much, he had no doubts whatsoever that he would soon return to England. And if love couldn't keep them together upon exhausting whatever good years he had to give, then the memories of the times they would soon share would have to be enough.

He unbuckled the thin belt from around her waist. The trousers slipped down around her ankles and she stepped out of them. She stood there, naked body outlined by moonlight, breasts rising and falling with each shallow breath. Her fingers went to his belt buckle, unfastening it diligently.

"I want you to know...I'm in love with you too," he whispered.

"I know."

Jillian reached behind and drew back the covers. When John finished undressing, they sat for a few moments, caressing one another. As they kissed, his fingers slipped through her hair and she eased back against the mattress beneath the weight of his body. His lips kissed the soft skin beneath her ear, moving to her throat, teasing her nipples, down to her smooth stomach.

Barnes threw the woman's purse on the table in front of Brewster. After a brief explanation, Brewster radioed for backup. The six of them would go in and they'd do so heavily armed. The break they'd been awaiting for three and a half years had presented itself. Two Jeeps. One helicopter. Six of the original eight agents. No longer did it bother Brewster that Mills was a celebrity. Celebrities die just as easily as anyone else. Besides, he had a score to settle. Not only with the woman, but also with Mills. That bastard had struck him hard enough in the balls to make him ache for a week. Killing Mills would be a pleasure.

CHAPTER 37

A soft moan escaped Jill's lips as her head sunk deeper into the pillow. He got to his knees between her parted thighs, his left knee taking most of his weight. She reached for him, guiding him to her. Raising her hips and pressing both trembling hands, one at each side of his chest as he entered her. Her hips rose to meet him again and again; his mouth came down upon hers; her hands slipped around his back, fingers sinking into hardened muscle as she drew him close, closer.

Andrews piloted the chopper to the shack, completely uninformed as to Barnes' discovery, yet highly speculative. Laurel sat beside him, puffing on a cigarette. He turned to her just as he brought the chopper down, and said, "Put that out! You keep smoking like that, and you'll die ten years ahead of your time."

"They found her," Laurel said for perhaps the twentieth time since they'd left the house – a five-bedroom home they'd rented four miles this side of Sandstone. The woman absolutely glowed. "I know it. I can feel it."

Andrews felt it too. Only his gut reaction was much different than Laurel's. He didn't care if she had a ten pack a day habit or didn't smoke at all. Tonight, she would die. So would the other four. He should have killed them all months ago. But he had waited. Because, when you make a sacrifice to your god, you make sure your god is watching.

So tonight, he would kill all five of them, basking in the glory that awaited him. He would live. He would live because no one would harm the Braedon woman, and in response, she would grant him his life – life eternal. Yes, he alone would save her. She would not die. At least, that was how Andrews imagined it to be. And of course, Andrews was wrong.

Jillian nestled her head to John's chest, listening for the moment when his breathing would become the calm steady breathing of a sleeping man. Slowly, she drew down the covers, exposing his legs. If not for the horrible scars his right leg would have appeared perfect. He had the muscle tone of an athlete.

She dreaded the pain, almost as much as she dreaded the creature she'd soon have to face. Pain, however, was the catalyst. In a hypnotic state, the suggestion of pain – auto-suggestive or not – would ordinarily snap a person right out of the trance. After Jillian's surgery, however, it only brought greater depths to the trance. Pain opened up her mind, gave her the ability to fight the affliction. The worse the pain, the better the results. And pain she would feel.

Being careful not to rouse him from his sleep, Jillian inched down in the bed. She placed both hands, ever so gently, on his leg, one above the knee and one below the knee – where the worst scarring had occurred. She dropped her head back, relaxing her eye muscles until both eyelids drooped. And relaxing them even further, she allowed them to close. Her favorite testing suggestion was that she smell roses. And when the fragrance of rose petals deceived her olfactory nerves, she knew she approached the desired state of mind. Yet, she had to go deeper, much deeper. Again, the auto-suggestive word was 'roses,' which she whispered aloud.

When Brewster told Andrews: "Give us thirty minutes, then bring in the chopper," Andrews bit down on his tongue to keep from panicking, and he bit down hard. This was not the way he'd planned it. But maybe it would work out okay. Certainly they wouldn't kill the woman before they got some answers. Or, perhaps they would. It was a chance he couldn't take.

"Kevin," he said, grabbing the man by the arm. He led Brewster away from the others and over to a corner of the room. "I thought I was going to be in on this."

Brewster yanked his arm free. "What's wrong with you? You *are* in on it."

"It's Barnes," Andrews said quietly. "Barnes is going to screw it all up. He'll go in, shoot first, and ask questions later."

"I heard that!" Barnes yelled from across the room. "Fuck you too, Andrews!"

"Listen to me, Kevin," he said, ignoring Barnes. "We want the woman alive."

"That's why I'm going in with a tranquilizer. The Braedon woman will be sound asleep before she even knows what hit her. We should be in position within fifteen minutes and should have her within another fifteen minutes. If you don't hear from me in thirty minutes, you'll know everything's gone according to plan. You'll fly in with the chopper after Mills and the kid are dead, and you'll fly out with the woman. Bring her straight to the house, got that?"

"If you want the woman to talk, the kid has to remain alive," Andrews argued. "That kid is our only weapon, and maybe our only defense."

Brewster nodded his agreement, and Andrews bit down on his tongue again. Not to keep from panicking, but to ward off a grin. He would have the woman all to himself. He was already solely responsible for saving the child, ensuring Jillian's gratitude. Turning matters further in his favor, from his position in the air, he could pick off the other five, easy as can be. It looked better than he'd dared hope, with one exception: The woman wouldn't be awake to witness the act that would prove his loyalty. Yet, in the end she would know. And that end would be a new beginning.

The way Jim and Richard had explained it several years ago, was that Jillian, while in a hypnotic state, could actually receive the nerve impulses of another person simply by physically touching that person. In return, as with a two-way radio, messages could be sent as easily as they were received. Right now, if she so chose, she could focus her thoughts and send a command that he wiggle his toes. And those toes would wiggle. Jillian knew, for she'd conducted such an experiment before. It was as if John's leg had become her leg. And the two areas where she felt the most discomfort were the knee and just below the ankle.

Since she didn't want to wake John, the message she now sent was for the leg to go numb. He would feel nothing, sense nothing. To test it, she concentrated while slipping one hand up and down his leg, and found that all feeling had gone.

The next step was to put up a mental block. Otherwise, the pain she would call upon would backfire, and he'd most certainly wake up screaming in agony. With that accomplished, the pain would do the rest. She wouldn't need to concentrate on the scars, the damaged nerves or the misaligned bone – as she had to do when repairing part of her own body.

The way the healing of others took place remained even a mystery to her. The amount of the healing seemed contingent upon the amount of pain she brought upon herself. Triggering the pain was like triggering a guided missile. And since only his right leg was linked to her mind, only his right leg would be healed. In other words, to erase the scars from his arm, stomach and chest, she'd need to link herself to those particular parts. However, she had no intentions of tampering with them.

There was another method, one she'd used on Jim, one that Dr. Neas had refused to take any part in. And that was to link her mind with Jim's mind. The result, startling as it had been, was not only an apparent cure to all that ailed him, but a reversal of the aging process, as well. She hadn't been able to erase the gray from his hair. Yet, Jim had looked ten years younger. His complexion had smoothed to that of a twenty-five-year-old man. His youthful muscle tone had returned. And, he'd felt ten years younger. Although he'd been a cigarette smoker for over fifteen years, Jim's lung x-ray suggested that even the effects of tobacco could be reversed to some degree. She had wondered many times since, that had she been able to heighten her own pain even more, if the age reversal might have been taken a step further. Was it possible to turn a full grown man into a child?

She believed it was. And she also believed that to do so in one sitting would result in her immediate death. As she had once told John, energy doesn't come out of thin air. It was physically draining.

The auto-suggestive word she used when calling upon the pain, was 'life.' She whispered that word aloud. Immediately, she felt a tightening of the muscles. Her head snapped back as if she'd been cracked in the face with a baseball bat. And indeed, the pain felt every bit as bad as if she had been struck that way. Teeth gritted against the pain, she repeated the word, again and again. Both eyes rolled back in her head until only the whites could be seen. Saliva dribbled from the corner of her mouth. Lips snarled. Tears streamed down her reddened face. Muscles stood out on her neck, blue veins so pronounced, appearing ready to burst. All at once, she buckled forward, agonizing pain bolting through every muscle, every nerve fiber. And the shrill scream that had been locked behind clenched teeth was unloosed.

Both Jeeps had been left behind the nearest mesa, about a quarter of a mile back. As Brewster and his agents approached the house, they observed no inside lighting. Smoke from one of the chimneys entwined with the crisp night air, drifting their way. The dirt road crunched lightly beneath their feet. Brewster's right hand shot up, and they came to a momentary halt. He eyed the single-story residence, inhaled deeply, and then proceeded forward. Quietly, they came upon the stone building.

Having been all through the house, Brewster knew the layout quite well. The master bedroom was on the northeast side, where they'd go in. Hopefully, Mills would be sleeping. And if that goddamn dog didn't give them away, the bedroom window could be pried open and Mills would be dead before the woman and her child had knowledge of the attack.

Brewster headed towards one of the bedroom windows, gun drawn, screwing a silencer in place when the woman's scream suddenly brought him to a halt. After nearly dropping the handgun, he regained his stride, filled with a mixture of determination and apprehension.

CHAPTER 38

John sat bolt upright just as Jillian collapsed to the bed like rag doll. His eyes darted to every dark corner, expecting to, but not seeing the demon that surely was responsible for her scream. Bear began to bark in another room. It was that same wild barking that had accompanied the monster's last visit. Yet, he saw nothing in the room that didn't belong here. He brushed the dark bangs from her face and despite the shadows, her faint smile became evident, as did the sweat glistening on her pale moonlit skin.

"Jillian," he said.

Her hand, weak and shaky, reached up and touched his face. "It's not safe," she said. "The nightmare...it's coming."

It partially occurred to him that he now rested on his knees and should be experiencing pain. Mostly, however, all he could think about was Jillian and the horror they would soon have to face. "Are you sure?" he asked.

"I need to be alone. Lock the door behind you."

"No," he whispered, gently stroking her cheek. He got to his feet and slipped into the trousers he'd left on the floor. "I'm not leaving you," he said, and then stared down at his leg. His eyes narrowed and filled with confusion.

Brewster laid a pneumatic dart rifle against the stone wall of the house. No longer did they have a reason to sneak quietly inside. The woman was there, in the bedroom. Brewster shivered with delight. He licked his lips, already tasting victory. The element of surprise would keep her panicked enough, allowing him not only to kill John, but time to grab and aim the dart rifle before she could comprehend the situation.

He waved an arm, indicating that he wanted Reese to join him at the window. Reese stood taller than he did by a good three inches. The man had a stomach of rippled hardened muscles, and biceps the size of the average man's thighs. Reese had to have his shoes special ordered, because size sixteen six E wasn't found in the average department store. When Reese stepped up beside him, Brewster took aim with the handgun. Through the narrow parting of the drapes, he zeroed in on Mills just as Mills leaned forward over the bed.

Tiny shards of glass from the window exploded into the room. At the exact same moment, John's arms shot up and he pitched forward. Jillian screamed as his body fell upon her. "John! *John*?"

She pushed back against the dead weight of his body, heart pumping wildly, adrenaline rushing through her system, terrified when her hand slipped in a sticky substance that could only be blood. "*No*!" she screamed, embracing him. "*God, No*!"

With trembling, bloody fingers, she reached for his neck, hoping to find a steady pulse thumping away in the carotid artery. She felt nothing. Nothing but utter panic.

Reese cleared the glass from the window frame with the butt end of his rifle. He laced his large fingers together to make a step for Brewster then Brewster went in, rifle slung over a shoulder.

Brewster went directly to the bed, where he grabbed a fist full of Mills' blond hair, and dragged the body off the naked woman, letting it fall on the floor with an audible double thud. He'd rehearsed his line at least a dozen times in the last half-hour. And with much delight, he looked down into the woman's frightened eyes and said, "I own you."

Jillian made a grab for the sheet, mouth gaped open. The entire situation was too much to handle all at once. She got to her knees on the mattress, where she could see the motionless body of John Mills on the floor. It couldn't be happening, but it was. She looked up at Brewster, head shaking, eyes wide and glassy and without any understanding.

"*Why*?" she asked, bringing a bloody hand up to cover her mouth, fingers trembling. "My God... *Why*?"

Reese had made his way into the bedroom, followed by Barnes. The three men stood together, looking down at the crying woman, who now rocked on her knees, still clinging to the sheet, sobbing, "Why?" again and again.

"I can't believe it's over," Barnes said, grinning. He turned on the nightstand lamp, then stepped over Mills' body, undecided as to whether he should kill the barking dog at the other side of the door.

Brewster yanked the bloody sheet from Jillian's grip and leaned forward so that his hand now rested on the bed. And as she crouched there on the bed, staring fearfully into his soulless dark eyes, he said, "We can do this the easy way, or the hard way. It's up to you. Where's your daughter?"

"Go to hell!" she cried venomously and spat in his face.

"I think that means the hard way," Barnes said and laughed.

Brewster backed away, wiping the spittle from his face before leveling the rife at the woman. "Say goodnight," he said to Jillian.

If these men were nightmare incarnate, she had the power to pull them back into the dream and out of existence. Even now, after the healing had spent much of her energy, there was enough left to undo these men. She could not, however, take them all on at once. Since physical contact was essential to eliminate them, they would catch on to what she was doing by the time the first man disappeared.

The effort would be futile. So, she closed her eyes, not only expecting, but also wanting to die. Which was when Brewster pulled the trigger, shooting a small dart into her neck.

The search for Valerie Braedon turned up empty. Under the circumstances, Brewster decided that the child had died during the blizzard. Either that or that Talbot guy had somehow smuggled the child out. Not only did they find no little girl in the house, but also they found no little girl's clothing.

They didn't pull the platinum albums from the wall, yet they took practically everything else of value that was easy to carry. Reese had silenced Bear permanently by putting a single bullet into the dog's brain, killing him instantly. Laurel and Reese had gone back to get the Jeeps, which they loaded as swiftly as any professional thieves could. There was the box from the spare room filled with precious jewelry. The candlestick holders, the vases, and the pewter statuettes...whatever they could scavenge. Barnes took a tapestry down from the living room wall, hoping it would bring a pretty penny from an antique dealer. Laurel went into the dining room, finding all the silverware in a drawer of the china hutch, stuffing every piece into a pillowslip. With the silverware loaded in the Jeep, Laurel returned for the china.

She carried out the first armload of china when Andrews landed the chopper. The man had arrived late, nearly twenty minutes late. Under the circumstances, since all had gone well, Laurel didn't care. Of course, had she known why Andrews was so late, she'd have shot him without hesitation.

Brewster had wrapped Jillian in the quilt from the four-poster bed and now cradled her in his arms as if she were an overgrown baby. One bare arm slipped from the quilt, hanging limply. Her head dropped back as he handed her over to Andrews.

Very carefully, very gently, as if she were made of eggshells, Andrews placed her in the back of the chopper, making sure he was covered well, then removed his overcoat, rolling it up, and placing it beneath her head.

"We all set?" Brewster asked, seeing that everyone but Andrews now stood outside by the two Jeeps. "Laurel, you ride with Andrews. We'll meet you two back at the house."

Barnes wanted a few extra minutes to plunder through Mills' bedroom closet; sure he'd find something of value in there. Brewster, wanting confirmation that Mills was dead, decided to go with Barnes.

Andrews took the chopper up into the purple night sky, alone with his god. To him, it all played out like a dream. As Laurel rushed below him, arms waving, yelling and demanding him to come back down, Andrews leaned partway out of the chopper with his AR-15, and cut her in half with a short burst of bullets. He then turned the weapon on Brewster, getting both Brewster and Barnes as they did an about-face on the porch steps. Both men, like puppets without strings, did a little dance, tumbling backwards, dead before hitting the porch floor. Reese came next – cut down as he drew his sidearm. And Carney, who'd ducked between the two Jeeps, got off three poorly aimed shots before the top of his head became one with oblivion.

Andrews hovered the chopper over the massacre below, shining the searchlight upon each dead body, looking for movement.

John pushed himself up with one hand to his knees, and then fell flat on the stone floor. The bullet had gone in just below his right shoulder blade on a diagonal path upward, and had exited straight through the collarbone, shattering it into splinters. The pain had reached an unbearable level, and yet the wound itself probably wasn't fatal.

No vital organs had been hit. But the bleeding was severe. He shuddered from the cold that now invaded his body. And the bleeding...

He lay face down in a puddle of his own warm blood, terrified, aware of the nearby helicopter. The shotgun remained in the closet, less than ten feet away. Again, he tried to push himself up, finding his right arm useless. Pale and sweaty, he eased himself over on his back, propping his head and neck against the bedpost to examine the wound. With his left hand, he swept the floor, grabbing the shirt Jillian had worn earlier. A lock of blond hair fell over his sweaty brow. The act of breathing had become not only painful, but also deliberate; he came nearly to the point of passing out. Before he could press the shirt to his shoulder and apply pressure to the exit wound, John had to correct the splintered bone fragments. He dropped the shirt on his stomach, and gritting his teeth, face twisting into a grimace of agony, he snapped the splinters that were beyond mending completely off, as if pulling broken twigs from the branch of a tree.

With the shirt pressed gently but firmly to his shoulder, he slid both legs under him, using the bed as an armless man might use a crutch. He got to his knees first, using his good shoulder and head for leverage then his good elbow.

Once he got to his feet, the dizziness hit him hard. It was then when he heard the roar of an automatic weapon being fired.

As he went to the closet, the bursts of gunfire ceased. He listened, noting only the sound of the chopper. Then, instead of going for the shotgun, John went for the window. From there, he could see absolutely nothing of the carnage outside. And yet, by the sound of it, he knew the helicopter was leaving.

John closed his eyes against the pain, both physical and emotional. Jillian was still alive. She had to be alive. They would need to question her first. As strong willed as she was, they wouldn't get anything out of her without the use of drugs...unless they had Valerie. Which – considering the way Brewster came here knowing what he'd find – was quite possible.

He leaned his bad shoulder to the door casing of the closet, enabling himself to free his left hand from the shirt-bandage to get the gun. When he turned around, shotgun in hand, the bandage fell to the floor. John swayed on his feet, the wound once again exposed and bleeding. He wasn't about to retrieve the bloody shirt from the floor, for the act of bending forward would surely bring him to his knees.

CHAPTER 39

The dream was a familiar one:

She's driving down a dark road in Jim's Volvo. To either side stands a wall of tall pine trees. It's a muggy night, and hot. The mist from an earlier rain swirls up from the asphalt in front of the headlights. She tries to adjust the headlights to high-beam, only to find the switch stuck.

She comes upon a curve in the road, yet fails to slow down, because she's on an important mission. The mission of motherhood. Vaguely, she remembers that Valerie has been crying. The child is teething – yes. And Jill's job is to find an all night store so she can buy some Ora-Jel for Valerie. Or, perhaps it's Jim who needs the medicine. Either way, finding an all night store is imperative.

But there's more.

She has an unshakable feeling that someone or some thing *is following her. And when she looks up, staring into the rearview mirror, she notices a pair of headlights that weren't there a moment ago. She gives the car a little more gas as she pulls out of the curve, then floors the accelerator. Something's wrong. Terribly wrong. And when she returns her attention to the rearview mirror...*

Opening the garage door took his every effort. He could hear only a faint thumping of the helicopter. His stomach still turned, his heart breaking from having to step over Bear's dead body in order to pass through the hall. As he stumbled towards the vehicle, his mind returned to the dead, mutilated bodies now littering his lawn and porch. Brewster was one of them.

When he got to the Land Rover, John eased himself onto the seat, once again struggling against a wave of dizziness. He grabbed the keys in the ashtray, inserted the proper key in the ignition, pumped the gas twice then cranked her up. The engine roared to life almost immediately. John pulled the Land Rover door shut as he sped off towards the sound of the helicopter.

Andrews circled the property twice then headed in the direction of Sandstone, flying low to the ground, which was something Brewster had never permitted him to do. Brewster preferred to fly several hundred feet off the ground, to distort the sense of speed so it didn't feel quite so fast. Andrews, however, preferred that sense of speed. Especially now.

Although he'd done his best to obey most laws, despite Brewster's orders, Andrews couldn't help but gloat over this most current thrill. Skimming just above the ground, heart in his throat, he could almost believe himself invincible. The woman was his, finally his. Perhaps he wasn't invincible now, but soon, very soon...

He kept his eyes glued to the ground below and in front of him, bringing the chopper up and over a rocky mesa, then rounding it on down, keeping within twenty yards of the ground. He could think of little else but his god and what she would soon do for him...

...Until something long and black slithered against the side of his face. Before he even noted its hideously deformed face, talon-like claws sunk into his shoulder. Andrews shrieked, covering his face with both hands, hunkering down as far as the seat would allow.

John had never traveled these roads at more than twenty-five miles per hour...until now. The rough terrain had him bouncing several inches out of his seat. Numerous times, the top of his head struck the headliner. With his right arm totally useless, he had to rely upon his left hand to not only steer the vehicle, but to shift it into low gear as well. No longer could he hear the helicopter. And yet, he didn't slow down, but pushed the Land Rover up to forty-five miles per hour in low gear. He went up and around Disaster Hill, the left side tires of the vehicle momentarily leaving the ground.

Andrews reached beneath his jacket for his sidearm, screaming, as the beast blew plugs of mucus from its pig-like snout. The goddamn thing actually grinned at him. Frantically, he brought the gun up, cowering against the control panel. He pulled the trigger. The blast reverberated in his ears. One blazing demonic eye disappeared from its socket, and a black, oily substance discharged from the hole. The beast screamed. Its tail smashed down on the unconscious woman behind it. Jillian's head tipped off the makeshift pillow as the chopper lost altitude in a steep pitched decline.

Andrews turned around, eyes screaming with fear, mouth open in a silent cry of terror, hand in mid air, as the chopper exploded into the side of a mesa.

John got to the paved highway and hesitated, fearing the direction he'd pick would be the wrong direction. Blood covered his chest and stomach, still oozing from the wound and soaking into his trousers. He panicked, hearing nothing but the soft humming of the Land Rover's engine and his own labored breathing.

Knowing he'd lost the helicopter, he headed in the only direction that made sense: towards Sandstone.

John put the transmission into gear, spinning up sand behind him as he made the left-hand turn. He hadn't gone a mile when his head fell back against the headrest. He swam in a sea of black dizziness. He no longer felt cold, just numb, and yet his body continued to shake, doing so right up until the moment the front tires left the road, and the vehicle slammed head-on into a clustered stand of Pinyon pines.

Seconds, minutes, or hours later, John opened the driver's side door and fell out onto the ground. He could hear sirens in the distance. Many sirens. A Chevrolet Camaro passed him by, and then stopped a hundred or so feet up the road. The reverse lights came on. The engine whined as the car backed down the road to where John lay. He lifted his head, left palm pressed to the dirt. He looked up at the gray-haired man who'd come to his rescue.

"Hold on there, buddy. I'll radio for help."

John waited for what felt like hours, listening to the exchange of garble on the radio.

The man, who appeared to be well over fifty years old, crouched down beside John, as John stared straight at the man's dusty cowboy boots. "Okay, buddy. Help's on the way. You're lucky there's an ambulance in the area. Bad accident off the road a mile or two ahead. Turns out they didn't need the ambulance. Good thing for you. Not so good for them. Was on my way there when I noticed your vehicle. Just relax."

"Who are you?" John asked, wetting his parched lips.

"Name's Farmer. Brett Farmer." Brett Farmer then reached into the breast pocket of his flannel shirt and pulled out a badge. The guy was a sheriff. Exactly what John needed.

"Listen to me," John breathed. He grabbed the man's sleeve with his bloody left hand, drawing him closer. "There's a helicopter. Stop it! Please!"

"I know. Damn shame. Must have been flying too low and didn't see the mesa. Looks to be no survivors." The man scowled, deep-set eyes narrowing. "Hey, you're that English feller. Can tell by your accent. You must be that import, the one the wife's been talking about. Sandstone's only celebrity. Mills, ain't it? John Mills?"

"Jillian," John uttered, dragging in a hissing breath. The pain in his shoulder had become a deep explosion of fire, burning down to the core. Nothing, however, matched the loss he felt in his heart. He wanted to die. He wanted to close his eyes for the last time and die.

Brett Farmer shook his beefy head. "Just relax. Don't wanna move or you might puncture a lung, or something. Ambulance should be here any minute. Lucky for you that helicopter went down. Otherwise, it'd take half an hour or more for an ambulance to get here all the way from Show Low. Not so lucky for them, though. Nope. Damn shame about that helicopter. Busy night. Yup. Real busy. You just relax. Everything's gonna be just fine."

John dropped his head on the ground, cheek to the dirt, eyes open, staring numbly at the patch of red on the asphalt from the Camaro's taillights, telling himself that she couldn't be dead. Only a few hours ago, he'd held her in his arms. They'd made love. She wasn't supposed to die. Not this way. Not in a helicopter. Not! In! A! Helicopter!

"Hey, buddy, you all right? Just hold on. Ambulance is coming. Hear that? Just hold on."

CHAPTER 40

"What's the count?" Lyle Guthrie asked as he walked through the smoking debris. He'd never seen such a terrible accident. And being an EMT for over seven years that was saying a lot. Sure, he'd been there to pick up the pieces after that bad wreck two years ago, New Year's Eve. Two dead, that time. One was decapitated. The other had been thrown through the windshield and was found ten feet from the vehicle, and fifteen feet from the vehicle and in a bush, and on the hood of the car. He wouldn't be at all surprised if he returned to Sandstone Corners and found another piece of that guy all dried up and hanging from the branch of a tree. Damn pity too. For that guy had turned out to be the mayor's son. And Mayor Blysdale was still in shock over it.

But this, this was absolutely sickening. They had removed the charred remains of what appeared to be a man from the wreckage and had it all (or most) packaged up in a body-bag for M.E. And then, there was That Other Thing. At first he thought The Thing was a pig. But no. It was too goddamn *big* to be a pig. Besides, what remained of the body looked all wrong. It had scales, large black scales the size of a fifty-cent piece cut in half. And that huge chunk of charred tail they'd found. Where in the hell did that come from? It looked more like something you'd find attached to a small dinosaur. And of course, there was The Claw. Charred as it was, if he had to make an identification of it, he'd swear it must have belonged to the largest bird on the planet since the age of the dinosaurs. Wild. Freaky. Lyle felt like puking his guts out.

"Hey," he said to Marge Townsend. "I asked about the count."

"Hard to say," Marge shot right back. "One human, dead. We might find more when we widen the search. I don't know what That Thing was. Thank God *it's* dead."

"Hey, Lyle," Roger Met called out. Roger, who had been just about to hang up his gun and badge when the call came in, knelt down on the ground about thirty yards from where most of the wreckage now lay.

Lyle rushed to where Roger indicated, nearly tripping over a rock, and then shone his flashlight down at what might have once been a quilt. It was rolled up, lightly charred on the outside, and stained with blood. He hunkered down. And together, he and Met uncovered a pale, naked woman.

Unlike the man, her body appeared, for the most part, intact. She had the smoothest porcelain white skin he'd ever seen. Absolutely perfect woman, with one exception: She was broken and dead. The quilt had evidently spared her from the flames. But it hadn't prevented the woman from getting her throat slashed open.

He was sure there were numerous internal injuries. Aside from the throat injury, he found no other explanation for the blood pooled in her mouth. And evidently, since she'd bled so much, the woman hadn't died instantly. Blood dried in and around her right ear. Her right foot had twisted and hung only by a few tendons. The woman didn't have a chance of surviving after crashing into the side of a mesa. Regardless, Lyle checked for a heartbeat. Nothing. He pulled back her eyelids, checking her pupils with a penlight. "Fixed," he said, shaking his head.

"What a pity. Pretty thing like that."

John slipped in and out of consciousness throughout the ambulance ride to Show Low. At one point, he'd reached up with his left hand, grabbed the EMT by the collar and gruffly whispered, "Save Ryan," through clenched teeth. Then his bloodstained hand dropped as he fell away into a restless daze.

Dr. Geffield was on duty in the E.R. that night. He was a tall man with a thin hook of a nose, who looked about thirty, despite being all of forty-seven. He had long fingered hands, and was just as skilled with a scalpel as John had once been with the keys of a piano. As the EMT rolled John through the emergency room doors, Geffield ran to greet them, already barking out orders. It wasn't every day that a man as well known as Mills graced Geffield's presence. When one of the nurses had announced that John Mills – *The* John Mills – was on his way in with a gunshot wound, Geffield knew immediately who the man was. He'd been a fan for a good many years.

Geffield checked the drip that had been started in the ambulance, got an update on the vital signs, and ascertained that his patient needed to be sent directly to surgery.

John, who had appeared unconscious when they'd transferred him from the stretcher, opened his eyes while lifting his head. "Need to...to use the phone."

"Later," Geffield replied.

John clenched his left hand into a fist. He wasn't playing games. At this moment, there was nothing more important to him than contacting Mel in Phoenix... provided Mel was in Phoenix *and* alive. Because, John had to know. He had to know if everyone he loved was dead. "Now!" he growled, dropping his head back. "God damn it. Now!"

"Mr. Mills, you're in no condition," Geffield said.

John's eyes narrowed, cheek muscle twitching. "You lay one hand on me ba-before I place my call, and you...you'll have…" He gritted his teeth, feeling cold and faint. "I'll slap you with a...with a lawsuit that'll leave you ba-begging in the streets."

Geffield backed off while ordering a nurse to bring a telephone.

When the nurse, Billie Sanchez, set the phone on the counter behind John's head, she said, "What number?"

"Call information. Phoenix."

After nearly tripping once, Lyle walked a little slower, shining the flashlight to the ground in front of him while watching his step. He found Marge over by the meat wagon.

Marge, the most beautiful woman he'd ever met, stared up at the stars, tears streaming down her lovely face. She had a tender heart, which was only one of the many reasons Lyle found her so attractive. At five foot six inches, two hundred forty-three pounds of mostly muscle, she had hands that could squash a watermelon. And those same hands were balled up at her sides as her bottom lip quivered and her large heart ached...because two people she'd never seen before were dead.

Lyle slipped a hand partway around her waist, tucking her rounded head beneath his chin. "Couldn't save them, babe. Wasn't anything we could do. We're only human, Marge."

"It ain't right," she gasped, sniffing a time or two. "If only we could have got here sooner. That...That poor woman might not have died."

Lyle considered himself cold-hearted by no means, but he knew he had to make a point, thereby letting Marge off the hook. Otherwise, Marge would cry herself to sleep tonight...if the woman found sleep at all. So, he walked around to the rear of the meat wagon, pulled open the double doors and waved an arm while telling Marge, "Come over here."

She came, wiping the tears from her face with the fingers of both hands. "Yes?"

"You know there was nothing we could have done for the man. The woman was in bad shape, too. I doubt she remained alive three minutes after the crash. Take a look and you'll see I'm right."

Marge shook her head, brown eyes filling with fresh tears.

"Come on. It's not as if you haven't seen a dead body before."

He caught the end of the stretcher upon which the woman in the body bag now rested. He pulled it about a quarter of the way out, just far enough so he could reach the zipper, which he now pulled along its tracks. "I'm telling you, Marge, the woman..."

He could have sworn the woman's throat had been laid wide open. Lyle let go of the zipper and rubbed a hand down the length of his tired face. He had the strangest urge to smile. Because...he finally understood the situation. He was in a dream. He had fallen sound asleep in his own bed, dreaming. It explained that pig-thing that wasn't a pig. It explained that long, thick chunk of tail they'd found. And it also explained why a woman whose throat had been laid open, now appeared unblemished in that area. Either that or he was so darn tired he was imagining things.

Lyle grasped the zipper once more, pulling it down the rest of the way. He told himself he had to be mistaken. And yet, uncertainty left him anxious. He wanted confirmation. But Dave and Roger, the two men who'd helped him load the body, had already left. He and Marge were the only two people still at the scene, aside from Sheriff Farmer who'd arrived not ten minutes earlier.

"Marge, you ain't gonna believe this," he said, gazing down at what should have been a foot hanging by tendons. Instead, what he observed was a perfectly normal foot in a perfectly normal position with the toes, all unmarred, pointing upward.

"What is it, Lyle?" she asked, still unable to force herself to look at that beautiful woman's torn body.

Lyle removed the penlight from his pocket while climbing into the rear of the ambulance. He made his way to the cadaver's head, walking in a crouched position. He pulled the left eyelid up with a thumb, shone the light then sighed heavily. Still fixed. Of course it was fixed. What else had he expected to find? He shook his head lightly, not wanting to answer that question. Next, he reached for the cadaver's neck, feeling for the carotid artery, and then letting go. The woman was dead, cold. Very dead.

"Lyle? Something wrong?"

"No, babe. Go ahead and get up front. I think it's time we get the heck out of here."

He went to the rear doors, pulling them shut. As Marge started the engine, Lyle took a seat, knees drawn to his chin, hands folded over his shins. He stared at the dead woman as a child might stare at a dark and foreboding closet from his not-so-safe bed. He considered pinching himself to make sure he was awake, only to decide he'd rather not know.

CHAPTER 41

The line was answered on the second ring. And Mel's voice, grumpy as it was, pleased John immensely. "What do you want?"

"Mel. I've been...Where's Valerie?"

"Sleeping, until the phone rang. What's up? You sound like shit."

"Been shot."

"Fuck," Mel breathed. "You're not shitting me, are you, man?"

"They're all dead. Jillian, Brewster...all of them. I'm in...the emergency room. Show Low. Got some..."

The phone slipped through the fingers of John's left hand. And the nurse who'd dialed the number retrieved the phone from the floor. She held it up, shrugging, as if asking Dr. Geffield what to do with it.

All Geffield said was, "He goes to surgery. Now!"

Billie brought the phone to her ear. She was a graceful woman of twenty-eight years, with long dark hair, perfectly twisted into a bun, and a smooth olive complexion. She shook her head, unsure of what to do, then said: "Hello?"

"Who is this?" Mel asked.

"Billie Sanchez. I'm an R.N. attending Mr. Mills. Who is this?"

"I'm Mr. Mills' brother," he lied. "Name's Mel. What's going on? "

"Well," Billie said, watching two nurses and a doctor roll Mr. Mills out of the room, "It seems that your brother was shot. I can't give you any more details over the phone, Mr. Mills. But if..."

Mel slammed down the phone, flipped on the overhead light, and sat Valerie up on the edge of the bed. This afternoon, during a three hour shopping spree, he'd purchased the child five complete outfits of winter attire and two pairs of shoes...all at John's expense. He dressed her in one of those outfits now. He didn't take time to match the clothing, but slipped a red turtleneck over her head, then held out a brown pair of trousers for her to step into.

"What's the matter?" she asked, dragging the back of a hand across both squinting eyes.

"We're going for a ride," he replied.

"To see Mommy?"

Pausing long enough to look into her sleepy eyes, John's words finally pounded home; the little girl's mother was one of the dead. Mel lowered his gaze, grasping the small shoe as Valerie slipped her bare foot into it.

After tying the laces of her little Nikes, he grabbed her by the hand, leading her to the door, which was when he realized he also needed to get dressed. Mel, for the first time since elementary school, had actually worn pajamas to bed. He looked down at the striped top and baggy bottoms he wore, wiggled his hairy toes, and thought to himself: Fuck it. The only things he needed were the keys to the Bronco and his wallet, which he found in the bathroom, in the pockets of the jeans he'd left crumbled on the floor.

John awoke in a semiprivate hospital room, his senses assaulted by a strong disinfectant. He felt groggy, listless. He had a bandaged shoulder, which indicated the surgery was over. And yet he didn't have the use of his right arm or hand.

His second waking thought hit him hardest. Practically everything he loved was dead: Jillian, his music, Jillian, Bear. It didn't matter that he would never play a guitar again; he'd never play anything on the piano other than a one handed rendition of *Chop Sticks*. What bothered him most was what all this would mean to Valerie. Five years old and she'd already lost both parents. It would crush her. No doubt, she'd become hysterical...or worse. The child had no family, which meant she'd be tossed from one foster home to another. John, being single, knew the state wouldn't look kindly upon his petitioning to adopt the child.

But he did have money, the kind of money that could buy the best damn attorney in The States. The only other recourse was to do it the illegal way. And Mel would help if it came to that.

John gazed out the window at the arrival of dawn. In these few short weeks, his entire life had changed. From wanting nothing more than complete solitude, to finally allowing himself to dream and feel again. As the sun rose higher, and the desire to join Jillian began to settle into his heart, the only movements he made were to blink his eyes, to breathe, and occasionally cough. An hour passed. Twice, someone had come into the room. A nurse, he supposed. The woman had lifted his wrist, seemingly oblivious to the fact that he was now awake, holding his arm for several seconds before disappearing through the door on a pair of soft-soled shoes.

With each added second, he felt more and more numb. It just didn't seem possible that Jillian was dead. His mind kept rejecting it. As he'd once told Mel: He'd close his eyes and see her face. Vibrant. Alive. Full of beauty. The only woman he'd ever met who actually quoted Sappho. One of the few people who he'd ever allowed to touch his heart. And now that heart remained beating, while her heart had fallen still.

He started to bring his left hand to his bandaged forehead, only to realize an IV attached him to a bottle of glucose. Numb. Barely coming out of the groggy stage of the anesthesia-driven sleep.

"You awake?" Sheriff Brett Farmer said, stepping into the room.

John turned his head on the pillow, and regarded Brett Farmer evenly. "Barely," he replied, his voice a gruff whisper.

"Been a long night," Farmer stated, looking down at the jeans he wore. "Supposed to be my day off, but I got a few questions. Found five bodies out by your place last night. First, I'd like to know who shot you."

"He's probably amongst the five bodies you found on my property."

Farmer pulled up a chair by John's bedside, and plopped his rounded butt into the cushioned seat. He laced his fingers together over his sagging belly and said, "You own an AR-15, Mr. Mills?"

"No, sir." He tried to lift his right arm, which seemed all but dead from the shoulder down. "Neither did I have the opportunity to...shoot back."

"Glad to hear it wasn't you."

John sensed doubt in the man's voice. Farmer had probably saved his life. Farmer was also a sheriff. So John had two good reasons for wanting to set the record straight. "I was shot and went down before I knew what was happening. When I made it outside, I found all five of those people the same way you probably found them, last night: dead."

Farmer shook his beefy head while flicking a thumb at his nose. "The motive behind the break-in appears obvious: Robbery. Looks like they were in the middle of loading up all your stuff when they were murdered. Every last one of them had fake ID. We're running the prints now."

"The guy in the helicopter," John said. He gazed up at the ceiling. "Must have been he who shot them."

"The man who flew off with your girlfriend."

John inhaled deeply, exhaled slowly. He didn't know the details regarding the crash or of the invasion into his home. He had blacked out. But Jillian had lived it. The blind terror she must have felt, virtually alone against all those men. He wanted to believe it was over quickly, that she'd felt no pain, and hadn't the time to hold out for the hope that someone would come to her rescue. John's heartbeat quickened, blood pounded through his head as he closed his eyes to fend off the tears. "Jillian."

Farmer bit down on one large, rubbery lip, brows furrowed. "Gotta ask you a rather strange question about that, Mr. Mills. We found something in the wreckage of the chopper. Can't seem to figure out what it was. Last night, you didn't by any chance see something well... something...something..." He shook his head, ruddy face turning a darker shade of red. "...something odd? An animal, maybe. Large. Looked kinda like a pig."

"No, sir," he replied. He hadn't seen it last night. Yet, he'd seen it before. Jillian's nightmare had evidently paid another visit. An untimely visit. Whoever the bastard was that had been piloting the helicopter, must have panicked when the monster appeared. It made sense, about as much sense as anything else did over the last three weeks. Knowing what had caused the helicopter crash, however, didn't make it any easier to digest. Had they come for her a day sooner or a day later, the nightmare wouldn't have happened. The helicopter wouldn't have crashed. And Jillian might still be alive. One day could have made all the difference in the world. One hour.

If it weren't so tragic, he'd consider it ironic: Jillian's nightmare had finally ended...and yet she wasn't alive to enjoy the new freedom.

John turned his cheek to the pillow, eyes stinging with tears. "I'm tired, Sheriff," he said solemnly. "Very tired."

"Sure you are. Got a few more questions for you. Guess they can wait another day or two." Farmer got to his feet, cowboy boots clicking against the tiled floor as he headed for the door. "Oh, one more thing. Spoke to your girlfriend, a few minutes ago. Were you aware she's wanted for questioning by the FBI?"

"Girlfriend?" John said. His heart raced quicker. He tried to wet his parched lips, but found no saliva. He pushed himself up on his left elbow, neck bent at an awkward angle, blood rushing to his face. "You spoke to her? Jillian? She's *alive*?"

"Jill Braedon. Found her out in the waiting room early this morning with her kid and some barefoot English guy dressed in striped pajamas. Got a man keeping an eye on her right now. Suppose she'll want to see you soon as visiting hours start. Less'n the FBI gets here first. Sure was a strange thing," Farmer said and shook his head. "The two people who brought her in seemed to a been under the impression she was dead. Had her in a body bag and everything. Talked to one of my men, who'd thought she was dead, too. Heard about things like that happening...way every once in a while. Never actually been involved, though. Just read about them in the paper. Nope...Kinda makes you wonder. Mighty strange." He placed both hands, one at either hip as he stared down at his snakeskin boots. When he looked across the room at John, Farmer's face had turned a pale shade of red again. "Mr. Mills...you don't, by any chance, have something you wanna tell me about all this?"

"No," John replied, nearly choking on his own voice.

Farmer shook his head again, lips pressed firmly together. "Thought that's what you'd say," he muttered, and then walked out of the room.

EPILOGUE

Because Jillian's only defense for fleeing the night of the fires was that she'd been running for her life – in effect, running for the past three and a half years from whomever had set the fires – the FBI concluded their questioning within a few hours. And since all the evidence had been destroyed in Fairshire's twin blaze, no motive could be established as to why Brewster and his men had wanted Jillian and her family dead. Neither did she offer any answers to that question. She'd been wise enough to use a string of assumed names during her three and a half year stint on the lam, which was probably why they didn't connect her to the many miraculous healings that had taken place from one end of the country to the other. The FBI couldn't hold her. All they had to go on was circumstantial evidence which placed her in the vicinity during the crime. And gut-instinct, that suggested she wasn't telling the whole truth; neither of which would stand up in court. Their only recourse was to let the woman go. And keep a close watch of her activities.

Within six weeks, she and Valerie had obtained legal passports, and were on their way to Dover. Since John had dual citizenship and the wedding was to take place on the following Saturday, visas were not required.

The wedding ceremony was formal. Of the three hundred, fifty-seven people who filled the cathedral, Jillian knew only three: Valerie, John, and Mel. By the end of the ceremony, she'd been introduced to countless others, including the infamous Uncle George. The red-carpeted aisle she crossed was lined with hundreds of roses. Her flowing gown, which had been custom designed, was a magnificent white, with a low-cut bodice inlaid with pearlescent sequins. The train was carried by not one, but five of the cutest little children in formal attire. Jillian graced her way to the altar accompanied by a selection of chamber music composed by Johann Sebastion Bach.

It was there, facing the man she loved, lean and handsome and most proper in his black tuxedo, where they exchanged their vows and kissed for the first time as husband and wife. But not before a rather lengthy delay on John's part to answer one particular question with the appropriate 'I do.'

When the Reverend Harold J. Wentworth said to John, "...in sickness and in health, for as long as you both shall live?" John gazed tenderly into Jillian's blue eyes. He hesitated to answer. Not because he wasn't sure; rather, because he was struck dumfounded by the meaning of that last phrase. Forever was a very long time.

Jillian flashed a nervous smile as the good reverend lightly cleared his throat. A hushed commotion swept through the cathedral as some of the guests shifted and leaned forward in the pews to get a better view. And John, who had never taken a commitment lightly, said: "I do."

As it turned out, Jillian's nightmares didn't end with the helicopter crash. She'd found that out the night after John Mills made a miraculous recovery and was sent home with the complete use of his right arm and hand. But they found a solution – something simple enough for a five-year-old child to have discovered.

That night, seven weeks ago, when John woke up to Jillian's screams, a mistake had been made: the bedroom door had been left unlocked. The demon that had been thought dead loomed over the bed, while John tried to hold Jillian back. And when Valerie, singing at the top of her lungs, filled with complete faith, opened the bedroom door, the demon vanished as if it had never been there. A simple song had done the trick...

...Which is why, should you visit the Mills' estate in Dover, England, you'll always hear, day or night, the sweet sound of music filling the rooms.

About the Author

Jamie Eubanks resides in Southern California, where she studies Martial arts, runs a small business and is currently working on her next novel.

CPSIA information can be obtained at www.ICGtesting.com
Printed in the USA
LVOW10s1504270315

432314LV00001B/6/P

9 781482 356182